CW00660483

Netta Muskett was born in Sev
Kent College, Folkstone. She h
at first teaching mathematics before working as a secretary to
the then owner of the 'News of the World', as well as serving as a
volunteer during both world wars - firstly driving an ambulance
and then teaching handicrafts in British and American hospitals.

It is, however, for the exciting and imaginative nature of her
writing that she is most remembered. She wrote of the times
she experienced, along with the changing attitudes towards sex,
women and romance, and sold millions of copies worldwide.
Her last novel 'Cloudbreak' was first published posthumously
after her death in 1963.

Many of her works were regarded by some librarians at the time
of publication as risqué, but nonetheless proved to be hugely
popular with the public, especially followers of the romance
genre.

Netta co-founded the Romantic Novelists' Association and
served as Vice-President. The 'Netta Muskett' award, now
renamed the 'RNA New Writers Scheme', was created in her
honour to recognise outstanding new writers.

BY THE SAME AUTHOR
HOUSE OF STRATUS

GIVE BACK
YESTERDAY

Netta Muskett

HOUSE OF
STRATUS

Copyright © 1969 Estate of Netta Muskett
Typography: 2014 House of Stratus

All rights reserved. No part of this publication may be reproduced, stored in a retrieval system, or transmitted, in any form, or by any means (electronic, mechanical, photocopying, recording, or otherwise), without the prior permission of the publisher. Any person who does any unauthorised act in relation to this publication may be liable to criminal prosecution and civil claims for damages.

The right of Netta Muskett to be identified as the author of this work has been asserted.

This edition published in 2014 by House of Stratus, an imprint of Stratus Books Ltd, Lisandra House, Fore St., Looe, Cornwall, PL13 1AD, UK.

www.houseofstratus.com

Typeset by House of Stratus.

A catalogue record for this book is available from the British Library and the Library of Congress.

ISBN 07551 4284 5
EAN 978 07551 4284 2

This book is sold subject to the condition that it shall not be lent, resold, hired out, or otherwise circulated without the publisher's express prior consent in any form of binding, or cover, other than the original as herein published and without a similar condition being imposed on any subsequent purchaser, or bona fide possessor.

This is a fictional work and all characters are drawn from the author's imagination. Any resemblances or similarities to persons either living or dead are entirely coincidental.

I

'MORE tea, darling?'

'Tea? No. Oh no, I don't think so.'

The man sitting opposite her in a discreet alcove of an Olde Worlde Tea Shoppe laughed, a teasing, indulgent note in his laughter in which the girl joined, rather shyly. Her cup of tea was untouched and the merest nibble had gone from the cake she had chosen at random half an hour ago.

'You're off your food,' he said. 'Don't happen to be in love by any chance?'

She laughed again, a sound of breathless wonder and happiness.

She was twenty, a pretty thing, and in love for the first time. The rose colours of life were an almost visible cloud about her.

She nodded with that touch of shyness which he found one of the most adorable things about her in a world of the hard-boiled.

'I think that might be the explanation,' she agreed.

'I hope it won't keep you indefinitely from eating,' he teased her. 'Not going to keep me waiting too long, I hope.'

Her face clouded a little.

'Not a minute longer than I must, but—you know, Giles, don't you?'

'That the family are adamant against your marrying anyone as ancient as I am, yes. We'll get over that. You'll see. Shall we go?'

She nodded again and picked up the expensive bag he had given her, and the gay, cheap little gloves which gave him an odd feeling of tenderness. He enjoyed feeling tender. He enjoyed everything about Alison, her youth, her shyness, the fairy-tale quality of her corn-gold hair, her blue child's eyes, her mouth that was a woman's.

Giles Paraway was in love, a condition in which he had not expected to be again, least of all with Alison Clurey.

Life had taken on a new charm.

'We'll go the long way round,' he said when he had paid the bill and slipped a hand under her elbow to take her across the street to where his car was standing, a long, low, racy-looking car that was perfect for a summer afternoon.

'I mustn't be too late, Giles,' she said with a little frown.

'All right. Hop in, sweetness, but it's got to be the long way. I've just got to kiss you again to make sure it's real. It is, isn't it?'

She gave her breathless little laugh again. She was wholly enchanted. Though she had told him prudently that they must not be late, he knew that he held her in the hollow of his hand, that she would go anywhere, do anything, be anything he wanted.

That was all right, for it suited him excellently to let things go as she planned them, not to alter her in any way, not to disenchant her. Nobody had ever been more careful or circumspect than he had been and intended to be with Alison.

But when he had reached the spot which had been in the minds of both when he spoke of 'the long way round', and stopped the car under the trees just off the road and taken her in his arms, he had to remind himself of his intention. She was so innocently tempting to a man, her arms clinging about his neck, her lips warm against his own, her body so soft and pliant and yielding.

'I do love you so utterly, Giles,' she whispered.

'Bless you for that, sweetness,' he said. 'I want you. You know that? Do you understand?'

'Of course. And I want you, desperately. Giles, you'll make it come true? Say you will!'

'*We'll* make it come true, darling, but you know I can't do much about it myself, don't you. I'll have to leave the persuading to you, or most of it. You're sure you want me to come this evening?'

'Sure. I can't stand it like this any longer. I'll tell Mum when I get home and then she'll realise it's serious and forever. Why do one's parents have to be so difficult? Why do they always try to manage our lives as well as their own? They married who they wanted to, so why shouldn't we?'

'It's a way they have, I suppose,' he said, smiling into her flushed face and kissing her again, lightly, barely touching her lips, her cheek, her small and rather indeterminate chin, pushing aside the hair that was like spun silk so that his mouth could reach her soft neck.

She gave a little shiver of rapture.

'They've got to consent,' she said; 'but, darling, if they don't, we shan't have long to wait, only three months. After my twenty-first, I can do what I like.'

'Yes, that's true, but we don't want it that way, do we? No runaway business for you, my sweet. Everything's got to be decent and in good order, white satin and all the rest of it, if that's the way you'd like it, and I take it you would?'

'Well, of course that's what I *really* want,' she admitted. 'Most girls do, and I'd never feel I was properly married without Daddy to give me away and darling Mummy shedding a few quiet tears. Giles, you'll love them. They're sweet, even though they do make me wild at times.'

He smiled.

'The important thing is whether they'll love me,' he said.

'But they will. They must. Once they've actually met you, they won't be able to help themselves and they'll realise how idiotic it is to have made all this fuss about it and that I couldn't possibly be happy with anyone but you. Oh, Giles—darling—*darling.*'

He held her closely and kissed her again. Then he put her resolutely from him. He knew temptation when he met it, and this was by no means the first girl he had kissed.

'Now I'm going to take you home,' he said firmly. 'Sit back there and don't dare to move again until I tell you to get out.'

She gave her happy laugh and sat back in her corner.

'You take such care of me, which makes it all the more idiotic of them to be so much against you,' she said.

'I can understand it. After all, on the face of it, I'm not very suitable, am I?'

'Just because you're a few years older!' she said scornfully. 'I hate boys. I always have done.'

He gave her a little crooked smile and, turning into the main road again, gave his attention to his driving.

Alison sat and looked at him, her heart in her eyes. Of course they would understand as soon as they saw him. How could they help it? He was so fine, so distinguished. She knew every line of his rather heavy, good-looking face, the strong mouth and chin, the grey eyes deep set and made the more fascinating to her because of the network of fine lines etched about them. For the same reason she loved the slight greying of his hair, dark hair with a strong wave in it which he tried sedulously but without complete success to brush straight.

A man among men, ran her romantic thoughts. No, a king among men. And at home they talked about her meeting and marrying someone of her own age! A boy of twenty-one! Had they no idea at all of what she was really like inside, what she wanted, what she *needed*?

It was Giles she needed, with every breath of her body, with every thought of her mind, for ever and ever.

She forgot to tell him to put her down at the corner, but he stopped where he always stopped, pulling in to the kerb, and smiling at her.

'Didn't you want me to stop here?' he asked.

'Of course. Just this once and after this—right to the house. You will come tonight, darling?'

'Of course. What time? Sevenish?'

'Better make it eight. It will give Mummy more time to flap round with the meal. It won't be anything very super, you know,

4

not giving her any time to get something special.'

'I'm coming for you, not food,' he said.

'You always say the right thing, don't you? Good-bye for a very little while, darling.'

'Shall I ring you first to make sure it's all right?'

'No. It's going to be all right,' she said positively, and he sat watching her until she had turned the corner and gone out of sight, hurrying, her head held high, short curls blowing in the wind.

She was certainly a darling. In every way he was in luck.

Luck?

He needed a break, and this was it.

Alison ran up the short path that led to the tall, old-fashioned house in the now quite unfashionable suburb in which the Clureys lived. Before the war it had been one of the best roads in the district, a road lined with trees, the houses detached or semi-detached and either owned or rented *in toto* by the sort of business man who started out late and came home early, or by doctors who had a Harley Street address as well.

The war had altered all that, the war and that insidious, intangible thing which, in the course of a very few years, can entirely alter the character of a road. Most of the people who had lived there when Simon Clurey, outwardly bold but secretly fearful, had borrowed most of the money to buy No. 11, had moved away. At one end of the road, where a bomb had fallen, a row of 'pre-fabs' had made their appearance and been received with horrified amazement by the occupants of the big houses bordering on them. Children played and shouted in the road where once a dignified calm had reigned, and more and more people fled from the outrage, selling their houses to people who could not afford to be so selective, or leaving them to be requisitioned by the local council and turned into an amazing number of small, inconvenient 'flats' which provided more street urchins and continuous lines of washing and aproned women gossiping at gates which had once admitted carriages and pairs.

The Clureys lived at a respectable distance from the pre-fabs, but even they occupied only part of the house now, a fact which was a constant source of regret and trouble. It had happened towards the end of the war. So many people were homeless through the bombing, and now that the Clureys could no longer afford to have a maid, the empty rooms at the top of the house gave their consciences so many jabs that one day Helena had gone to the housing committee and offered the use of her top floor.

'Just till the war is over,' she added.

'Of course, Mrs. Clurey. That's understood,' the harassed woman at the improvised desk had agreed at once. 'It's only a temporary measure, and we are most grateful for your help. May I send someone right away?'

Helena, full of the milk of human kindness, had agreed and hurried home to finish clearing out the boxes, bits of broken furniture and junk which had accumulated in the attics. There was no time to do any of the painting and distempering she would have liked to do.

'Don't you worry about that, ma'am,' Mr. Oliver had said cheerfully. 'Me and the missus are dab 'ands at anything like that. We'll be as snug as a bug in a rug, won't we, Flo?' to the big, untidy-looking woman who so far had had nothing to say, though her small, observant eyes had missed nothing.

'O' course we shall,' she agreed, 'and it's only temp'ry.'

Temporary?

That had been nine years ago, and the Olivers were still there, a thorn in the Clureys' flesh but utterly immovable since they were protected by laws which gave Simon Clurey, their landlord, no rights at all. He wanted full possession of his house; he needed it as his children grew older, but there was nothing he could do about it and the Olivers sat tight.

It was not as if they stayed on the top floor either. Indeed, how could they? In her compassion for people who had no homes, and in the class-levelling comradeship of the war, Helena Clurey had overlooked the practical issues involved, the lack of amenities on the top floor. Simon had had a tap put up there for them, but that had merely been a small additional convenience to them, affording no relief to Helena, for the Olivers had overflowed by necessity into her bathroom, her kitchen, were always, or so it seemed, on the stairs or in the hall or hanging out washing in the garden.

'Well, we gotta do washin' same as anybody else,' said Mrs. Oliver with a sniff when asked diffidently if she could not limit her use of the garden clothes lines to one or two days a week.

When he came out of the army, in which he had had an undistinguished career, ending up as a lance-corporal, Simon had added a sink and a gas cooker to the tap on the top landing, which had kept Mrs. Oliver more or less out of Helena's kitchen, but nothing could be done about the bathroom, or the use of the stairs and the front hall, and when Mrs. Oliver started to produce children, a pram took up permanent residence inside the front door. In the space of a few years there seemed to be young Olivers everywhere, playing on the stairs, sliding down the banisters, racing in and out of the Clureys' rooms, churning Simon's well-kept lawn into a morass and pulling up his flowers, whilst day in and day out, lines of washing waved in the breeze and wore down Helena's protests until she protested no more. It was easier and less uncomfortable to let the Olivers do as they liked than subject herself to the biting tongue of Mrs. Oliver, who had quickly revealed herself as very different from the placid woman she had first appeared to be.

The young Clureys, growing older, took up the battle and waged it with unrelenting vigour. In vain the Clureys had tried to beat a retreat and find somewhere else to live. There just was nowhere else to go. There was no other house to rent and no money to buy one and no redress to be found. Simon Clurey, a solicitor's head clerk earning a comparatively good income, did not belong to the class of society for whom housing laws were made. He was told that if he could find as good accommodation for his unwanted tenants as they had in his house, he could get rid of them, but no such accommodation could be found and they made no attempt to find any for themselves. Why, indeed, should they? asked the Olivers. They were all right with their three attics and the run of the house at the very low rent which Helena, in her large-hearted compassion, had asked when they came to her homeless. They could not even increase the rent.

No, there was no reason at all why the Olivers should put themselves out, and they didn't.

Alison was thinking of this, for the thousandth time, as she put her key in the lock, moved the now dilapidated pram which stood right across the hall, and picked her way distastefully amongst several small, unwashed Olivers who were amusing themselves with an old fork, picking out as much as they could of the little pieces of mosaic tiling set in what had once been a pattern on the floor.

What on earth would her home look like to Giles when he made his first acquaintance with it that evening? He was not coming until eight o'clock, at which time she and her brothers, at the age of the Oliver children, had been tucked up in bed, their toys put away and the house dignified and tidy and quiet. It would be none of those things tonight, of course, though she made up her mind she would somehow clear the Oliver brats themselves out of the way before he was due.

Mrs. Oliver was hanging over the banisters, as usual, a drab in her torn, shapeless overall. Surely she was not going to have *another*?

'Hullo, dearie,' she said cheerfully. She was completely uncrushable. 'Bit late tonight, aren't you? 'Ad a long day?'

'No,' said Alison, tight-lipped. 'Isn't it time you took the children upstairs, Mrs. Oliver?'

'Time? W'y, it's on'y just past six,' said Mrs. Oliver, bristling at once.

'They're not supposed to be playing down here at all.'

'Give the pore little blighters a chance. W'ere else are they to play? Yer dad makes a stink if they're in 'is precious garden, and yer mum won't 'ave 'em out in the front, and with them lorries in the road, it ain't safe in the street. Got to play somew'ere, pore little beggars, ain't yer, lovey?' to the eldest of them, who was now climbing up the stairs, not on the treads but by way of the spaces between the banister pillars.

'Why can't they play in your own part of the house?' asked Alison.

'It's as 'ot as 'ell up there. Besides, wot 'arm are they doin'?' demanded Mrs. Oliver, preparing as always to do immediate battle.

'For one thing, they're picking up the tiling with that fork, and you know my father relaid it all only last week. Take your things and go upstairs to your own rooms,' said Alison to the children, beginning to pick up their scattered toys and throwing them into a cardboard box. 'Put down those bits of tiling. They're not yours,' snatching a handful out of one of the dirty little hands.

The child set up a howl and Mrs. Oliver came downstairs, cuffed the culprit and made it howl more loudly and shooed the other two in front of her with indignant looks at the girl who stood her ground.

'Go on, kids,' she said. 'Go on up to yer own stinkin' 'ot place. Not good enough fer the likes of them, you aren't. Let me tell you, Miss 'Igh an' Mighty Clurey, as things is changin'. You've 'ad your day, you an' your sort, and it's our turn now. Less than vermyne – that's wot 'e calls you, and e's about right too. He, he, he! Vermyne, that's wot 'e says you are,' and she disappeared up the stairs, leaving dirt and bits of stick, one or two broken toys and some ice-cream papers for the Clureys to pick up.

Alison collected them distastefully, felt furious when she saw how much of the mosaic had been picked out, and wondered if she could find a rug to hide the depredations before Giles came. There was certainly no time to fit the pieces in again, even if they did not have to be cemented.

Raucous sounds came from the living-room which had to serve the Clureys for both sitting- and dining-room now that each of the three children had to have a separate bedroom. The original drawing-room had been turned into a bedroom for

Helena and Simon, the three younger members of the family occupying the three bedrooms on the first floor with the Olivers on the floor above them.

Alison opened the door. Though it was used for so many purposes and the furniture was shabby and the carpet threadbare, this room was always home to them all, untidy and cluttered and beloved. At one end of the table, littered with books, John Clurey sat with his pencil between his teeth, one hand ruffling his thick fair hair into still greater disorder whilst with the other he beat time to the 'melody' blaring from saxophones and drums.

'Hullo, ducks,' he said as his sister came in. 'Been having fun with the Olivers?' the vernacular for the constant warfare.

'Fun, do you call it?' asked Alison wrathfully. 'Johnno, it really is the limit, isn't it? Can't we do *anything* about them? After all, it is supposed to be our home, though nobody would think it from the way their horrible brats are always littering up the place. What *can* we do?'

'I could always organise a fire and burn the place down,' suggested John blithely.

The ubiquitous Olivers did not worry him as much as they did the rest of the family. At thirteen, he had far more interesting things to think about, and he and his contemporary cronies even derived a considerable amount of pleasure from baiting their unwanted tenants and working out ingenious ways of making their life uncomfortable for them.

There were seven years between him and Alison. There had been another girl in the gap who had died in infancy, secretly mourned after sixteen years by Helena, and Brian, the eldest, was twenty-two.

'That would leave us without even this apology for a home,' said Alison. 'I'm absolutely sick of them and their beastly kids and the smell that comes out of what they call their flat is enough to give us typhoid or something. Not that I suppose it will matter to me much longer.'

'Why not?' asked John suspiciously, for the Clureys were a

devoted and united family and none of them had ever suggested going away.

'I'm going to be married,' said Alison, trying to make it sound off-hand without succeeding.

'Golly! Not to the Caraway Seed?' he asked, goggle-eyed.

'I do wish you wouldn't call him that. It's rude, to say the least of it. His name is Paraway, and you know it Giles Paraway.'

John gave a whistle.

'But, Allie, you can't! He's old.'

'He's not old, though of course he's older than I am. I can't stand *boys*,' said Alison hotly.

'No, but there's a difference between what you call boys and the Cara—I mean, Paraway. What do the parents say?'

'They don't know—yet. But I'm nearly twenty-one anyway, and in three months I can do what I like.'

'I know, but—I mean—they wouldn't like that a bit, marrying someone they don't like.'

'How can they not like him when they haven't even met him?

'It's only because they know he's older than I am that they have made such a fuss about my going out with him. Anyway, they're going to meet him. I've asked him to supper.'

'When?'

'Tonight,' said Alison defiantly.

'Golly. That will about tear it. Do they know?'

'Not yet. Where's Mum?'

'Out shopping with Aunt Ruth.'

Alison stretched out a hand and turned off the wireless.

'How you can do your homework with that row going on I can't imagine,' she said.

'It helps me to think. Besides, there's a Sinatra record coming on after this.'

'That crooner,' said Alison contemptuously.

John laughed and burst into a loud, tuneless song about his baby.

'I suppose you imagine you've got what Sinatra's got,' said his sister scathingly.

'Well, haven't I? And what's more, I've got poisonality, Sister. Poisonality! The stuff that makes women swoon,' spreading himself over his books with his hands stretched out and his eyes rolling.

'You'd make them swoon all right,' retorted Alison, going up to a picture on the wall, a print depicting a lurid battle scene, and turning it over to reveal another picture on the other side, that of a calm, pastoral landscape far removed from thoughts of war.

The picture was one of the family jokes and was constantly being turned from one side to the other, according to the various tastes in art.

John grinned and returned to his homework.

'I say, Allie, if it takes ten men working for fifteen hours a day three days to dig a trench thirty yards long, how long would it take half as many men to dig three and a quarter times as much?'

'Can't be done.'

'Gotta be done. It's my homework.'

'Still can't be done. Twenty thousand men would go on strike if *one* man worked fifteen hours a day, let alone ten men. Sure it doesn't say ten *women?*'

'I'm not going to get involved in any sex argument,' said John loftily.

'Johnno, be a sport Nip upstairs and clear up the bathroom and the whatsit, will you? It's sure to be in a foul mess—and bring the key down with you so that the Olivers can't get in there again.'

'What are they going to do?'

'They can use the outside one for once. Better take another packet of paper up too. Their kids use it for drawing paper or something. There's never any there. What's for supper?'

'Fish, I expect,' said John disgustedly.

'I wonder we don't all grow fins. Here's a new packet,' taking one out of the cupboard in the corner.

'If I do, will you help me with my 'rithmetic?'

'Oh all right, if I've got time.'

'Why, what time's the Caraway Seed coming?'

'John, you're to stop calling him that! The name's Paraway—
Mr. Paraway to you.'

'I might as well start calling him Giles if he's going to be
joined to the family in holy wedlock. Do you think he is?'

'I don't know—yet. I think so. Yes, I'm sure. I've definitely
made up my mind about it, whatever the parents say. Johnno,
don't be mean tonight, will you? Don't make things more
difficult for me by any of your silly jokes. I suppose you wouldn't
like to go to the pictures?' hopefully. 'There's a ghastly-looking
thing on at the Regal, all blood and gangsters, right up your
street—judging from the posters. Have one and ninepence on
me.'

'If you're trying to bribe me, young sis, it'll be worth more
than one and ninepence when he's actually coming here.
Besides, I've seen it. It's jolly good. Hardly anybody left alive in
the end.'

A tap at the door interrupted them, and it opened to admit
Mrs. Oliver's frowsy head.

'Hullo, kiddies. Mummy not in?' she asked, as if there had
been no fiery altercation between her and Alison a few minutes
ago.

They glared at her.

'No,' said Alison frigidly. 'Do you want something, Mrs.
Oliver?'

'No. 'Salright. I'll pop down again when yer mum comes in.
It's a bit o' liver Mr. Speed let me have and we've still got a bit
of the joint left over so I thought yer mum might like this,'
showing them a revolting-looking parcel done up in newspaper
with the blood oozing through it.

Neither of them offered to take it.

'We don't eat liver,' said John aggressively.

Mrs. Oliver gave a little laugh and shook her finger at him.

'Naughty, naughty! I saw yer mum buying some last week, so

I know that's one of your little jokes, Johnno—'

'The name is John if you *have* to use it,' said the boy stolidly.

'Oh well, I'm almost one of the family as you might say,' laughed Mrs. Oliver. 'I do 'appen to know as yer dad dotes on a bit o' liver. Never mind. I'll pop down again presently. I'm sure to 'ear yer mum come in.'

'We can count on that,' said John rudely.

'Oh, aren't you a one?' said Mrs. Oliver, taking her reluctant departure and leaving the door open behind her.

John shut it with a bang.

'Poisonous old baggage—and I could say worse,' he said.

'Now, now, little man!' said Alison, wagging her finger at him in imitation of the departed visitor. 'Remember that you're not at the moment at the school where they specialise in turning out perfect little gents!'

'She's a dog's wife. Wish we could think of some way of getting rid of them. Why doesn't Dad just chuck 'em out and see what happens?'

'Can you imagine Dad chucking anyone out? They'd only have to tell him a hard-luck story for him to give them our part as well.'

'Well, I'm bagging your room after you—' began John, going out into the hall.

'Ssh! There's Mum,' said Alison quickly, as the key turned in the front door.

Mrs. Clurey came in, weighed down by a heavy basket, her elegantly dressed sister behind her.

'Thank heaven I'm home!' she said. 'That you, Allie darling? Dad's not in yet, I hope?'

'No, only John and me,' said Alison, taking the basket from her.

Helena caught sight of the packet in John's hand as he started up the stairs.

'Oh, no!' she said. 'Not another packet! Why, I put one in there yesterday. What on earth do they do with it?'

'I expect she's saving it up for Christmas presents,' grinned

John. 'Hullo, Aunt Ruth. Do you want to have first go, or will you go out to the back?'

Ruth Mallow laughed.

'Get away with you, Impudence,' she said. 'How badly you bring your children up, Helena,' but the tone and the glance that accompanied it showed that she was very partial to her sister's children, specially John.

'What on earth have you got in here, Mum?' asked Alison, carrying the laden basket into the living-room.

'My dear, that's what made me so late. They were selling tins of fruit at Galloway's and there was a dreadful queue. My feet are simply killing me!'

'All for a tin of fruit!' said Alison. 'As if it mattered! Sit down and I'll get your slippers. I suppose you haven't had any tea either?'

Her tone was affectionately bullying and Helena Clurey smiled at her lovingly. As if she wouldn't half kill herself for a tin of fruit or anything else that meant pleasure to any of her beloveds.

'Yes, I have,' she said. 'Ruth simply insisted on taking me into the new tea-rooms. They're quite nice, though the girls are a bit B.B.C. Thank you, darling. That's lovely,' wiggling the toes which Alison had freed from the shabby shoes which had not been a good fit even when new, but they had been marked down in the sales.

'She wouldn't let me send for the car,' said Ruth Mallow, stretching out her own beautifully shod feet and admiring the set of her very sheer nylons.

'It would have meant Hump getting home by tube,' said Helena.

'That wouldn't have hurt him for once. I don't believe in spoiling men,' said Ruth serenely. 'As for that wretched tinned fruit, I told you Hump could get you as much as you wanted.'

'Yes, on the black market and at a price,' retorted her sister.

'Idiot. Hump wouldn't have charged you more than you paid in the shop.'

'Well, you know what Simon feels about black market things,' said Helena.

'Then why tell him? I never tell Hump what it isn't good for him to know. Don't turn into a prig, Hel.'

'Oh well, we've got the fruit anyway,' said Helena.

'And at the price of your feet. How you survive your sort of shopping is a mystery to me. I should be dead, standing in those queues and then carting all the stuff home with me. I telephone for what I want and have it sent.'

'If I did that, I'd miss lots of little things you never even know about,' said Helena.

'So what? I'm not turning myself into the domestic beast for anybody. They say an army marches on its stomach, whatever that may mean, but no husband's stomach is going to march on me. Besides, I keep the shop people sweet with a little bit of baksheesh at the right time and I don't think I miss much.'

Ruth smoothed down the skirt of her immaculate grey suit with a contented air.

'For one thing, I couldn't afford all those tips,' said Helena as Alison fitted her second slipper on her, 'and even if I could, Simon wouldn't like it. You know how he is about tipping. He says it is degrading to the human species either to give or receive tips, quite apart from the attempt it makes to get more than one's fair share of either goods or service.'

'Oh well, thank heaven I'm married to a man without principles,' said Ruth cheerfully. 'The odd half-crown is a wonderful easer of life's burdens, and Simon ought to be able to afford it now, with Alison off hand and Brian getting himself this wonderful job.'

'He hasn't exactly got it yet,' said Alison, 'but of course he will. It's been promised to him, privately, if nothing goes wrong, and it can't very well, can it? He really did pass top in the exam, and there's nothing that can go against him in his reputation or anything. I mean he isn't a communist or anything.'

'I should hope not,' said Ruth. 'When are you going to set the Thames on fire, young Johnno?' as the boy came back into the room and hung the key he had purloined on a convenient nail.

'Me? Never,' he said disgustedly. 'I'm sick of hearing what a wonderful brother I've got. Blah, blah, blah.'

Alison laughed.

'Jealous, little man?' she asked, and was rewarded with a cushion flung at her head.

'Now children, children,' laughed their mother. 'Johnno, put your books away, there's a dear.'

'I haven't finished my home-work.'

'Well, you must finish it after supper. I want the table.'

'What's for supper?' he asked, not averse to the delay.

'As if you didn't know! Fish,' said Helena, getting up to go into the kitchen.

'Oh, Mum, isn't there anything else? Just for tonight?' asked Alison.

Her mother gave her a surprised look. Alison rarely bothered about what she ate.

'Why, darling?' she asked.

'Well—Mum—if it's all right with you,' said the girl, colouring nervously, 'I've asked someone to supper.'

'Oh, Allie, who?'

'It's—Giles, Mum. Mr. Paraway."

Helena stopped short.

'I wish you'd told me before, dear,' she said with a little frown. 'I'd have made a special effort, got a hare or something. Must it be tonight?'

'I've asked him, Mum. I thought it'd be all right—and the fish will do quite well. He's not a bit fussy."

'Then he's different from most of the genus man,' said Ruth briskly, which comment Alison ignored.

'I'll manage then,' said Helena. 'After all, everybody lives on fish nowadays. I can scrape up enough fat for a few chips and make an apple tart.'

'Chips. Good egg,' said John. 'Can I have about six pounds all to myself?'

'As many as I've got fat for if you peel and chip them

yourself,' said his mother, and he threw the rest of his books into the bottom of the cupboard and took himself off to the kitchen whistling, pausing to turn the picture round as he went.

'Do you mind if I go and tidy myself first, Mummy?' asked Alison, absently turning it back again. 'I'll set the table when I come down. May we use the best cloth?'

'Of course, dear—and see if there are enough clean table-napkins whilst you're upstairs.'

II

'NICE child,' said Ruth when Alison had gone. 'If I'd had to have children, Helena, I'd have chosen your lot, though of course Brian is the outstanding one. Where did he get all his brains from? Not from our side of the family, and though Simon's a dear, you can't say he's a genius.'

'Perhaps not, but he's the way I like him,' said Helena. 'Could we have peas with the fish, do you think?'

'Personally I hate vegies with fish, but people do all sorts of things nowadays, so I should think so. It'll help the fish down. Shall I shell them for you? I needn't rush off for a few minutes.'

'No, sit down and talk to me. You'll mess yourself up. Just let me get a basin and I'll do them in here.'

'You want a new suit yourself, old dear,' said Ruth when they had settled down again, Helena with the basin and the bag of peas in her lap.

'I know, but at the moment it's more important for Simon to have one – I can wait,' said Helena serenely.

'You know, Hel, there are things about your life, most things in fact, that I simply couldn't stand. All those children—'

'Only three, dear,' laughed her sister.

'And always being short of money and all the work you have to do. Look at you now, tired out and with a dinner to get ready. You're a slave to them all—and yet somehow I always feel that you and Simon are the only two people I know who've really made a go of marriage. Of course Hump and I get on all right. That's to say we don't quarrel *all* the time. He goes his way and I go mine and we don't threaten to divorce each other more than about once a week, but you and Simon have got something.'

'Could be love,' said Helena quietly, smiling a little.

'Story-book stuff. After twenty-odd years?'

'Perhaps it's because we're very ordinary people and we've never asked or expected perfection from each other, and neither of us has tried to own the other, body and soul, as some married people do. And we've shared everything, the bad things and the things we have to go without as well as the good things, even the work! Simon would never think of just throwing himself down in a chair when he comes in unless I can do the same, though of course I don't save up anything I can get done during the day. He even does the ironing with me! I think that makes a lot of difference to a marriage, the little things, the sharing. We weren't married in a church, you know, but he would never have had to swear he'd cherish me and all that because he's done it, always.'

'You don't look very cherished to me at the moment,' said Ruth drily, and Helena smiled again.

'But I am,' she said softly. 'I think one thing that's helped is that we've never tried to be different from what we are. Most people choose a husband or a wife because they admire them as they are, and then as soon as they get married, try to change each other into something quite different. Simon and I like each other as we are—but no one could help liking him as he is. For one thing, he's so—tolerant. He believes in people too, and that's a big thing when you live with it, always to be believed in, to be given the benefit of the doubt, if there is any.'

'Yet you didn't marry him for love, did you?' asked Ruth suddenly.

Her sister looked up sharply, startled.

'What makes you think that?' she asked.

'My dear Hel, I've always known that it must have been Mother who fixed up the marriage for you and got you safely tied up to someone *she* thought suitable for you. So respectable, my dear! And such good connections! Though I can't believe that even Mother, all that time ago, could have known just how good your connections were going to be.'

Helena frowned.

'I don't want to think about that,' she said. 'I prefer to pretend that it can never happen.'

'You can't shut your eyes to it, though. It's bound to happen. I even saw something in the paper about it the other day.'

'Why on earth can't they let us alone?' asked Helena crossly.

'You can't expect them to. It's the silly season for newspapers. No major war on at the moment, and the gossip writers have to find something to say, and after all, when it does happen, they'll have plenty to say. Obscure solicitor's clerk becomes a baronet and all that.'

'It does annoy me so much that they've managed to tack all that on to Brian's success,' said Helena. 'It's his own achievement, and it's nothing to do with Curtis and that rubbishy title. It detracts from what he's done himself. Besides, we don't want the title. It's too ridiculous for people like us to have it.'

Ruth laughed. She was faintly envious of this thing which her much more unworldly sister would have liked to repudiate.

'Well, when Sir Curtis Clurey dies, you'll get it whether you want it or not. What a pity Mother isn't alive. She'd have loved it. She couldn't possibly have known that three in succession, *three* mark you, would be wiped out so as to leave the way clear to Simon, but can't you imagine how she'd have fluffed about it and taken the credit for having got you married to a future baronet? Sir Simon Clurey. Sounds quite nice, doesn't it? I don't care what you say, Helena. I *know* you weren't in love with him when you married him, though I've never been able to understand how you let yourself be married off like that. You were always the pretty one, and you had dozens of much more attractive and marriageable men than Simon after you. Do you ever look back on those days, Hel? The fun we had! I always remember one man in particular who used to hang around you. Geoffrey Something. What was it? Pullen? Pullet? Pellet! That was it. Geoffrey Pellet. Remember him?' with a reminiscent smile.

Helena stooped to pick up some pea-shells that had fallen to the floor.

'What on earth made you think of him?' she asked.

'I don't know. He just came into my mind, thinking of those days. You were quite besotted about him, weren't you? And Mother simply wouldn't hear of your getting engaged to him, though when Hump and I got married and went out to India, you swore to me that you were going to marry him and come out to us for your honeymoon. And then, blow me, the next thing I knew was that you'd married Simon Clurey of all people! I could never make out why.'

'It could be because I wanted to,' said Helena.

'Boloney! You were potty about Geoffrey Pellet and you couldn't have fallen out with him and in with someone so completely different as Simon, all in a few months. Do you know what I always thought?'

'No, and I don't particularly want to. After all, it's ancient history. Nearly a quarter of a century ago.'

'Heavens, don't talk in centuries! What I think is that Geoffrey let you down and Mother pushed you off to Simon on the rebound. The miracle is that it's all turned out so well. You may love old Simon now, and I honestly believe you do, even after being married to him all this time. That's fantastic in itself! But I'll never believe you married for love.'

'Does it matter, anyway?' asked Helena. 'I've been so happy with him that everything that happened before we married seems to have happened to someone else, not to me at all. All I know is that not for a day or an hour have I ever regretted marrying Simon and—oh well, why are we getting girlish and lyrical about it? Simon and I have made a good life together, and a happy home for our children, and that's all there is to it.'

'Well, as I say, it's marvellous,' said Ruth, fitting a cigarette into a long holder and lighting it. 'I expect you actually *prefer* Simon to any other man you know, after twenty odd years!'

Her sister laughed.

'You're a cynic, Ruth.'

'I'm married to Humphrey Mallow, my dear, and that's

enough to turn any woman into a cynic. I wish I were the one coming into the title and the Clurey estate. I mean—for you—' looking round the homely, littered room with the unmistakably frank appraisal of a sister.

'I know. You don't have to tell me. It *is* absurd—me with the chores to do and a basket always hanging on my arm or an apron round my middle. Lady Clurey! Lady Sink would be more appropriate.

'I suppose the children know?'

'Yes, though we never talk about it and of course we none of us know Sir Curtis and we've never been there. When his second son died, he wrote to Simon and asked him to go, but he wouldn't. There was still the third son, the one who was killed in the air crash, and we couldn't see the point of going. As Simon said, they'd never taken any notice of us before, and he wasn't going rushing off to The Holt to be looked over in case the unbelievable happened, as it did happen afterwards.'

'And he didn't ask you again?'

'No. We wrote, of course. One had to. It was such a terrible tragedy, losing all three of his sons like that. But he didn't reply, though Simon had a letter from the solicitors. I believe the poor old man went slightly mental. Who could wonder? I always hoped he would marry again and have another son, but he didn't.'

The door came open suddenly. It was Mrs. Oliver again.

'Oh, you *are* in, dear?' she asked. 'I didn't 'ear you come in, but as you know, I never like to push my nose in w'ere I'm not wanted. Good evening, Mrs. Mallow, and 'ow are *you*? I believe I caught sight of that naughty 'usband of yours the other day, but don't ask me wot 'e was doing or with'oo because that would be tellin'!' with a roguish smile.

Ruth gave her an icy stare.

'Indeed?' she asked.

Mrs. Oliver bridled and coloured.

'Of course it's not my business,' she said primly.

'I couldn't agree more,' said Ruth, and picked up a newspaper.

'Did you want something, Mrs. Oliver?" asked Helena.

'This bit o' liver," said Mrs. Oliver, offering the even gorier parcel. 'I wondered if you'd like it. Mr. Speed smuggled it over the counter to me, and as I'd got a bit of me joint left, I thought to myself, "That'll just do nicely for Mrs. Clurey," I thought and I popped it into me basket—'

Helena took it gingerly and put it down on the table on a folded newspaper.

'That was very kind of you,' she said. 'How much do I owe you?'

'Oh, I couldn't dream of takin' anything, just between friends,' gushed Mrs. Oliver. 'Wot's a bit o' liver between you and me? You take it, dear.'

'Thank you, Mrs. Oliver, but naturally I wish to pay for it,' said Helena firmly, taking some money from her bag. 'Will this be enough?"

Mrs. Oliver snatched at the money in high dudgeon.

'Oh well, if that's 'ow you feel about it, of course,' she said.

'I do,' said Helena. 'Did you want me for anything else, Mrs. Oliver?'

'Oh no. No, not at all, I'm sure,' said the woman, and retired with obvious reluctance, leaving the door open behind her.

Helena got up to close it with a sigh.

'If ever I have to live at The Holt, the one thing I'll be glad about is getting shot of the Olivers,' she said.

'My dear, they'll be dropping in on you even there, their livers clasped in their hands,' said Ruth. 'It's a good thing Sir Curtis doesn't live just round the corner, or I bet she'd pay a social call on him, for of course she knows. That sort always do.'

'I simply can't imagine myself living anywhere like The Holt,' said Helena. 'In fact, when death duties are paid, I doubt if there will be enough left. I've no idea whether there's much money there or not, but if I ever do live there, there will be one thing I'll be glad not to have to do—make beds and wash up. I shan't mind popping a duster over my tiara and rolling up my velvet and old lace whilst I put a spot of polish on the ball-room floor if only someone will wash up and make the beds. There, I've finished the peas and I should think John's done as many potatoes as even he can eat by this time,' and she went into the kitchen with her basin.

As she did so, Alison reappeared to have her frock fastened at the back.

'Go in and ask Aunt Ruth, dear,' said her mother. 'My hands are messy and I must start the fish. Perhaps I can cheer it up with a nice sauce. What time did you tell Mr. Paraway?'

'Supper at eight, I said. Mummy, it *is* all right, isn't it?'

Helena managed a rather twisted smile.

'Of course, dear, so long as we don't let you down. You know we've been wanting to meet him.'

Alison gave her a little hug.

'You're a darling,' she said.

Ruth looked her up and down appreciatively.

'That's nice,' she said. 'Your mother and I have been reminiscing. *We* used to put on blue when we had a new beau coming. Gracious, the child's blushing! How enchanting! I didn't think any girl could blush any longer. What's he like, this Giles of yours? You did say Giles?'

'Yes. Giles Paraway. I suppose you couldn't stop for supper, Aunt Ruth?'

'Good gracious no. I gather that the fish will only just go round as it is. Why do you want me particularly?'

'Well, you're—you're a bit more—*worldly* than the parents are. It might make it easier for him, and for me.'

Ruth laughed.

'I suppose I am to take that as a compliment, but what is wrong with their other-worldliness in this affair? Don't you think they're going to like him?'

'That's just it. They don't want to like him. You see, he's older than I am. That's absolutely the only thing they could possibly have against him because they don't even know him.'

'How much older?' asked Ruth.

'Well—quite a lot. Aunt Ruth, it doesn't matter. I mean, I

couldn't possibly get on better with anyone than I do with Giles and I've never liked *boys*,' infusing a world of disdain into the word. 'They seem—well, sort of half-baked. Giles is so finished.'

'You haven't told me how old he is,' Ruth pointed out.

'Well, round about forty,' admitted Alison reluctantly, though she knew that he was in fact forty-six, 'but not a bit like forty really.'

'Well, if he isn't "finished" at forty, it's quite time he was. My dear, forty's much too old for you, twice your age, in fact. I don't wonder that the parents don't feel too keen. What is he? Who, I mean?'

'I don't quite know, except that it's something to do with finance and he always seems to have as much as he wants to spend. He's got two cars, for instance.'

'Mm. Not been caught by the glamour of that, have you?'

Alison flushed, annoyed.

'Of course not. I'd feel just the same about him if he hadn't a penny and we had to go by bus everywhere. I didn't think you'd be beastly about him, Aunt Ruth. I thought you'd stick up for me.'

'Well, that's a tall order without seeing the man or knowing anything about him. Naturally I want you to make a good marriage, not a hole-and-corner affair, living in a rabbit hutch and doing your own chores the way your mother's always had to. You don't have to marry a man twice your age, though, to escape that fate. Doesn't it occur to you that before very long you'll be in the sort of position where you'll meet all sorts of new people, different men?'

'You mean if Sir Curtis Clurey dies?' asked Alison distastefully.

'I mean *when* he dies, and that can't be long. Alison, my dear, hold your horses for a bit, especially if the parents disapprove of this man when they've met him. Does he know, by the way?'

'About Sir Curtis, you mean? Yes, he does.'

'Did you tell him?'

'No, he seemed to know.'

'Mm. How did you meet him, by the way?'

'He came to the office. He had some business to do with Mr. Mackerley.'

'And made a pass at the typist?'

'You make it sound rather beastly. It wasn't a bit like that. Mr. Mackerley had to keep him waiting and we talked and he told me about some pictures he'd seen—'

'Movies?'

'No, some by a new French painter. Gardet. Do you know him?'

'No, my love. I'm profoundly ignorant about painters, other than the house variety. So he took you to see them?'

Alison nodded, a faraway smile coming into her eyes.

Ruth got up from her chair and began to gather her effects together.

'So that was that,' she said. 'And he knew already about Curtis Clurey?'

'I don't like the way you keep saying that,' said Alison with spirit. 'As if a potty little title and whatever the Clurey estates are worth could matter to a man like Giles!'

Ruth Mallow gave a deprecatory smile.

'Sorry, Allie dear, but you know how down-to-earth I am and my general opinion of men. There's no reason in the world why he should not love you for yourself alone. You're pretty enough. You know, you're exactly like what your mother was at your age. We've just been talking about our young days before either of us got married.'

Alison's face was still mutinous and withdrawn.

'I hope you won't put ideas about Giles into their heads,' she said. 'It's bad enough without that.'

Ruth patted her cheek.

'There, there, my pet. As if I should do anything to hurt you or make you unhappy! You've always been my favourite. All I want is for you to be happy. Now I must fly. Forgiven me?'

Alison submitted to her kiss without returning it. If she had to fight them for her love, she would fight them all.

After her aunt had gone, she went into the kitchen.

'Can I help you, Mum?' she asked, but her face and voice kept her mother at a distance.

'No, dear, except by setting the table. Luckily I could get brill today and I had a tin of shrimps so I can make a shrimp sauce.

'Had we better start with soup? I could furbish up something from a tin.'

Alison's face began to change. Helena looked hot and worried, her hair, only a little darker gold than her daughter's, straggling wispily and her still neat figure encased as ever in a much-washed overall.

'You're being so sweet, Mum,' said the girl. 'No, of course we don't need soup. The fish will be lovely the way you do it, and Giles isn't a fussy sort of person at all. Mum—you will try to like him, won't you?'

'Darling, you know we shall do our best,' said Helena. 'You know how we feel about him, though, don't you? Being in love is so marvellous when you're young, and we want you to have the best, to have someone's first love. You know how unlikely a man so much older than you—I mean, dear, there must have been women in his life before. What' do you really *know* about this Mr. Paraway? Is he a widower or—or anything?'

'Or divorced, you mean?' asked her daughter with the calm candour of her generation. 'No. No, he's never been married and though I dare say it isn't easy to believe, there really hasn't been anyone in his life before. He waited to meet me,' with a sweet turn of her voice that twisted Helena's heart.

The young in love are so terribly vulnerable!

'All we want is your happiness, darling,' she said gently, 'and if he can give you real happiness, what is there for any of us to worry about? Better set the table now so that it'll all be ready when he comes. Daddy's a bit late, isn't he?'

'He may have had to wait for a bus. Can't you leave things now and get yourself dressed? I want you to look nice.'

Helena laughed.

'Get along with you. I won't disgrace you in front of your Giles. You wouldn't like us to put on evening dress? I doubt if

Daddy's will meet round him now, and mine's pre-war—'

Alison joined in the laughter and hugged her mother.

'He'll adore you whatever you wear,' she said, 'but don't take that literally and appear in that ghastly overall. Wear your brown.'

'As it's that or the overall, I probably shall! Go and set the table, my duck. I've raked out the best cloth and run an iron over it and there are just enough plates without chips or cracks.'

Alison gave her another brief hug.

'I'm so lucky to have you for a mum,' she said. 'We mustn't forget to get Johnno washed up at the last minute.'

Helena was just finishing her rapid toilet when she heard her husband come in and called out to him from their bedroom.

'That you, dear? Have you had a bad journey home?'

'No, I was kept a bit late. Tell you presently. My, my!' coming into the bedroom and seeing her in her best dress. 'Have we got a date?'

He was a small man, scarcely more than Helena's own five-foot-three, inclining a little to corpulence in his middle forties, his greying hair receding at the temples, his grey eyes twinkling with kindliness. That, most people felt, was the keynote to Simon Clurey's character, sheer human kindness. There was nothing distinguished about him, nothing clever beyond normal intelligence, nothing even remotely good looking, but he had friends wherever he went and nobody had ever heard another say a bad word about him.

He put his brief-case down on the bed and gave his wife a husbandly kiss and then stood back to admire her.

'Yes, I'm afraid we have got a date,' she said.

'We haven't got to go out?' he asked, dismayed.

'No. Someone's coming. Alison's friend, Giles Paraway.'

'Hm,' was Simon's only comment. 'You look very nice, my dear. Have I seen that dress before?'

She laughed.

'Only about fifty times. It's the one Ruth gave me for the birthday before last. Shall I wear my Ciro pearls, do you think?'

trying them round her neck.

'I think so,' he said, fastening them for her. 'Sorry they had to be imitation, dear. I've always thought how much I'd like to be able to give you real ones.'

'These are just as nice, and I'd be terrified of losing real ones,' she said contentedly. 'Am I all right? I don't want Allie to be ashamed of me.'

His kind eyes wore their special smile for her.

'She couldn't be that, ever,' he said. 'The only thing she need worry about is that he might fall for the mother instead of the daughter. When you take a bit of trouble over yourself, it's incredible that you should have grown-up children. You look about thirty. Even less.'

'That's arrant flattery,' she said, laughing, but she took another look at herself.

At forty-one, though there were faint lines in her face, her bright hair showed no dimming, and she wore it short for convenience and speed. It set naturally in smooth waves close to her head, deeper gold than her daughter's and her eyes a deeper blue. There was less strength, though, than Alison's face revealed. Her chin was less determined, her mouth softer under the small amount of make-up which Alison insisted upon and had shown her how to apply.

'I'm not looking forward to meeting the fellow, but I suppose it's about time we did,' said her husband. 'Do you think I ought to shave again?'

'I don't think you need do that, but I should put on the other suit, and one of your best shirts,' said Helena.

He grinned.

'Funny to be dressing up for one of the kids' friends,' he said. 'I suppose Brian will be the next. I caught sight of him the other day handing a rather luscious-looking peach into a taxi, but I didn't tell him I'd seen him.'

'I hope she was young, anyway. Alison's so anxious for us to like this man, but I'm sure we shan't, not a man of his age. She says he's forty, so I expect he's a bit more. It's all wrong, Simon!

She's so *young*, not only in age but in herself, so young and fresh. I can quite believe that he's in love with her, but what colossal cheek to want to *marry* her! What can he possibly have to give her which could compare with her quite heart-breaking youth and innocence?'

'I feel just the same about it, but I don't see that there is anything we can do. If we don't have him here or let her see him openly, she'll only be forced into an underhand affair with him. The best we can hope for is that she'll think better of it the more she sees of him. By the way, they rang me up from The Holt today.'

She gave him a look of consternation.

'Simon! Whatever for? Nothing's happened, has it?'

'No. Curtis is obviously not going to get any better, though. It was his solicitor. He's making a new Will and he wanted some details. He thinks I ought to go down, but as I told him, it's very difficult just now with that big case we're working on, the Hind business. I said I'd go as soon as I could.'

'Poor dear, you're going to hate that. The whole thing's upsetting. Why do we have to have this forced on us when we don't want it? Why couldn't it have been somebody who would really enjoy it? Ruth and Hump, for instance. Ruth would love to be 'my lady' and she'd look the part.'

'Nobody would look it better than you, love,' he said tenderly. 'The one thing that makes it at all acceptable to me is that at last I shall have something to give you.'

'Oh, Simon—dear Simon!' She put her arms about his neck and laid her cheek to his. 'As if you haven't given me everything in heaven and earth already! What more could anyone give me than what we've got? Each other, our home (most of it anyway!), the children. No woman was ever richer.'

'Thank you for that, darling. I feel that, too, but I'd like you not to have to work so hard, to have a little more fun, and clothes and things.'

'What about you then? Do you think, Simon, that if Curtis does die and we get The Holt, you can give up the office?'

'Depends on what's left when the Treasury have had their rake-off,' he said. 'Anyway, the old boy's not dead yet, so it's a bit gruesome to be making plans. Which shirt shall I put on?'

'I've put one out for you. I'd better go and finish off the meal now. Fish, of course.'

She was glad to have her mind occupied with immediate matters. A few months ago, a few weeks even, life seemed to be so pleasantly set along the familiar channel, the contented monotony of so many family lives, not too much money but enough to live on without extravagance. Simon had been for many years with a good firm which would eventually pension him, and Brian, after winning a scholarship to Cambridge, was working for a science degree. Alison was heart-whole and care-free, whilst Johnno – well he was just Johnno, healthy and grubby, noisy and rather idle like most thirteen-year-olds, and she, Helena, looking after them all, was the heart and the hands and the feet which had made their house a home.

And now?

There was this almost certain change for Simon, who, as Sir Simon Clurey of The Holt, in Hampshire, could scarcely go on being Galton, Somerley and Co.'s head clerk; Brian had come out so brilliantly in his examination that he had been offered an imposing job in a Government Research Department and Alison was mixed up with this Giles Paraway, a man old enough to be her father; and she herself, Helena Clurey, would be turned into 'her ladyship', which seemed to her fantastic and absurd. She saw herself turned out of her beloved home and thrust into a position where she would feel insecure and ridiculous. Even Johnno would be touched by it, for it would cut across the fierce friendship with his bosom pal, 'Stinky' Morris, whose father was a local greengrocer but who, in these levelling-off days, had won a scholarship to the school where Simon had to pay fees for John.

The raucous shouts of John and his pal at the bottom of the garden reminded Helena that she had better get him cleaned up, and she went to the kitchen door to call him in.

'Can Stinks stay to supper, Mum?' yelled John, climbing down from a tree and unconcernedly tearing his shorts.

He seldom employed the quieter tones of his voice. He would have been a welcome guest in a house of the deaf. In an ordinary household he was overpowering.

'Good heavens, no. There's scarcely enough fish to go round as it is—and no second helpings, mind.'

'But I'm starving, Mum!' he objected.

'You'd better have a few slices of bread and marg first then, to take the edge off. There's some peanut butter, if you want it.'

'Good egg. I say, Mum, fancy the Caraway Seed coming! Bit of a lark.'

'Now, Johnno, behave yourself, won't you? Don't make Allie ashamed of us. It's so important to her.'

He grinned. He was no Adonis, and he had a broken front tooth and more than a sprinkling of freckles, but Helena felt a sudden rush of affection for this, her youngest. Here as yet was no problem. All he needed was plenty of food and soap and water.

She gave him a little hug, her brown dress protected by the overall again.

'Bless you,' she added to her adjurations. 'You're such a comfort to me!'

He stared at her, submitted somewhat reluctantly to the hug and pulled himself free as quickly as possible.

'That's all right, Mum. I'll be careful,' he said. 'Cross my heart,' and he was away up the stairs, whistling loudly.

'Don't use my towel!' called Alison as he passed the door where she was carefully setting the table. 'Mine's the pink one, yours is the filthiest one. And don't use the clean one I've just put out either!'

'All right. Keep your wig on,' said John, and at that moment the door-bell rang.

'Oh, Allie! I'm not quite ready,' said Helena, appearing at the kitchen door. 'You go. And keep this door shut. I'll be in in just a few minutes. I'm in a dither!'

Alison gave a little excited laugh and prepared to go to the door.

'Everything will be all right. You'll see,' she said, and the kitchen door closed as she opened the front one.

Giles Paraway came into the hall, glanced round and then took her in his arms.

'Not too early am I, sweetness?' he asked against her lips.

'You couldn't be. Oh, darling, it's so lovely to have you here, so lovely!'

He set her free and produced some flowers, a great sheaf of pale pink roses in the cellophane wrapper which proclaimed their quality.

'I've brought these for your mother,' he said.

'Giles, how thoughtful of you! She'll be thrilled. She won't be a minute. Put your hat and coat here, will you? We don't possess such a thing as a hall cloak-room. Come in here,' opening the door of the living-room. 'This is the room we live, move and have our being in. I told you we didn't live on a grand scale, didn't I?'

'But this is just what I'm craving for,' he said, going with her into the now tidy room, the litter of books, sewing and various hobbies pushed away out of sight and the table inviting with the lace-edged cloth and sparkling glass and cutlery. 'This is what I've never had. A home. A home!' he repeated softly, his deep voice taking on one of the cadences which made the heart turn in her breast.

'Darling,' she said softly, 'to think that *I've* got something to give *you*!' and she nestled against him, her head on his shoulder.

It was like that that Simon Clurey, coming in from the bedroom, saw them.

He frowned instinctively, his usually kind and gentle eyes wearing an almost ferocious expression for a moment. The wolf stealing into the fold to snatch his lamb, his best-beloved of the three, though he always tried to hide the fact. Then with a resolute effort he threw the feeling off and came forward. Giles Paraway, seeing him across Alison's bent head, smiled and gently released her, going to her father with outstretched hand.

'Mr. Clurey?' he asked, and there was a note of slight, amused surprise in his voice. 'Why, we've met! Do you remember me?'

Simon Clurey knit his brows in thought for a moment before he shook his head regretfully.

'No, I'm sorry. Should I?' he asked. '*Have* we met, Mr. Paraway?'

Giles laughed ruefully.

'I'm not feeling flattered,' he said lightly, 'but indeed we have. In the offices of Galton, Somerley and Co. I had some business with one of the partners who happened to be engaged, and as the matter was somewhat private, I waited in your office That was—oh, some weeks ago now.'

Simon began to remember, vaguely. Though there was a comfortable waiting-room at Galton Somerley's, important clients were often put into the head clerk's room to wait, but Simon, always busy and absorbed, took little notice of them.

'Yes, I—I believe I do remember,' he said. 'Stupid of me. Anyway, may I atone for it by making you very welcome, Mr. Paraway? What about something to drink, my dear?' turning to Alison, who had watched the little scene in some confusion, not knowing whether it would further her cause or not.

'Of course, Daddy,' she said at once and went to the sideboard cupboard with little hope of finding anything there that would come up to the sophisticated tastes of Giles Paraway. All she was likely to find would be a bottle of inferior port, part of whose contents had been left over from the previous Christmas, and possibly some 'cooking' sherry.

'There's not much here,' she said with an embarrassed laugh. 'We're not drinkers, I'm afraid, Giles. There's some port of the variety called "style" and the sherry Mummy puts in a trifle.'

'My dear, we've still got a bottle or two of that very excellent sherry your Uncle Humphrey gave us for Christmas down in the cellar,' said Simon. 'Just a minute. I'll get it,' and he opened the door into the hall.

'No, Daddy, not you,' said Alison quickly. 'Those steps aren't safe. You know you nearly fell down them last time. I'll get Johnno. John's my younger brother and a holy terror,' looking at Giles with a smile, 'but even he has his uses! Johnno!' calling up the stairs.

'Hullo,' responded John's voice from above.

'Johnno, we want something from the cellar. A bottle of sherry,' she called.

'Right ho! Coming,' and he arrived at a great speed down the banisters, extremely clean for once, his hair plastered down with what Alison rightly concluded was her setting lotion. He grinned at Giles, who responded with an equally friendly grin.

'This is Alison's friend, Mr. Paraway,' said his father. 'John, my younger son. John, go down into the cellar, will you? I believe there are still one or two bottles of Uncle Humph's sherry down there.'

'Yes. Two,' said John, the only member of the family who had intimate knowledge of the dark and fearsome catacomb under the house from which at one time overworked scullery maids had lugged up buckets of coal far too heavy for them. For years now it had been left to the spiders, who had been sharing it temporarily with Humphrey Mallow's sherry.

'Be careful,' said Simon anxiously, as the boy took the key which Alison had in her hand and opened the little door under the stairs. 'This house suffered a little from bomb damage towards the end of the war,' he explained to Giles, 'and though the War Damage Commission enabled us to do the repairs, for some reason their generosity stopped short at the cellar steps, which I've never myself renewed. Some of the steps are just not there, but you see how my son overcomes what is rather a difficulty to the rest of us!' as John detached one end of a rope which was hanging inside and swung on it, monkey-like before sliding down it out of sight.

Giles laughed.

'I should say he was not unduly disturbed at the niggardliness of the War Damage Commission,' he said. 'The Government's gift to boys!"

Alison, still keyed up, loved him all over again for the easy way in which he accepted what must, to him, seem an odd way of life.

'There are actually the remains of the steps,' she said, 'but we don't like Daddy going down them, and John loves it, so why spend money on repairing them?'

'Why indeed?' echoed Giles with a smile for her. 'Ah, here comes the returning adventurer,' as John's head reappeared, followed by his body with the dusty bottle sticking out of one pocket.

His father retrieved it hastily before it could fall.

'Better dust yourself down, old man, before your mother catches sight of your best suit,' he advised him. 'Allie, get the glasses, will you, dear? I'll lock this dungeon up again.'

Whilst Giles strolled back into the living-room, followed by the superficially dusted John and in a moment or two by Simon, Alison popped her head round the kitchen door.

'Nice smell,' she said. 'Mum, we've got a bottle of sherry out of the cellar and Daddy says get glasses. How many have we got?'

Mrs. Clurey looked up from the sauce which she was stirring, a considering light in her eyes.

'Let me see. There are two in the sideboard cupboard, and I've got one out here that Daddy takes his medicine in, and—I expect I can rake out another. That makes four, and Johnno can have orange squash in a tumbler. Go back to them, darling, and I'll just take off my overall and bring the two in with me. I'll have to wash them.'

She set the now finished sauce back from the heat, covered it carefully, and washed Simon's medicine glass and a small tumbler which would have to do. After all, if this man Para way was going to become a member of the family (which God forbid!) he would have to get used to a shortage of unnecessary things.

Then she took off her overall and, with the two glasses on a small tray, opened the door into the living-room.

'Oh there you are, my dear,' said Simon, going towards her to take the tray from her hand.

But he was too late.

The first thing she had seen as she opened the door was Giles Paraway.

For a second she remained rooted to the spot, the glasses sliding across the tray as it tilted in her hand.

Then it fell with a little crash of breaking glass, and amongst the shattered fragments, Helena herself dropped to the floor in a dead faint.

III

RUTH MALLOW, returning to the very comfortable home provided for her (gratis and for nothing, he sometimes told her) by her stock-broker husband, found her mind still caught back into the days when she had still been looking for a rich husband and Helena for the fairy prince of her dreams.

What really had happened to throw lovely, innocent, romantic Helena into the arms of Simon Clurey, very prosaic, unexciting arms which had yet held her fast for nearly a quarter of a century? How long? Twenty-two years? No, must be twenty-three because the newspapers, congratulating young Brian on his outstanding success, had given his age as twenty-two.

Of course, she herself had stuck to her own husband even longer, but then poor old Hump had always had something to give, something solid and enduring and extremely comfortable by way of his business acumen, which brought in even during the lean years of war enough to maintain his wife in the state which she expected and demanded. He had done more than that. Long out of love with her himself, but liking an untroubled life outside business hours, he had closed his eyes and ears to various little indiscretions which had kept life pleasantly endurable for her throughout the years. So long as she ensured the discreetness of the indiscretions, with none of the public gossip which might affect his private relations with desirable people, he harboured no resentment against her, having his little bits of fun himself if he so desired.

Yes, she reflected, it had been an easy and comfortable affair, her marriage with Humphrey Mallow – so completely different from the way poor Helena lived with Simon and three brats.

How *had* that started?

It had started on the day Helena left school, not quite eighteen years old and far less than eighteen in experience or knowledge of life.

Pauline Thorwell (pronounced Thorrel, she was accustomed to say when having to write it down) was a woman who knew what she wanted and intended to have it, and from her nursery days Helena had been the one singled out by her for a 'good' marriage. Ruth, three years older, had had none of the fragile, wild-rose beauty of the younger sister. Ruth was tough both in appearance and in fibre, dark-haired, with glinting brown eyes which could look almost as black as sloes, and a tongue which at school had earned her the sobriquet of Ruthless.

Ruth, decided her mother, could practically be left to look after her own future, with the modicum of guidance into the right channels so that she met the right sort of man – by which Mrs. Thorwell, pronounced Thorrel, meant men all set for financial success. She herself had been left a widow on a small pension whilst the two girls were still at school, Ruth fifteen and Helena twelve, and she had struggled, using up her capital, to pay their school fees at an expensive school and to send each in turn to the exclusive finishing school in Lausanne to which, in the still affluent days of the late nineteen-twenties, other girls in a similar social position to that of Admiral Thorwell's widow went.

'You must meet the right people from the start,' she had told Ruth when they were working out the ways and means necessary to let her have her year there and keep Helena another two years at her expensive school.

Ruth had agreed. She was as determined as her mother that she would make a financially successful marriage. She had hated the economies which had to be practised in order to keep up appearances after her father's death and had not the least intention of subjecting herself to such a regime once she had a home of her own.

After she came home for good, Mrs. Thorwell strained her dwindling resources to the point of exhaustion to provide her with a London season. The wife of an old friend of the Admiral's presented her to the Court of King George the Fifth.

'I shall never be a beauty,' said Ruth, surveying the effect of her court panoply, 'but I hope I shall never have to look as idiotic as this again. Helena will look marvellous, of course, but by that time I hope I shall have got myself married and relaxed.'

'You look very distinguished, dear,' her mother tried to console her.

'Distinguished by my long nose and blackberry eyes, and my legs too long for my body,' said Ruth, giving a vicious little kick to her train. 'Well, come on. Let's go.'

It was some months after that that Ruth spoke of the man she had almost made up her mind to marry.

'How much do you know about Humphrey Mallow, Mother?' she asked thoughtfully.

Mrs. Thorwell glanced up from her embroidery frame.

'Mallow? The Downshire Mallows?' she asked.

'I think so. Could you find out about them?'

'Of course. Has he asked you yet?'

'Not in so many words. I don't think he knows yet that he's going to,' said her daughter with a laugh. 'It's at a stage when I can bring it on or fend it off.'

'I'll find out,' said Mrs. Thorwell.

'Don't be too long. He's the sort to go like a bull at the gate once he sees the gate and I want to get fixed up before there's any chance of Helena arriving to queer my pitch. I want her kept out of sight until I'm at least engaged, if not actually at the altar.'

'Of course, dear,' her mother agreed readily. 'I'll find out about the Mallows at once. Have I met him?'

'Yes. He was at the Cressets' the other night—big, clumsy brute, thick fair hair, nose a bit flattened. Probably done a bit of boxing.'

'Oh yes. I remember,' said Mrs. Thorwell with heightened interest, for the large young man had come with the Aubyns, and Terence Aubyn was one of the young men whom she thought might do nicely for Helena. He would get the title eventually, and his father had had the good sense to marry an American who had brought a dowry of dollars to prop up the fine old property she was marrying.

Her inquiries about Humphrey Mallow proved satisfactory, however.

'Yes, he *is* the Downshire Mallows, my dear,' she told Ruth. 'Not the least possibility of a title there. He's too far away. But there's plenty of money. His father and two old aunts have most of it at the moment, but it will all come to him under various Trusts. I believe he works at something too.'

'Yes, on the Stock Exchange,' agreed Ruth. 'In spite of his looks, he's got a flair for that sort of thing and will make money on his own, though of course it's always a comforting thought that there's money behind him which he won't have to make. I think perhaps I'll have him, Mother, if it's all right with you.'

'I don't really think you'll do better,' advised Mrs. Thorwell. 'As you say, you want to get settled before Helena comes home—not that I should pick out anyone like Humphrey Mallow for her.'

'Quite. The trouble is that there isn't a great deal of choice nowadays, with all the taxation and death duties and so on which leave the real old families with nothing, not even their homes or their ancestors' portraits. Still, with Helena's looks, surely you'll be able to get *something* worthwhile?'

'I hope so, though she won't be too easy. Perhaps I've made her *too* unsophisticated? She's really quite shy and gauche. I can only hope Lausanne's done something for her,' with a sigh.

Ruth got her Mallow. She was already engaged to him by the time Helena arrived.

Helena, with three other girls under the care of Sister Marie-Claire, had a newspaper cutting about the engagement in her bag.

She had left their reserved compartment already three times during the short train journey between Folkestone and London, and Sister Marie-Claire was a little worried.

'Are you sure you are quite well, Helena?' she asked. 'Did you eat something at lunch perhaps that did not agree?'

'Oh no, Sister. Everything at lunch agreed with me very well, thank you,' said Helena, colouring a little with excitement and enjoying her small private joke, for meeting Geoffrey Pellet had been one of the things which had been very agreeable at lunch. The other three girls and the little nun had all been affected by the rough crossing, but Helena was a good traveller and had no wish to spend the time in the private cabin reserved for them. Besides, she had a healthy appetite and had no intention of missing her lunch, so though Sister Marie-Claire was aware that she was neglecting her duty in allowing one of her charges to go out of her sight, especially to eat alone in a public room, she was too ill to do anything about it. Besides, Helena Thorwell had always been one of the quietest and most trustworthy of the twenty 'young ladies' in the convent finishing school.

So Helena went off to find the dining-saloon, pleasantly conscious of this first step towards emancipation from school thraldom, and had taken her place at one of the rows of long tables indicated by the steward. Though there were a great many empty places, a young man came to take the chair opposite hers, and as they were alone at the table, it was difficult not to allow herself to be drawn into conversation with him.

He was an extremely good-looking young man, tall, slim, with nice dark hair which had a wave in it, a sunburnt, lean face and very white teeth revealed by his ready smile. She was not quite sure what they had talked about, but afterwards, greatly daring, she had stayed on deck with him to watch for the first signs of the white cliffs until, with the boat beginning to slow down and to indulge in a series of hoots, she had declared her urgent necessity to join 'the others' and had fled down to the cabin where Sister Marie-Claire, unsteadily on her feet again, was relieved to see her.

The young man was on the train. She could not believe that he was actually *waiting* for her, but the fact remained that when Sister Marie-Claire had ushered her charges into the compartment, there he was in the corridor just outside where Helena was sitting, and the gesture of invitation he made was unmistakable.

That had caused her first discreet withdrawal from the compartment, and the second one, and the third one, and now the fourth one which had drawn the anxious questioning from the nun.

This must be the last time, she decided regretfully, but as it would not be long before they reached the terminus, it would be the end in any case.

'Sister Marie-Claire's having a fit,' she informed him when she found him waiting, as before, in the corridor of the next coach. 'I shan't be able to get out again.'

'Meaning that this is the end?' he asked, and the tone of his voice set her romantic young heart racing madly.

'It'll have to be,' she said in a whisper, forcing her eyes from the compelling gaze of his.

'Not unless you want it to be. You don't even know my name, do you? It's Pellet, Geoffrey Pellet. And yours is what? Angel? Titania? Aurora?'

She laughed.

'How absurd you are! Nothing so romantic, of course. It's Helena Thorwell, though it's spelt T-H-O-R-W-E-L-L. Look, I'll show you. My sister sent this yesterday. It's a cutting from one of the evening papers,' and she produced it from her bag.

He studied it. The newspaper reproduction did not do either of them justice, making Humphrey Mallow look even more like a prize-fighter and Ruth Thorwell more like a witch, but the letter-press underneath left no doubt of their identity.

Miss Ruth Thorwell, daughter of the late Admiral Lessway Thorwell, and of Mrs. Thorwell, with her fiancé Mr. Humphrey Mallow.

That's really why I'm going home,' said Helena. 'I'm supposed to stay at school until I've actually had my eighteenth birthday, but I'm going to be Ruth's chief bridesmaid and it would be silly to go back for just a few weeks afterwards, wouldn't it? I'm looking forward to it. Mother's going to spread herself with a wedding at St. George's and a reception at Claridge's. It'll be fun.'

He digested this piece of information, looked again at the newspaper cutting and again at Helena's piquant, wild-rose face, charming in spite of what her almost nun-like garments did to her. The Reverend Mother insisted on her young ladies wearing clothes like this whilst they were under her care. Helena's long navy blue coat hid her shape just as the pull-on felt hat hid the soft golden mop of hair, but Geoffrey Pellet had eyes which could pierce such disguises.

They had pierced it in Helena's case.

It was absurd and fantastic and incredible, he told himself, that he should be falling for this raw little schoolgirl, her feathers still damp from emergence from the egg, and yet he knew he was in imminent danger of doing so – especially when he found that a paragraph in the newspapers and a wedding at St. George's, with a reception at Claridge's, were part of her social background.

'I shall have to go back or Sister Marie-Claire will be coming to look for me,' said Helena nervously.

'When am I going to see you again—Helena?' he asked, and as he spoke he covered with one of his big, beautifully kept hands the one with which she was holding the rail along the side of the corridor. She gave an instinctive little jerk as if to resist it. Then she let it stay there. She had never experienced any feeling at all akin to this. She wanted it to stop and wanted it never to stop.

'When, Helena?' he insisted.

She lifted blue eyes to his, childlike eyes and yet eyes in which was the faint dawn of the woman.

'How can we?' she asked unhappily.

'We can if we want to. Do you want to, Helena?'

She nodded her head and looked away from his eyes.

Then tell me how. Look, I'll write down my telephone number – and my name in case you forget it. You ring me up and tell me where you will be at some certain time, in the park, or a picture gallery or a museum or somewhere. If I'm not in (I live in rooms at this address), the housekeeper will take a message. You need not give your name, if you don't want to, but she is very discreet. You will, won't you?"

'If—if I can.'

'No, that isn't enough. Of course you can if you really want to. Promise me?'

After another moment or two of hesitation, in which the thought of her home, of her mother, of Ruth, passed through her mind, she gave another nod.

'All right,' she said desperately, 'I will.'

'That's a girl. You will—who? Say my name, Helena. I keep saying yours.'

'Geoffrey,' she said shyly, and he smiled, squeezed her hand and let her go.

Back in their compartment, the others were arranging their hand luggage.

'Ah, Helena, you are come,' commented the little nun. 'I think you must tell Madame your mother that you are a little deranged, isn't it? She will give you perhaps some chlorodyne. Chlorodyne—that is how you say it? It is for this derangement the best.'

'Yes, *ma sœur*,' said Helena meekly, but her heart danced.

Chlorodyne as a cure for romance! And who, at not quite eighteen, wants a cure for that?

For that was what Geoffrey Pellet was to Helena – Romance with a capital R with long, luscious curves to the letter and a tail that wandered on, away into the future, into the delightful, rose-coloured mists that veiled that wonderful vista.

Romance.

She had no idea how she was going to elude the watchful eye

of her mother who, against all the trend of a modern age of feminine advancement, believed in the guarding and cherishing of a young girl, especially one who looked like Helena, until she had safely been led to the altar (in St. George's, of course) and handed over intact, with the bloom still unimpaired, to someone approved of, picked out for her if possible, by that watchful guardian.

But for once Mrs. Thorwell was too much engrossed in her elder daughter's affairs to be always on the watch, and Helena managed to elude her, finding it actually quite easy.

'Helena, you'll simply have to go for your fitting without me today,' said her mother with a worried frown two or three days after the girl had come home. 'I must be here when Humphrey's aunts come to call but it won't matter if you're not. I'll send for a taxi for you and it can wait and bring you back.'

The Thorwell domestic economy did not run to a car and this was not an occasion when Humphrey's could be put at their disposal.

'That'll be quite all right, Mother,' Helena assured her gaily, and as soon as the taxi was out of sight of the house, she signalled to the driver to stop by a telephone call-box.

'I shan't be a minute,' she said as she popped into it and took from her bag the cherished scrap of paper with Geoffrey's number on it.

He was in, and delighted to hear her voice.

'I've got to go to the dressmaker's for a fitting,' she told him, 'but it need not take long and I could meet you somewhere for about a minute.'

'Good. I'm glad you only say *about* a minute. Where will you be?'

'Berkeley Square.'

'All right. Do you know where Cook's is? You can't miss it, anyway. I'll go into the entrance hall there now and wait for you. Don't be long.'

'Absolutely no time,' she told him blithely, and found so little fault with her bridesmaid's dress of pale hyacinth blue organdie that in less than ten minutes she was outside again and almost running in the direction of Cook's.

He was waiting for her, and her heart gave a leap at sight of him. She had been faintly worried in case she should be disillusioned when she saw him again, but she need have had no fear. There he was, tall and handsome, immaculate in town clothes, his smile as charming, his manners exquisite even to Helena who was used to good manners.

He did not make it awkward for her by asking, as so many men do of their women, 'What would you like to do?' or 'Where shall we go?', nor would she have had any answers to such questions. Where did one go with a man at three o'clock in the afternoon?

He signalled a taxi, put her into it and gave the driver his instructions.

'Where are we going?' she asked, intrigued.

'The British Museum,' he said.

She chuckled.

'What on earth for?' she asked.

'It's one of the most wonderful places in London to be alone in, except for the various officials loitering about and they don't take any notice if you don't ask them questions. You'll see. Lovely to be with you again, Helena. How do you feel about it?'

'The same,' she said shyly. 'I mustn't be very long, you know. I'm supposed to have kept the taxi waiting so as to get home immediately my fitting was over, but I got through that in such quick time! I told Mrs. Lander (she's our fitter there) that everything was lovely – perfect – not a stitch or a line to be altered, and was out again like greased lightning.'

'So you can spend with me only the time you might reasonably have spent being awkward with your dressmaker?' he asked in mock chagrin.

'Oh well—only about that time,' she said, 'but there could have been a hold-up in a traffic jam, couldn't there?'

He laughed and took her hand in his, peeled off its glove and put its palm against his cheek.

'You're very sweet,' he said, and that was the fatal moment for Helena Thorwell, perhaps the most fateful moment of her life, for in it she passed out of her own keeping and into that of a stranger to her, another self she had not known dwelt inside her, a wayward, passionate woman who in that instant changed all the rules and values by which so far her life had been guided.

She was in love with Geoffrey Pellet.

He had been right about the privacy of the British Museum for lovers at their stage of loving. In one of the deserted rooms, flanked by tall glass cases of whose contents she had not the least idea, they might have had the whole vast place to themselves. Sundry officials knew they were there, but as their only duty was to see that no one did any damage to the treasures under their care, or perhaps to direct inquirers to some other part of the museum, they had no wish to interfere, and this was by no means the first couple who had come here for the sole purpose of being together.

So, protected by the treasures of the ages, Geoffrey Pellet and Helena Thorwell talked a little, laughed softly, and presently, unable any longer to be with this lovely, enchanting girl with no closer contact, he put an arm around her and drew her to him, lightly, easily so as not to frighten away the thing that was being born in her eyes, born for him.

She started to draw away from him, her breath coming quickly, but he held her with his light pressure and she stopped struggling, though her eyes were frightened.

'No—no—you mustn't do that,' she said.

'Why not? I'm not going to hurt you and you know what's happened to us, don't you? Don't you, Helena, you utterly enchanting thing?'

'No,' she said with a little gasp, but she did. She knew what had happened to her, anyway. She had fallen in love.

'But you do know,' he insisted. 'We're in love—in love, my darling!'

'We can't be. We don't know each other. We've only just met.'

'How much does that matter? I think I knew the first moment I saw you. That's how it happens, Helena, when it's real. Two people meet, they see each other, across a crowded room perhaps, and they look into each other's eyes and he says, "This is the one", and—what does she say? What did your heart say when you saw me? You know, don't you? You for me, and I for you. Isn't that how it happened? It had to happen some time, somewhere, and we are two people to whom it's happened so soon, whilst we're still young, whilst we've still got all life in front of us. Suppose we hadn't met now, hadn't met until we were years older, one of us or both of us already married to someone else? It does happen. It's always happening, and people are so helpless when it does. But not us, my little beloved. For us it's all loveliness and happiness.'

She was only vaguely aware of what he said. She was listening to his voice, the deep tones of it which seemed to draw up the threads of her very being until he held them in his hand; she was aware of his arm about her, of his masculinity which had invaded and conquered her world of women and was making her aware that that had not been her world at all but only the outer atmosphere in which she had lived and dreamed and waited – waited for this.

Only the very young can have these thoughts, know this enchantment, before reality brings unbelief and doubt and cynicism.

She scarcely knew she turned her face towards him until she felt his lips on hers, very gently, and lightly, touching them and letting them go.

'Geoffrey—Geoffrey,' she whispered, intoxicated by her own joy.

That was the beginning of it. But it was not the end, as at first Geoffrey Pellet had intended it to be, for he soon found that the totally unpredictable had happened to him and he, too, was in love, wholly and madly in love.

In years he was twenty-three, five fully-lived years more than her eighteen years of dreaming unrealities, and his first experience with a woman had been when he was sixteen and the middle-aged wife of his employer had seduced him in the room at the back of the little shop where he was supposed to be selling books, toys, and cigarettes. Since then he had tasted many joys of the kind, but he told himself that this was the first time he had been genuinely in love, the first time he had desired anything of a woman but her warm, willing body in bed. He had become too much of a connoisseur to enjoy the sort of furtive fumbling and quick, wary consummation into which he had been initiated on the broken-springed couch in the grubby room behind the shop.

But it was exciting to know that he could feel for a woman as he felt for Helena, that he could desire more of her than just a momentary possession.

They met as often as she could devise it, and as Mrs. Thorwell became more and more wrapped up in Ruth's wedding preparations, it became increasingly easy. Not being officially 'out', she was debarred from many functions which took Ruth and her mother away for long hours at a stretch, dinner-parties, dances, the opera, or one of the unending visits to Humphrey's enormous family ramifications.

'I'm afraid it's terribly dull for you, darling, being left alone so much,' said her mother, 'but once the wedding is over, I'll make it all up to you. You'll see. We'll be on our own then, just you and I, dear.'

'That's quite all right, Mother. I don't mind a bit, really,' Helena assured her with perfect truth.

'There may be something nice on the wireless, dear,' said Mrs. Thorwell, who never listened in.

'I dare say there will,' agreed Helena – but she seldom knew it if there were.

Mrs. Thorwell had had to import one or two additional servants during this busy time, with its bout of entertaining, but they had quite enough to do, they assured themselves and one another, without worrying what Miss Helena was doing. She gave them so little trouble when she was in that they never knew if she went out, and she was far more careful than Cinderella about getting in again.

They quickly grew beyond the British Museum stage. He managed to acquire a small sports car, tenth-hand and dilapidated and not very reliable, and in it they roamed into heaven itself, into the country-side so close to London for those who knew where to find it, or further afield or even as far as the coast when she knew there was enough time. And with every hour spent with him, love became overwhelming, the one real thing in a world of the useless, unimportant matters which did not contain Geoffrey.

Yet, deeply passionate as she showed herself to be, he found there was an impassable barrier set against the full possession of her which he so ardently desired. In the midst of her ardour for him, the sixth sense that is in women warned her and drew her away from him physically and mentally. He realised that, desire her as he might and experienced though he was, there was a strong fibre of resistance in her which would never yield to him except through marriage.

And how could he marry Helena Thorwell? Because Ruth's marriage was a comparatively important one, Humphrey having good social connection and no lack of money, Geoffrey had an exaggerated idea of the Thorwells' position and was under no delusion about the place to which he would be relegated if he were openly to aspire to marriage with Helena.

He had long risen above the shop which had provided him with his first job after leaving the grammar school which could in no way compare with the sort of schools to which people like the Thorwells sent their sons. Endowed with a flair for seizing an opportunity when it presented itself and for squeezing out of it its every possibility, he had been successively a clerk in the office of a small suburban newspaper, to which he had contributed (secretly and without the knowledge of his employers) such 'copy' as he had been able to find or even invent, a free-lance journalist making a speciality of sporting events not covered by bona-fide 'regulars', and an assistant in various capacities at a greyhound racing establishment. At the time of meeting Helena, he had even acquired two dogs of his own and a small share in a horse which, if it would never win the Derby, yet brought in various small sums in prizes and much more substantial gains by careful betting against it. His recent visit to France had been in connection with this, and at the moment he was in possession of a somewhat precarious means of livelihood from such sources, though he told Helena glibly that he was 'in the city, financial, you know'.

Helena did not know, did not care.

When the date of the wedding was only a few days off, she conceived the idea, long nagging at her mind, of introducing him into her own circle so that when the opportunities afforded her by her mother's preoccupation were over, she could still see him.

'Will you come to Ruth's wedding, darling?' she asked him, cuddled up as close to him as she could get whilst he drove homewards from a magical day at the sea.

Her hair was still wet, and she was letting it dry in the wind, its soft tendrils blowing every now and then against his cheek and firing to still greater heat his desire and need for her.

'But how could I? They don't even know of my existence,' he said.

'I'll send you an invitation card. I know where they are, in Mother's bureau. You'll have to have one because there will be a crush, and everybody's asked to show their tickets. Will you, Geoffrey? Please, darling, please!'

'Well, if you think it will be all right,' he said doubtfully, though for some time now he had been wondering whether it would be possible to get into the Thorwell circle. He did not really believe that they would ever let him marry Helena, but he believed in the long shot. One never knew what might come of it.

'Of course it will,' she said happily. 'I'll send you a card and tell you all about what to do and so on. It will be rather a grand affair, you know,' with a furtive glance at the grey flannels and old sports coat which he usually wore for their outings.

He caught the glance and grinned.

'Don't worry, sweetheart,' he said. 'I shall know what to wear and I promise I won't let you down.'

She laughed, embarrassed but relieved. How silly of her! Of course he would know.

She stole an invitation card with great ease and sent it to him, inserted his name unobtrusively into the long typed list which the typist from the bureau had prepared, and put against it the mark which meant that the invitation had been accepted, and warned Geoffrey not to ruin her careful work by accepting it himself.

He complimented her on her manoeuvres.

'I couldn't have done better myself,' he said, smiling.

'It's rather awful of me,' she admitted. 'It's not really a bit like me to deceive Mother, and if it were for any less worthy cause, I might feel a bit ashamed of it. I know it will be all right, though, once Mother has met you. She won't be able to help loving you.'

Geoffrey was not so sure, but he didn't say so, and when he caught his first glimpse of her, radiant and like a flower in her hyacinth blue gown, he was determined to have her, whatever the obstacles. She was, he thought, the loveliest thing in all that galaxy of beauty, real and artificial.

Ruth had said so too, rather ruefully, before they set out for the church.

'Nobody will look at me once they have sighted you, you fiend,' she said, though she was certainly looking better than she had imagined she could herself look in her bridal white.

Helena, peeping about her on her solemn way up the aisle behind the long train of satin and lace, saw him and allowed herself the ghost of a smile. As if she might for one moment have doubted his ability to outshine all other men! Moss Brothers had done well for him, though they had told him regretfully that all their best outfits had already been allocated, and his attire as a wedding guest was beyond reproach.

The moment came when she had to present him to her mother, however, for it was no part of her programme that this golden opportunity should be lost, and she enlisted her new brother-in-law's aid.

'Hump, be a darling,' she said, seizing a suitable moment. 'I'm going to introduce someone to you. Will you introduce him to Mother without mentioning me? Look, he's over there, the tall man talking to the woman in brown. His name's Geoffrey Pellet.'

Humphrey laughed.

'What are you up to?' he asked. 'Who knows him?'

'I do. His name is Pellet, Geoffrey Pellet. Oh, Hump, will you?'

'All right, but don't get me into anything, will you? Fetch him over.'

It was not quite as simple as she had hoped, however, for once the introduction had been made, she could not bring herself to leave Geoffrey's side for long, and later in the day, when all the wedding guests had gone and she and her mother were alone in their own house again, Mrs. Thorwell referred to him.

'Darling, who was that man Pellet?' she asked. 'I had a few words with Humphrey and Ruth about him, but they were quite vague and I don't think they really knew him at all. How did he get there?'

'He must have been invited,' said Helena, 'mustn't he? I liked him, didn't you?'

'You made it only too obvious that you liked him,' said Mrs. Thorwell with an edge to her voice. She was very tired and was suffering from the inevitable reaction and she had been annoyed with Helena. 'What I want to know is, just who is he?'

'He—he's in the city, I think,' said Helena vaguely, but she was too inexperienced in the art of dissembling to hide from her mother a suspicious embarrassment.

'Well, you must be careful not to make yourself conspicuous on future occasions,' said Mrs. Thorwell severely. 'I must ask

Humphrey when they come back what he knows about him, as of course it is very important for you not to make wrong contacts or get yourself associated with the wrong sort of man. You're very young still, but girls marry young nowadays and one cannot be too careful. I asked several people, very discreetly of course, but nobody seemed to know him.'

Geoffrey did all the right things, called with his card and flowers for Mrs. Thorwell, and at his second visit was shown into the drawing-room, where he stayed only the conventional ten minutes or so and devoted his attentions to the mother rather than to the daughter.

But whatever might have been Helena's hopes, and her assurances to Geoffrey, it was quite clear that his entry into their circle of friends was not to be encouraged. Mrs. Thorwell had managed to keep her daughters in a guarded seclusion as far removed as possible from the emancipation she regretted so deeply, and Helena was too newly released from the thraldom of school to take her life and her pursuits into her own hands. Nothing, however, would stop her from seeing the man with whom by now she was so wildly in love that nothing else was of any importance in her life. She existed for the snatched hours she could spend with him, and it was impossible that her constant manoeuvring, her unexplained comings and goings and her frequent absences, could for long escape her mother's notice.

When Mrs. Thorwell discovered that her daughter was having a clandestine affair with the man of whom she was already suspicious and disapproving, the storm broke in earnest and Helena was whisked away into the country and told she would have to stay there, in the house of an intensely disliked aunt, until the London season opened again and she could be officially 'brought out'. Mrs. Thorwell had had regretfully to decide that Helena could not be presented at Court, as Ruth's wedding had left her with too straitened means for all that a court presentation would involve, but as this was no longer an absolute essential, Helena would have to do without it. Fortunately, with her looks, it should be easy for her to make a good marriage, by which her mother meant marriage to a man of birth *and* means.

In vain Helena protested. Mrs. Thorwell was adamant.

'You will stay with Aunt Alice at least until Ruth has more time and can help me to look after you since you are so regrettably unable to look after yourself.'

'It's quite unfair, Mother,' said Helena hotly. 'You've nothing against Geoffrey at all, except that he isn't connected with the one or two families *you* like. You've got an early Victorian outlook. Nobody bothers nowadays who other people are, so long as they're decent and can behave properly.'

'You're very young and very foolish, my dear,' said her mother. 'The fact that birth and breeding are no longer essential as an *entrée* into some of our best homes and families need not influence what I choose to do, and I do not choose to have my daughter running about with a man of whom nobody knows anything at all, not even what he does for a living. Once and for all, this friendship is *over*. I forbid you to have anything further to do with this man. Please understand that.'

She wrote despairingly from Aunt Alice's dull house in the country, popping out late at night to post her letters at the box at the corner of the road and intercepting the postman every day before he could put the letters into the box at the front door.

It's too absurd and old-fashioned (she wrote angrily). *Mother lives a century behind the times. Fancy shutting me up here as if I were a Victorian daughter and you the Local Villain! But she won't keep us apart, darling. She can't. Nothing can. Somehow I shall be able to see you, in spite of her. Perhaps when I see Ruth again, we can think of something.*

But when she did see Ruth, it was to learn that she and Humphrey were going to India, partly on a visit to some of his relations but chiefly in connection with a big business deal which, if it came off, would be very considerably enriching.

Helena poured out to her all the tale of Geoffrey, but Ruth was preoccupied with her own affairs and did not want to be involved in those of her sister. Also, she was in full agreement with her mother on the advisability of any girl brought up as they had been choosing a husband with care and not as a heart-throb only.

'Of course I don't know anything about him,' said Ruth, 'and he may be all right, but what does he *do*? What is he? Who is he? You can't just chuck yourself away like this, without an idea what sort of landing you're going to make. I should hang on a bit. See what else comes along.'

'You're pretty beastly, Ruth, considering that you've married the man you wanted,' said Helena miserably.

'My dear child, I didn't go all gaga over Hump as you seem to have done over this man. I looked him well over first and when I decided he came up to the mark in the more important things, I let myself get fond of him. You're doing it the wrong way round.'

'How cold-blooded you are, Ruth! Aren't you in love with Hump at all?'

'In love? My dear! I've told you. When I found he came up to standard, I let myself get quite fond of him. It's just as easy to be fond of the right man as the wrong one, and there are lots of men just as attractive as Geoffrey Pellet and much more marriageable.'

'I shall never love any other man. He's my whole world and if I don't marry him, I shan't marry at all. I might even go into a convent,' said Helena dramatically, who had only just thought of that as a possible threat if they still tried to keep her apart from him.

Ruth laughed.

'Not you, my dear,' she said. 'Besides, you'd soon create such havoc amongst the priests that they'd be only too glad to get rid of you again. Now don't be an idiot, Hel. I'll tell you what. As soon as Hump and I get settled in Bombay, why not come out to us on a visit? Hump will pay your fare. There are sure to be heaps of eligible men out there to make you forget this man Pellet, and I'll vet them first for you.'

'If I do come out, it will be for my honeymoon with Geoffrey,' declared Helena, a statement which her sister brushed aside with a sceptical laugh.

To her disgust, Helena was sent back to Aunt Alice as soon as the Mallows had sailed, and it was then that she first met Simon Clurey.

IV

SIMON CLUREY, who was twenty-two, had been articled by a benevolent uncle to a London firm of solicitors, but when it became apparent that he would not pass the necessary examinations, he had been found a job with a slower-moving country firm and conveniently forgotten. He was the sort of quiet, painstaking, reliable young man who, though he might never get very far, was invaluable as a solicitor's clerk. His parents were dead, and the uncle who had paid for his education felt he had done all that could reasonably be expected of him, and he plodded comfortably along with no definite thought of the future until Helena Thorwell broke on him like a burst of sunshine out of a dull sky.

They met at a church bazaar. Helena, left in charge of her aunt's stall, was trying to sell the usual collection of useless embroidery and hideous knitted garments whose purpose she could not begin to divine. She had, however, been doing a brisk trade with the men who had been dragged there by their womenfolk against their will and who had gravitated to her stall like needles to a magnet.

Simon knew who she was. He had seen her vaguely in church, but she had not been laughing and sparkling as she was now and this was the first time he had really *seen* her. He had been given a job selling tickets for the sideshows, but had been relieved for a few minutes and had wandered out aimlessly amongst the stalls.

'Have you come to buy?' Helena asked him when he paused, irresistibly. 'Could I sell you this, for instance?' holding up a large woolly garment. 'Don't ask me what it is, but I feel it must be male.'

He did not look at the garment but only at her, dazzled and lost.

'You're Miss Thorwell, aren't you?' he managed to stammer at last. I'm Simon Clurey,' though he had no idea why he should think her interested in his name.

'Do you live in Bickford?' she asked, for the sake of something to say.

'For the time being. I'm with Prentiss and Co. The solicitors, you know.'

'Oh, I know. My aunt goes to them. Is that how you know me?'

'No; I—I saw you in church once,' said Simon, his fair, freckled skin colouring uncomfortably.

Miss Alice Thorwell wrote to her sister-in-law a few days later to say that Helena had made the acquaintance of . . .

quite a nice young man, Simon Clurey. No money at all, but there are excellent family connections and I think the friendship might be good for the child. He seems a very steady, sensible young man and not at all likely to lose his head or get her involved in anything. It will be years before he is able to think of marriage, so I do not think any harm can be done by allowing the friendship.

Mrs. Thorwell made a flying visit to Bickford and with Alice's connivance managed to meet young Simon Clurey and agreed entirely with her sister-in-law's opinion that there could be no possible danger to Helena in the friendship.

In spite of that conviction, however, Simon, head over heels in love for the first time in his life, asked Helena if she thought that at any time, even in the far distant future, she would ever be able to marry him.

She had a moment of panic, almost as if the very suggestion that she might be persuaded to marry someone else heightened the barrier between herself and Geoffrey. Then she refused him, gently.

'It's terribly nice of you, Simon,' she said, 'but I really don't want to marry anybody, not for ages anyway.'

'I know, but I can wait. I'm good at that,' he said with his slow, kind smile which, to her great annoyance, always did something to her, something which Geoffrey, with all his charm for her, could not do.

When her mother came down again she listened to another discourse on her future whilst keeping her secret safe.

'There is no objection to your seeing this young man Clurey,' said Mrs. Thorwell, 'but don't encourage him to think you might marry him. It's a pity he is such a remote off-shoot of the family that he has no money at all and no hope of any, as the Clureys are a good family with an old baronetcy. I know I must sound hard and calculating, Helena, but my own experience of life has shown me quite clearly that the life of the wife of a poor man in this country is no sort of life for a woman. To be without money is sheer misery for a girl brought up as girls are in our circle, and I have only your best interests and happiness at heart when I try to guard you against what I know would mean misery for you. Be friendly with Simon Clurey if you like, but don't encourage him. There are one or two men I want you to meet as soon as you come home, so meantime don't get entangled here.'

'I'm not at all likely to get entangled with Simon,' said Helena, sick with apprehension at the way her mother had obviously thrust out of her consideration all thought of Geoffrey.

'You know the man I want to marry, Mother,' she added in a low voice. 'It's quite useless pushing other men at me. I only want Geoffrey.'

'I thought we had finished with all that nonsense,' said Mrs. Thorwell brusquely. 'Really, Helena, have you no more pride in yourself and no common sense? I'm disgusted with you. Once and for all, I will not have any further mention of that man's name. The regrettable thing is *finished* and you may as well make up your mind to it.'

Helena had nothing to say. She had never been able to stand up to her mother. All her life she had been in complete subjection to her much stronger will. Ruth may have been able at times to get her own way, but as her way was seldom different from her mother's, such a battle of wills seldom occurred.

Outwardly Helena submitted, as she had always done, but within her seethed a most unusual and uncharacteristic fever of revolt, and when Geoffrey wrote that he would try to come to Bickford for a few hours, her mind was made up.

They met in a quiet road a little distance from the station. Helena was supposed to have gone to the monthly meeting of the Women's Institute, of which her aunt was the president, but by a fortuitous circumstance, Miss Thorwell was in bed with a bad cold and suitable regrets had been sent.

Helena watched the train come in and then, her heart beating wildly, she had walked along the road as she had arranged with Geoffrey and stood waiting for him in the gateway to a field.

As soon as she saw his tall figure swinging along with the breezy stride she knew so well, she ran to him and into his arms, clinging to him, the tears running down her face.

'Oh, darling, darling!' she sobbed. 'Never let me go again. Take me with you. Take me away now, this very minute. Once Mother gets me back home, I shall never see you again. I know I shan't. She's so determined and once she makes up her mind, nothing ever alters it. Please take me away. Please, darling. It's the only way.'

It was not what he had intended. He had been forced to conduct the affair in a clandestine way, but he had not wanted to bring it to this sort of conclusion. He was on fire for her, however, and the feel of her arms about him, her utter and delicious surrender to him, sent prudence to the winds.

'All right,' he said at last. 'All right. We'll do it, sweetness. How? When?'

Smiles chased the tears.

'Now,' she said. 'This very minute. Look, I've brought with

me just what I shall need for the night,' showing him a bulky handbag stuffed to its limits. 'Once we're married, darling, they'll have to accept it, and then I can have the rest of my things. There's a train back to London at ten-past four. We can wait here till it's signalled, and then dash to the station. I've got a ticket. It's really Mother's, the return half of her ticket when she came down last week. I stole it from her bag and she thought she had lost it. Haven't I been clever?'

'Wonderful, darling,' he said, taking the ticket from her fingers which trembled with excitement and realising that this time fate, in the form of Helena's determination, had taken charge of the situation. 'You're sure nobody will see you and stop you?'

They can't. It will be too late. And how can the man at the station keep me from going on the train when I've got a ticket? He wouldn't dare, and we can send a telegram to Aunt Alice as soon as we get to London so there won't be any public hue and cry after me. Oh, Geoffrey, I've been so *miserable*, and now it's heaven, isn't it? How soon can we be married, do you think?'

'I don't know, but I'll work it out. It may be a week or two, and of course it will have to be in a registry office.'

'I know. I'd have liked to be married in a church, not with all the fuss there was at Ruth's, of course, but just the two of us. Still, that doesn't really matter, does it?'

'No, of course not. Nothing matters except that we shall be together.'

'For always—always! We're going to be so happy—so happy! I could jump over the moon!'

As she had said, there was nothing to stop them, and in little more than an hour they were in London and in a taxi, going to the small hotel where Geoffrey said she would be safe until he could make arrangements for them to be married. He made no suggestion of staying there with her, as she had been half afraid he might, shrinking from the thought but prepared now to accept anything he decreed. She had sent off her telegram to her aunt, but could not bring herself to communicate in any way with her mother until after the marriage. She was still filled with the fear that even at the last moment she would in some way find her and drag her back. Once she was actually married, she could do nothing about it, nothing.

Geoffrey's care of her was beyond reproach, though her fears kept her in the hotel and almost entirely in her room until the morning when he took her in a taxi to a grimy little office in a house in a back street, and after a procedure which she did not even try to understand, she was out in the street again, a shining gold ring on her finger and Geoffrey looking down at her with a new light in his eyes – her husband!

He had told her that his business was taking him immediately over to Paris, and she had received the information with delight.

'A honeymoon in Paris! It's probably what I would have chosen if it had been an ordinary wedding,' she told him happily, and even when they were installed in a dingy, third-rate hotel in a quite unknown quarter of the gay city, her spirits were not damped.

'I know it isn't what you're accustomed to, my sweet,' he told her apologetically, 'but just for the moment, and until your mother gets over the shock of it, it's best for us to stay out of sight and reach. She'd find us at the Crillon or the Meurice in no time.'

'She certainly would,' agreed Helena happily, 'though she couldn't do anything about it now, could she? We're married. I'm your wife, Geoffrey. Your wife! I can scarcely believe it even now. Kiss me, darling. Kiss me so that I know I'm really awake and not just in a beautiful dream about you!'

The beautiful dream lasted for some weeks, though it began to be a bit dim, its fabric just a little frayed at the edges as Geoffrey's first lover-like attentions to her became the less enraptured interest of a husband. They had no settled home, which she longed for, though he promised her they should have one 'when they got back to England'.

'I've got a lot to do over here, darling,' he told her, though she never knew what he did. 'Once I've got things squared up with the agents and things, we'll go back to England and have a home. You're quite happy, aren't you?'

'How could I be anything else when you're being sweet to me?' she asked. 'You're happy too, aren't you, Geoffrey?' rather wistfully.

He caught her in his arms and kissed her with the passion which could so satisfy and enrapture her, which could assure her, even in the midst of her bewilderment at the way they lived, her ignorance of what made up his life outside their hotel bedroom, that she had been so right to take her destiny into her own hands as she had done and lay it trustingly in his.

She tried not to mind the long hours, sometimes even days, when she was left alone. She spent a good deal of her time sewing, making things in readiness for the home he always promised her 'soon', and when they left Paris and did even more wandering with still no sign of going back to England, she resolutely kept her thoughts away from the memory of the ordered life she had known before, the comfortable home, her friends and the many things with which she had so pleasantly filled her days.

They were well lost, she told herself, since their loss had meant the gain of Geoffrey, of being his wife, of learning from him, wrapped in his arms, how much a woman's life can hold when she is in love and beloved.

But she began to long intolerably for some more settled existence, to wish that he would so arrange his affairs that she could make a home for him to which he would come and go as other husbands did.

'Couldn't we stay here a little while, darling?' she asked him when they seemed to be settling in a small town on the coast of Brittany, staying not in an hotel this time but in a cottage set right above the rocky sea coast, with the waters of the Bay of Biscay tumbling in white spray on the silver sands below them, and the blue sails of the sardine boats like fairy lace dipping and swaying as they came home in the evening, or lay at anchor, a web of gauze, when the sun was setting.

Perhaps it was being in a house instead of an hotel, the homely care of fat Madame Dulez, the noisy play of the children as they ran in and out, the cheerful home-coming of Père Dulez when the fishing-boats were in – or perhaps only that she was tired; but there was a deep longing in her for something settled and permanent in her life with Geoffrey as she wound her arms about his neck and laid her cheek against his.

'Well, perhaps we might,' he said cautiously, and she seized on the half-promise with joy.

'Oh, I did so hope you'd say that because I've got a secret. I've found a home for us, a real home, Geoffrey!'

He held her away from him and looked into her face.

'A home? Here? Where?' he asked.

'I'll show you. Come out with me now. Oh, Geoffrey, it's so darling! You'll love it,' and still with that wary caution about him, he let her persuade him to go down the rickety staircase and out into the cobble-stoned street to where, farther along the cliff, a tiny stone-built cottage hung precariously on the edge, almost falling over and yet still with its air of sturdy independence. A small garden bright with such stalwart flowers as would withstand the salt and the wind encircled it, and an old, apple-faced Breton woman opened the door to them even before Helena had danced up the path and knocked.

Inside was a primitive kitchen-living-room with a tiny lean-to behind it, and stairs which were little more than a step-ladder led to the one bedroom, low-ceiled so that Geoffrey had to bend his head to go through the doorway. There was nothing else, but everything was spotlessly clean, the walls whitewashed, the simple wooden furniture of the solid, enduring peasant make that had survived generations of human beings and would survive generations more.

The big bed was covered with a patchwork quilt, much washed so that the colours had faded, and turned down over it was a sheet of hand-made linen, coarse but white as snow. Rag rugs lay on the uneven floor of polished wood, and on a wash-stand stood a basin and ewer of old Breton *faience*.

'Isn't it sweet?' asked Helena, her head drooping against his shoulder. 'And we can have it, Geoffrey, for as long as we like, and the rent's too absurd. The old lady downstairs is going to live with her son in Quimper, but she wants to keep the cottage and not have to sell it.'

'And you'd like it here?' he asked her unbelievingly, with a sudden vision of her mother's home in London, its elegance and comfort, the well-trained maids and the calm dignity of Mrs. Thorwell as she had received him in frosty, well-bred courtesy.

'I'd love it!' said Helena. 'A little home of our own, Geoffrey!'

'But you'd never be able to stand it, my dear, cramped into this hovel. Why, one couldn't even have a bath!'

She laughed.

'Oh, but one could! Wait. I'll show you,' and she ran down the steep stairway again and took him into the lean-to at the back of the living-room and showed him with pride a large tin tub turned up against the wall, with a pail beside it.

'Look, this is what they call a *chaudron*. At least that's what it sounded like,' showing him an iron pot set over a small open arrangement of brick and stone which had at one time held a fire. 'I suppose it's what they call in England a copper, though I've never seen one. Madame Meunier explained it to me. You light a fire of sticks and things here, and when the water is hot, you bale it out with something or other – oh, this bucket – and pour it into the bath and then you let the fire go out. It's quite simple and it would be such fun having a bath in that!'

'Well, it's not my idea of fun,' said Geoffrey, but in the end her enthusiasm overcame his distaste for uncomfortable living and he agreed that they would try the cottage 'for a week or two'. Actually it suited his convenience at the moment, for he might have to stay in the district for some time, and it would be as well to have Helena settled somewhere where she would be reasonably happy and also have something to occupy her if he had to leave her for a few days at a time.

She was enraptured, and as the old woman was only too anxious to be gone, they moved their small wardrobe into the cottage and Helena proceeded to turn herself with difficulties of which she made light, into what she called a 'housewife'. Madame Meunier's daughter, Yvonne, agreed to come in every day for an hour or two to help her, but she was determined that she would find out how to do everything herself. Under Yvonne's guidance, she learned to clean and wash, to sew the sort of things someone else had always sewn for her at home, to cook the simple French dishes on which the Bretons themselves lived, even to bake delicious bread in the old, wood-fired oven beside the open range in their one living-room.

She was ecstatically happy, and if sometimes, especially when Geoffrey was away, she thought of her home and her friends, of Ruth far away in India, even of her mother of whom, at this distance of place and time, she was having softened memories, she forced the thoughts from her mind and told herself that for all she had given up, Geoffrey and their love made up abundantly and satisfyingly. She would not go back to that life, to its emptiness of Geoffrey, even if she could.

She had written to her mother, once only and from Paris, without giving an address. She had told her that she was married, and utterly happy and regretted nothing except that, in order to achieve that happiness, she had had to go away like that.

It isn't that I'm not grateful, Mother (she had said). *I am, and I always shall be. I know you must have given up a lot, gone without a lot, to keep Ruth and me at school and to send us to Lausanne, and I know how much you wanted me make what you would think a good marriage. But nobody could give me happiness but Geoffrey, and I hope that some day you will be able to forgive me and that we can meet again and be friends.*

Yes, she had certainly wished that, but she had never written again, sure in her heart that her mother would never forgive her, never receive her as Geoffrey's wife, and to be Geoffrey's wife was all that really counted with her.

But as the autumn came on, and the little cottage showed the worst instead of the best it could do, when the wind howled about it and the sea dashed up until it seemed it would actually sweep in, and the garden became a quagmire so that even to go outside to get wood soaked her feet through in their thin shoes, when it was an exhausting battle to go out and buy food after Yvonne went away to be married without being able to find anyone else to take her place – when the fire would do nothing but smoulder sulkily and send clouds of smoke into the room, when it became impossible to get the fire under the iron *chaudron* lit at all so that even the once-hilarious baths were impossible – when Geoffrey's absences became more frequent and prolonged and she got one heavy cold after another – when all these things happened, she doubted the wisdom of having persuaded him to have this little home, after all.

And, worst thing of all, they had begun to quarrel; not the little tiffs which had come and gone like puffs of summer wind and could be made up, entrancingly, in each other's arms in the big bed under the patchwork quilt, but real quarrels, with bitter words and recriminations and no making up in the big bed.

Those quarrels frightened her. She felt she did not know Geoffrey any more. She could no longer make him laugh at her struggles and mistakes. She could not even coax him into smiles with her arms about him and her kisses inviting his. He even, one evening when he had come home after three days of absence, pushed her away and complained peevishly of the rich smell of the onion soup, with the toasted cheese on croutons lying succulently on the top of it, which he had always before told her was the food of the gods.

'Don't we ever have anything but onions?' he asked her. 'God, I'm sick of the smell of them!'

'I'm sorry, darling, but if I'd known you were coming home tonight, I'd have gone down to the village. I could go down now. There may be a tunny boat in, in spite of the storm.'

He looked out of the little window with its fresh muslin

curtains which she was always washing and ironing. Though she had felt sick and tired all day, probably with another cold coming on, she never neglected the little house or let it be other than clean and sweet, in spite of the unequal battle against smoke and soot. The rain was lashing the glass, and it had been as much as he could do to fight his way against the wind from the bus which had brought him in from the nearest station, Quimperlé, five miles away. Since coming to France, he had not had a car, a fact of which he was beginning to complain, giving Helena to understand, without actually saying it, that he could not keep both a wife and a car.

'No. Never mind,' he said. 'Is there any cheese? I'll make do with that.'

'Oh, darling, I used it all up for the soup,' she said. 'There are some eggs.'

'All right, if I must,' he said ungraciously and slumped down in the one easy chair, a crazy basket-work affair that groaned under his weight and lurched sideways so that he had to get up again and wedge under one leg the block of wood which usually steadied it. 'No chance of a bath, I suppose?'

Her eyes widened with fear – fear of what he would say if she could not get that awful fire alight. She had already tried to light it several times, desperately wanting a hot bath herself in the hope of throwing off the cold which she knew infuriated him. As if she could help it when she had a cold!

'I'll try, dear,' she said as cheerfully as she could, and went back into the lean-to, once so delightfully novel and romantic to her, now neither novel nor romantic but just plain hell.

He called out to her after about ten minutes, irritably.

'What about those eggs?'

'I'll do them, dear,' she said.

She had forgotten all about them, and there was no more paraffin in the evil-smelling oil stove which she used for a 'quick' meal and she had to stop to fill it and slopped paraffin over the stone floor and then washed her hands as best she could in cold water before she put the eggs on to boil.

He tasted one and pushed it violently aside. She was outside struggling with the fire again.

'This egg simply reeks of paraffin,' he called out angrily. 'Good heavens, isn't there *anything* you can do? I suppose I'd better go down to the *Coq* and *buy* myself some food,' and he picked up his Burberry again and flung out of the house, banging the door behind him and sending fresh clouds of smoke across the room and up into the bedroom above.

Helena collapsed in a little heap on the floor amongst the half-burnt sticks and the remains of the paraffin and wept. If only she did not feel so rotten. If only the wind would stop for five minutes! If only Geoffrey had not come home tonight but had waited till the morning! Nothing was quite so bad in the daylight.

She thought of her bedroom at home, of the soft carpet and the comfortable bed, a cheerful fire in the grate, the bedside lamp in its frilled pink shade, and Florence coming in with a little tray with something delicate and inviting arranged on it for her, her mother following quietly with a couple of aspirins and an injunction to her to get into bed and stay there until the next day, with a promise of the doctor if she did not feel better. Nothing to do but lie down in her luxurious bed and sleep, or read, or just lie there and indulge herself!

She pulled herself out of such dangerous dreams, gave a last vicious little kick at the fire which had defeated her again, and dragged herself upstairs. She could not even bring herself to swallow a few mouthfuls of the onion soup, and she had no energy to heat a glass of milk or even to fill a hot-water bottle from the water in which she had boiled Geoffrey's eggs.

She pretended to be asleep when he came in a long time afterwards, but a fit of coughing destroyed the illusion and he spoke to her irritably.

'Don't say you've got *another* cold!' he said. 'I never come home without finding you sneezing and coughing.'

'I don't have colds because I like them,' she snapped at him. 'It's the damp and the draughts and all this unending rain.'

'Well, I can't help the rain, but who wanted to come to this beastly cottage? I certainly didn't. We could have gone back to Paris if you hadn't insisted on taking this place for three months.'

'I wanted a home,' she said. 'I hate living in hotels.'

'A home! Good lord, some home! Filthy little hovel—'

'At least it isn't filthy,' she said with spirit. 'It's always clean and it isn't my fault if the fires won't burn. I do my best, and you don't do anything to help—'

'What do you expect me to do? Your work as well as mine? I suppose I might have known how it would be once you had to do anything for yourself! Your mother was right. You ought to have married someone who could give you servants to wait on you and blow your nose for you—'

'That's unfair, Geoffrey. You wanted to marry me—'

'I did not,' he said coldly and cruelly, standing by the side of the bed and looking down at her, taking in every detail of her, the dull, lank hair that needed to be cut, the white face with streaks of dirt on it, her eyes and nose reddened by her cold. Good heavens, what a sight she looked! 'I did not want to marry you. I was in love with you, heaven knows why now, but you forced my hand. You begged me to take you away. You had even got your railway ticket, and your night-dress packed in your hand-bag. You gave me no choice. I *had* to marry you, and you know it.'

She lay there staring at him, unable to believe that he was saying these things to her, that it was not some horrible nightmare from which she would wake to find herself sleeping in his arms as she loved to do.

'You—you can say—that?' she asked in a whisper.

'Well, can you deny it? Isn't it true?'

She closed her eyes against the look of actual contempt there was in his.

Yes. Yes, it was true, in actual, bare fact. She *had* begged him to take her away. She had come prepared to go with him, her night-dress in her hand-bag and her railway ticket already bought.

But it hadn't been like that. It hadn't been the way he was making it out to be. It hadn't been!

'You loved me,' she said dully, opening her eyes again. 'You loved me and wanted to marry me.'

'Perhaps, but not then. Not like that. Only when I was ready to get married, and I wasn't. Not then. It was a confounded nuisance, if you really want to know.'

'I don't want to know—but perhaps it's best that I should, even though it's a bit late,' she said in a jerky, horrified whisper. 'Oh, if only you hadn't! If only you hadn't married me at all, Geoffrey!"

He stood quite still, looking down at her with an expression in his eyes which she could not fathom, a calculating, considering look.

Then he spoke, curtly and with no feeling at all in his voice.

'Well, I didn't,' he said.

She struggled into an upright position, her hands pressed down on the bed holding her, her eyes wide.

'Didn't—what?' she asked in a whisper, staring at him.

'Didn't marry you,' he said.

'You—you—you can't say that, Geoffrey. You're only saying it to hurt me. To frighten me. Of course we're married.'

'We're not. That was a fake. It wasn't a registry office at all, and the man who did the job for me was a pal of mine. He owed me something and that was the way he paid it. You had to know some time, so you may as well know now. You're not my wife and I'm not your husband,' and he turned on his heel and left her.

Through the dazed chaos of her mind, which was incapable of one clear thought, she heard him go down the creaking stairway, heard him moving about for a few minutes in the room below, and then the door slammed and the sound of his footsteps on the stone path below were swallowed up by the rain and the wind.

She lay quite still, incapable of movement, her mind beginning to form thoughts again as it tried to grapple with the hideous, the incredible thing he had just told her.

She did not doubt it. She could not. There had been cruel truth in his eyes, in the curt words in which he had told her.

Not married at all. Not Geoffrey's wife. For nearly ten months she had been living a lie, living with a man to whom she was not married, a man who had just been amusing himself with her.

Geoffrey's mistress.

When the tears came, they racked and exhausted her, and after a long time she fell into a sleep which was rather unconsciousness than the peace of normal sleep, and her dreams were peopled with nightmare horrors from which she woke without knowing whether they were real or fancied.

In the morning she was too ill to get up and Geoffrey had not returned – or at least, if he had, he had not slept beside her. His pillow was undented and she knew by instinct that he was not in the house.

She did not know how long she lay there, but later in the day she managed to crawl out of bed and put on a dressing-gown and feel her way stumblingly down the stairs.

He had left a note for her on the table. She could scarcely read it. The letters danced before her eyes and mixed themselves up, but at length she got the gist of them.

He was not coming back, he said. He did not think she would even want him to now that she knew the truth. He was leaving her as much money as he could spare and he suggested that she got In touch with her mother and went back to England. He would not trouble her again.

Not trouble her again! Not *trouble* her!

She put her head down on the table and laughed and cried and at last stumbled to the chair and lay there panting, every breath giving her a sharp pain in her chest, her head feeling ten times bigger than her body and burning hot, though her feet and hands were icy.

It was late in the afternoon before Madame Dulez, who had

promised to bring the little English *Madame* some of her special home-baked bread, knocked at the door of the cottage and then, not receiving an answer, pushed it cautiously open.

What she saw galvanised her into immediate action. It was common knowledge in the village that the little English lady was often alone in her cottage, her *Monsieur* quite reprehensibly staying away for days at a time, but to leave her like this! Since the comings and goings of everybody, especially of the English couple, were always known to everybody, Madame Dulez knew that *Monsieur* had come back last night on the bus from Quimperlé, so what was the little *Madame* doing here by herself and ill, obviously very ill?

She ran back to her own house for Yvonne, who was visiting her, and the two of them carried the now unconscious Helena up to her bed, made her comfortable with extra blankets and hot-water bottles, forced some hot soup and brandy between her lips, and then, as she showed no sign of returning consciousness, sent for the doctor.

Dr. Daudet, kind, fussy little man, shook his head over her, said she ought to be taken to a hospital but also that it was impossible, but impossible, you believe, to move her! Yvonne had to return to her husband, but Madame Dulez said she would remain, and Yvonne stayed whilst she ran back to her home to announce her plans and bring with her a big basket of necessities, and then she settled down to nurse Helena back to life.

Before he left, the doctor discussed with her the strange position in which the English girl was left, for she must have felt ill the night before and yet the husband had left her, and there was no sign of him.

'This I have found,' said Madame Dulez, giving him the note which Geoffrey had left, 'but I cannot read it.'

Dr. Daudet's knowledge was not profound, but it was enough for him to understand the purport of the words, and he explained them to Madame Dulez with much tut-tutting and many '*mon Dieu*'s.

'It is clear that something must be arranged for the poor young lady,' he said, and Madame Dulez agreed.

But what? They knew nothing about her, and even if the so vile husband could be found, of what use? She must have other friends, English friends.

'She calls for her mother, the poor little one,' said *Madame*, in tears herself. 'But how do we find that one? What is it that one can do?'

Apparently there was nothing that they could do other than give her the most devoted care and nursing, but it was a week before they could be sure that she had struggled back to life and that memory had returned to her tormented mind.

The doctor stood by her bedside with her thin wrist in his hand, big spectacles on the end of his nose, his short hair *en brosse* above his benevolent face.

It was a relief to him that she could speak to him in French, and he talked to her with gentle authority.

'Your husband, my dear. He will not, you think, return?'

She shook her head, turning her face away.

'But you can reach him? You know where I perhaps can write to him a small letter?'

'No. No. I don't know where he is and I don't want anyone to write to him ever,' she said with such determination in her voice, for all its weakness, that he shook his head gravely.

'That is not well, my dear young lady,' he said. 'That is not at all well. You have had a little quarrel, perhaps, but now—now is no time to keep a little quarrel alive. Now is a time for such things not to be remembered any more, a time when you need each other, a time when all wives need their husbands. You know that, my child?'

His look and tone conveyed his meaning to her, with utter horror.

'You—what is it you are saying? What is it?' she said urgently.

He took her hand and pressed it.

'Yes. I think you know. It is a little one. You are *enceinte*, dear *Madame*. Yes, yes. That is so.'

She knew it was useless to protest, useless to deny it, though until this moment it had never occurred to her. The thought had never crossed her mind even as a possibility.

It was true. There was the sickness, her general feeling of lassitude, and as dates flashed through her mind, she realised with a sick certainty that she was pregnant. In the constant travelling about of the first few weeks, and then the excitement of settling into the cottage, she had ignored the signs which ought to have warned her.

She clung to the doctor's hand.

'I can't have it. I can't. Don't make me,' she implored him, but all he did was to pat her hand, smile reassuringly at her and tell her that everything would be all right, that she must be brave, that it would be a wonderful and beautiful thing to have a little baby of her own to love.

He left her still weeping, still insisting that she could not, would not have the baby.

Dr. Daudet and kind Madame Dulez watched over her and fussed over her, talked to her and tried to persuade her that everything would be for the best, and she knew she was trapped and helpless. There was nothing she could do about it, even if she were strong enough to get up and go about her ordinary life, go to one of the big cities where surely they knew about these things, to Paris, to London—

London.

The sick longing to be back there returned to her with all the force of her loneliness, her fear, her anxiety about the future. What could she do? Where could she go?

She had insisted on Madame Dulez taking the money which Geoffrey had left carelessly thrown on the table with his note and which Madame Dulez had brought to her and shown her as soon as she was well enough to know what it was.

She pushed it back into the rough, work-hardened hand.

'Take it. Take it, dear Madame Dulez. Pay yourself for all the things you have bought for me – and the doctor – and there is the rent of the cottage—'

And after that, there would be nothing left, not a *sou*. What was she to do? She realised that it would be a long time before she could work, and even then, how could she earn a living, even in England? And here in France it would be even more impossible.

She lay there with the tears of weakness running down her cheeks, and the old Frenchwoman smoothed back her hair gently.

'*Chérie*, you have a *maman*, isn't it so?' she asked. 'She will come to you. It is right. Always the *maman* will come, always,' and in the end, desperate and at the end of her tether, she wrote the few difficult lines, the hardest thing she had ever done in her life.

Dear Mother,
I know I have no right to send this to you, but I am ill and desperate. Geoffrey has left me and I haven't any money at all and I don't know what to do or where to go.

Helena.

She did not know what to expect, whether her mother would do anything for her or even write. What she least expected was that, two days later, her mother would walk into the room.

'Well, Helena?' she said unemotionally, but at the sight of her, the sound of even those uncompromising words in an utterly detached tone, Helena threw herself to the side of the bed and caught at her mother's hand and laid her head on it and burst into tears.

'Mother—mother—'

Mrs. Thorwell was inexpressibly shocked – shocked at the ravages of illness which had robbed the girl of every vestige of her beauty, shocked at the dreadful room in the dreadful little house, at the thought of her daughter alone and uncared for except by a poor peasant woman with dirty hands and lined, careworn face and rough, uncultured speech in a *patois* which she could scarcely understand.

In a hard, ambitious way, she had loved her daughters but since Helena's flight, she had schooled herself to think of her as someone dead, dead by her own hand and through no possible fault of her, Pauline Thorwell. But the hardness was not proof against this desperate need, this pitiful humility of the child who would not remain dead, who would not be forgotten.

She hesitated and then laid her other hand on the girl's head and let it rest there, awkwardly, for a moment.

'That will do, Helena,' she said. 'No more tears. As soon as possible we must get you away from here. Until then, of course, I shall stay with you. When you are able to do so, you must tell me anything more you want me to know so that we can decide what is the best thing to do for you.'

'Yes,' said Helena weakly, and let herself drift on the tide of that blessed knowledge that she was not alone any more, that someone else was going to tell her what to do and where to go.

But first she had to tell everything, and she told it to her mother frankly, crudely, lying there with her eyes fixed on the darkening square of the window, her voice a dull monotony, unemotional, almost as if she told a story of things happening to someone in whom she had no interest.

Mrs. Thorwell listened, sitting upright in the chair which Madame Dulez had brought for her, offering no comment or interruption. The last vestige of colour drained slowly from her face. That was all.

When Helena lay silent again, still without moving, her mother drew a deep breath. It was even worse, in some ways, than she had imagined, but she seized on the one thing which might yet save something from the wreck of what had so short a time ago been a lovely, laughing, happy girl.

'Well,' she said at last, 'there's one thing for which we can be thankful. You are not married to this man.'

'I don't see what difference that makes,' said the girl drearily.

'Of course it makes a difference. All this can eventually be put behind you and you can marry. Some decent man, of course.'

'What decent man is going to marry me, even if I could ever bring myself to have anything to do with another man?' asked the flat, hopeless voice. 'The best thing to hope for is that I shall die.'

'Nonsense,' said Mrs. Thorwell briskly. 'Don't let me hear any more of that sort of talk. Of course you're not going to die. *That*, with all the publicity it would bring, would make things quite impossible for us, for Ruth and me. For once in your life, Helena, you are going to think of other people rather than yourself. As soon as you can travel, I shall take you back to England. I must make suitable arrangements. First I must see this doctor. He's French, I suppose?' with the note of distrust in her voice inescapable to so many British people where professionals of any nationality are concerned, distrust mingled with a little pity for such unfortunates.

Helena said nothing. She did not mind what they did for her, since they were not going to let her die.

A week later they were on their way home. Thinking about it afterwards, Helena marvelled at the way in which her elegant mother, used to comfort and to servants all her life, had adapted herself to the travesty of life in the little, comfortless cottage. Madame Dulez did everything possible, but it must have been a week of sheer purgatory for Mrs. Thorwell, with no hot water, no proper sanitation and only the most primitive of life's essentials. Yet she never complained and was courtesy itself to the overawed peasant woman and the fussy little doctor, paid them well as she accepted their services, and finally drove away in a hired car with Helena wrapped in rugs and propped up with pillows, leaving behind her ample compensation for their trouble, and frosty thanks in her excellent, Parisian French which the old woman scarcely understood.

Helena did not ask where they were going, but after the long, tiring journey, she found herself back at Bickford in Aunt Alice's best spare room.

'You're not going to leave me, Mother?' she asked, almost the first thing she had asked of her mother since she had appeared in the cottage bedroom. She was afraid of meeting life again, and at least her mother knew all about her.

'Not until you are up and about again and we can make suitable plans,' said Mrs. Thorwell.

She was kind and considerate in every way for the girl's comfort, but Helena knew she would never forgive her.

Well, what did it matter? What did anything matter now?

But whatever plans her mother might have made in her own mind, the actual events which followed had never figured in them, for they had not included Simon Clurey.

Simon came back into the fabric of her life a day or two after she had been prevailed upon to get up and go out.

The bad weather had broken by that time, giving way to one of the periods which even an English winter knows at times, bright, frosty days and clear, starry nights. Helena slept through the latter with the aid of sleeping-tablets which her mother produced for her. There was no need, Mrs. Thorwell said, for her to see a doctor again yet. Time enough for that later. And the morning came when Mrs. Thorwell insisted on her getting up and going out, down to the village with her to do some shopping for the household.

It was then that they met Simon Clurey.

He was in the shop where Mrs. Thorwell was paying a bill for her sister-in-law, and his eyes brightened with surprise and pleasure at sight of Helena.

'I heard you were here,' he said, 'but I understood you were ill and I didn't like to call. Oh, I do hope you're feeling better.'

'I'm much better,' said Helena shrinkingly, and presented him to her mother, who was pleased to be gracious to him.

He walked back with them, and perhaps the idea was already born in Mrs. Thorwell's mind, for she asked him to come to tea with them later in the day, an invitation accepted with instant delight on Simon's part, though Helena showed no interest.

For several days after that, he haunted them, bringing Helena flowers, waiting on her assiduously, so obviously besotted with love for her that it was no surprise to Mrs. Thorwell when, red-faced and diffident, he confided in her that the greatest hope of his life was that some day Helena would change her mind and agree to marry him.

She spoke briskly to the girl about it as soon as they were alone.

'You are very young still, and so is this young man,' she said, 'and I gather that he is not in a position to marry yet, but I have no doubt that can be arranged. He must be found a more lucrative position than the one he has here. I will speak to your father's solicitor, Mr. Galton, about that. He will probably be able to introduce him to a good London firm. It is not at all what I should have chosen for you, of course, but as you have ruined your life and your future in this way, we must accept the position and make the best of it.'

'You're not suggesting that I marry Simon Clurey, Mother, are you?' asked Helena, roused at last.

'I am. I imagine he is prepared to marry you at once, and I shall not object. It will be a very quiet wedding, here in Bickford at a registrar's office, and when the child is born, it must of course appear to be a premature birth.'

'You mean I am to foist off this child on Simon? Is he to know?' asked Helena, stupefied.

'No. There is no necessity. It will be a premature child. Of course the marriage must take place at once. I had arranged to go out to Ruth for a few months but of course I had to alter my plans on your account. I shall now tell him that it is imperative for me to go, and naturally I want to be here for your marriage, and he is so much in love with you that he will not make any trouble about it. You are extremely fortunate, Helena, more fortunate than you deserve, if I may say so. Now Simon is calling later on. I have arranged that, and Aunt Alice will invite him to dinner. We will give you an opportunity of being alone with him, and you had better tell him that I am going to Ruth immediately. I hope I can trust you to manage this properly?'

'But, Mother, I *can't* marry him. He means nothing to me, but even apart from that, the baby—it would be such an awful thing to do to him—'

'Then what do you propose to do about the baby? Have everyone know about it? Have it hanging round your neck for the rest of your life? And how do you think you're even going to exist? I have very little money, Helena, and I do not intend to share what I have with you for the rest of my life. It's very unlikely that you will get a chance like this again. However careful we are, however clever we are in getting the child adopted, these things get about. You have caused me quite enough trouble and anxiety and you must take this really wonderful opportunity of atoning for it. Simon Clurey is a presentable young man, and if he has no money and few prospects, at least he is a man of our own class, of good family and good repute. I insist on your doing as I ask, Helena, so let us say no more about it. As a matter of fact, I have given him to understand that you will accept him, so it will not be difficult for you.'

Weak and battered by life, terrified of the future, sick at the thought of the child within her womb, she found herself that evening allowing Simon to take her silence, her half-refusal, her tears, for an acceptance of the stumbling, difficult proposal he made her.

He let her cry against his shoulder.

'Darling, please don't. Don't cry,' he kept saying to her, smoothing her hair with a gentle hand. 'I have spoken too soon. I ought to have let you get better first, but I'm so much in love with you and I want to do everything for you, look after you, take care of you. I'll do anything in the world that you want, anything. Only let me do something. I can't bear to see you ill and not to be able to look after you. I know I've got precious little to offer anyone like you, but I can offer you the devoted love of my whole life. There's never been anyone else for me. There never will be. You will, darling, won't you? You don't need to say anything. Just let me go on holding you like this, and I know it will mean that you will come to me—be my wife—'

She let herself be lulled by his voice into a state of acquiescence without actually realising what she was doing. After all she had gone through, the death of her love for Geoffrey, the fear and the loneliness followed by her mother's cold, businesslike care of her, Simon Clurey's gentleness, his obvious adoration of her, the promise he held out to her of his love and care for ever, it was heaven to let herself drift without thought of the harbour.

And she drifted still, thrust forward by her mother's forceful determination, the special licence, the anxious tenderness of Simon Clurey, until she stood beside him before the registrar and saw him place on her finger, from which her mother had long ago taken Geoffrey's ring, the gold band which proclaimed her a wife again – Simon Clurey's wife.

Mrs. Thorwell had been as good as her word about bettering his position.

Mr. Galton, solicitor and lifelong friend of her husband, had not only found him a position; he had found one in his own office, advancing him for the sake of that old friendship to a place on his staff which it would otherwise have taken him years to achieve.

It was still, Mrs. Thorwell felt, a poor substitute for all the glowing things she had planned and predicted for Helena, but at least it was security and a decent cover for the girl's abominable behaviour in wrecking her own life.

Always afraid, however, that Helena might yield to her inconvenient conscience and tell Simon the truth, she dare not leave her alone with him. She cancelled her proposed visit to Ruth, finding some reasonable excuse, gave the young couple a suite of rooms in her own house, and became Helena's watchdog, constantly warning her, threatening her, stiffening her resolution.

And by the time the child, a boy, was born, she felt that the battle was won. Helena would not tell him now.

Fortunately the baby was very small and at first weakly, so that it was not difficult to sustain the fiction that it was very much premature. As luck would have it, Simon was away from home at the time of the birth, sent by his firm to get information which could not be obtained in London, and by the time he arrived back, he was given the news that he was a father.

Mrs. Thorwell herself told him. She could entrust to no one else this most delicate part of her planning. Helena had had a bad time and was too weak yet to be a danger, but the nurse and the doctor were not deceived, of course, into thinking the baby was before its time. But Mrs. Thorwell had already made a very handsome present to the nurse besides offering her a considerably higher fee than the one she usually received, and the doctor was a strange one, a young man with a new practice, who had not been slow to grasp the essentials of the case. When Mrs. Thorwell, who had sent for him, told him that the family doctor was old now and preferred not to take maternity cases (which was the providential truth), and that she preferred in any case to have a young, up-to-date doctor at her service, he was only too glad to accept without comment her assertion that the baby was 'very much too early, of course'. It would be of great help to him in his profession to have anyone like Mrs. Thorwell as a patient, and so long as he could avoid making a positive statement about the length of the pregnancy, it was not his business what his patient and her mother said about it.

But Mrs. Thorwell determined to be on the safe side by telling Simon herself.

'It was all very unexpected, of course,' she told him. 'These things do happen, especially with a first baby. Helena had a little fall the other day. Someone had quite criminally left a brush on the stairs. You know what servants are. Fortunately it was near the bottom of the stairs, and I did not think anything of it, but obviously that is what did the damage.'

'You're sure she's all right?' asked Simon, itching to get up to her.

'She's very weak. Very weak indeed. But the doctor assures me that she will be all right in a few days, though of course she must not be excited or tired in any way.'

'Of course not. May I go to her?' asked Simon.

'I had better go up first. Then I'll call you. You haven't asked about your son, Simon!' with an arch smile.

'Oh! Oh yes, the baby. Is it all right?' he asked, but it was obvious he had not wrenched his mind away from Helena.

'Perfectly all right, fortunately. Small, of course. Not quite six pounds, but quite healthy—'

She saw that he was not listening or caring, and they went upstairs to Helena's room, finding her lying awake, her lustreless eyes fixed on the ceiling.

'Simon is here, my dear,' she said quietly, and the staring eyes flinched for a moment, but she said nothing.

That will do, nurse, thank you,' said Mrs. Thorwell to the woman who sat sewing by the window. 'I will call you when Mr. Clurey goes.'

'Yes, Mrs. Thorwell. He won't stay more than a few minutes?'

'No. I'll see that he does not.'

When they were alone, Helena's eyes came to her mother's face.

'I can't see him,' she whispered.

'Of course you can—and must. He will want to see the baby, too. Fortunately it is exactly like you, a quite absurd resemblance.'

'I feel so—mean about it,' said the girl restlessly.

'That is natural, of course, but don't weaken now. There's nothing to be gained by it and everything to be lost. You understand that?'

'Yes. Yes, I understand,' and she turned away and closed her eyes and opened them again to find Simon entering the room with Mrs. Thorwell still watchful in the background. She dare not leave Helena at such a moment, her whole powerful will exerted to keep her daughter from ruining everything she had been at such pains to build up.

Simon went on his knees beside the bed and laid his cheek against Helena's inert hand. His eyes were wet.

'Darling—beloved—oh, Helena,' he said brokenly. 'Are you going to be all right?'

She looked as though a puff of wind would blow her away.

She smiled, and Mrs. Thorwell turned her eyes away with a feeling of profound thankfulness. For once Helena was going to be sensible.

'Of course,' said the girl weakly. 'Don't worry—about me, Simon dear.'

There was silence between them, the man kneeling in adoration, his cheek and then his lips pressed against her hand.

Helena felt stifled, but rather by her own sick shame and remorse than by Simon's closeness. A passion of gratitude to him kept her silent, though everything inherent in her bade her tell him the truth. When presently the nurse came in and brought the baby, saying that after 'one peep', Simon must go, Helena knew that, whatever it might cost her, she must keep silent for ever. To ease her own conscience of its burden would be to deal a death-blow to the man who loved her with his whole faithful heart, and who stood looking down at the child.

'It's—it's so small,' he said, awe-stricken.

Mrs. Thorwell spoke crisply behind him.

'One would expect that with a baby born so prematurely,' she said. 'We had better go now, Simon. I expect you can see Helena again before she settles down for the night.'

With another loving look at his wife, he tiptoed away and Mrs. Thorwell heaved a sigh of relief. At last, at last, she could begin to believe that all would be well.

'It's quite absurd, the likeness of the baby to Helena,' she said as they went down the stairs.

He smiled.

'I'm so glad,' he said. 'You're sure Helena is going to be all right? I don't mind telling you I'm thankful it's over.'

'She'll be quite all right,' Mrs. Thorwell assured him serenely. 'Helena is very strong, you know, though she has that fragile look fair people so often have. She probably won't have a premature confinement like this another time.'

'Another time?' echoed Simon, aghast. 'I simply couldn't subject her to this again. I could never let her have another child.'

But of course he did—Alison, who was born a year later, Helena's secret atonement to Simon for Brian, little Paulette four years after that, and John after another four years.

During those years, she neither saw nor heard of Geoffrey Pellet, and gradually she ceased even to think about him.

It was strange that Ruth should have remembered him and spoken of him that day, so many years afterwards.

Strange – because within an hour or two of that unwelcome reminder, Helena found herself face to face with him.

V

WHEN Helena came back to consciousness after the shock of finding herself face to face with Geoffrey Pellet, it was to find her family grouped about her anxiously, Simon with a glass of water at her lips, Alison fanning her and John standing, goggle-eyed and frightened, at the foot of the couch on which they had laid her.

She struggled to a sitting position and, her mind clearing, looked round with an expression in her eyes which they interpreted as no more than embarrassment at having fainted in the presence of an invited guest.

Alison spoke soothingly.

'Don't worry, dearest,' she said. 'Giles realised that you were not well enough for any entertaining, and he's gone. He'll telephone to ask how you are.'

Giles.

Yes, of course, Giles Paraway. Not Geoffrey Pellet at all – and yet she closed her eyes again and knew she had made no mistake. Whatever Alison called him, he was Geoffrey Pellet.

Simon's voice broke in on her agonised thoughts, kind, anxious.

'We sent for the doctor, dear. He should be here any minute now. How are you feeling?'

She passed a hand across her eyes.

'I'm all right,' she said. 'It's nothing. So silly of me. I never do things like this. I don't want the doctor. There's nothing the matter with me.'

He pushed her gently back against the cushions.

'We shall soon know,' he said; 'but it's because it's such an unusual thing for you to do that of course we must know why. That'll be the doctor now. Let him in, John, will you?'

Dr. Hewlett, an old friend now and the one who had seen John into the world, gave her a puzzled smile.

'Been overdoing it, have you?' he asked. 'You women never seem to know when you've had enough. No man would ever stand up to the work you housewives do. Why do you do it? If you formed a trade union and struck for reasonable hours and any wages at all, half my job would be gone. Into bed with you, and stay there for at least a couple of days. No use my saying a week, I suppose?'

'But I'm perfectly well,' she protested. 'There's nothing at all the matter with me and I don't do any more than any other women, and not nearly as much as some.'

'And you merely fainted for fun? Just to give us all a fright, I suppose?' he asked, a finger on her wrist. 'Get into bed and I'll run the rule over you.'

'There's the supper—' she began, but Alison interposed.

'Who wants supper until you're settled?' she asked. 'I'll come and help you, and Daddy and John can get their own supper for once. Come along, dearest.'

When the doctor saw Simon before leaving, he was still puzzled.

'There's nothing the matter with her, as far as I can tell,' he said, 'but she's probably over-tired and women simply will not take any rest until Nature steps in and forces them to. She's much too young for the menopause. I suppose she's not pregnant? If so, it is too early to make up our minds. Make her rest and I'll look in—say—Friday. I don't think there's anything to worry about.'

Simon did worry, of course, and so did Alison, but the girl was still so wrapped up in her love-affair that within a few days she was hoping to hear her mother offer an invitation to the man she knew as Giles Paraway to pay another visit to her home.

Desperately afraid, Helena made no such suggestion, but

there came an afternoon, when she was up and about again after the enforced rest, when, casually picking up the telephone receiver to answer a call, she heard his voice speaking to her.

'You, Helena? You know who this is, don't you?'

She could not speak. Her face went white and she caught at the edge of the table, her mouth making unintelligible sounds.

'Upset, are you?' he asked in the well-remembered, indulgent, amused voice he had used to her in their early days together. 'A pity you passed out like that. You're better now, I hope? But of course you are, as you are able to answer the telephone. I want to see you. How and where do we meet?'

'I—I don't want—to see you—ever again,' she managed to say.

He gave a little indulgent laugh.

'No? Well, I'm sorry about that, because of course we're going to see each other, and often, I hope. Shall I call?'

'No. No!' she said. 'I don't want . . .' and her voice trailed away as the door opened and Brian, her son, came in.

Blindly she replaced the receiver and gathered herself together with all her will-power.

'Hullo, dearest,' said Brian, putting an arm about her and giving her a hug. 'Feeling better? You don't look too good yet. I didn't know till I got Alison's letter yesterday or I'd have run down sooner.'

He was finishing off a special course at the university whilst awaiting confirmation of the appointment which was such a feather in the cap of such a very young man.

He was, as he had always been, a faithful replica of his mother, the same fair hair, the blue eyes a little more grey perhaps, but the shape of his face, his expressions, his movements, so much like hers that she had never been forced by anything about him to remember the man who had been responsible for his being.

Now she remembered it, with horror and self-loathing, for the first time for many years, and unconsciously she drew herself away and dropped down in a chair.

'I—I'm quite all right,' she said.

This hideous nightmare I Would it never end? What would it do to them all before it did end?

Brian looked at her in concern.

'I couldn't agree less,' he said. 'Oughtn't you to be in bed, or resting or something? Why don't you keep Alison at home for a few days? Or get someone in?'

She managed to smile reassuringly.

'I really am all right, dear,' she said. 'I couldn't possibly expect Alison to take time off from her job, and these daily women are so unreliable, and they never want to do anything but a little light dusting. Really, dear, I'm all right. It's lovely to see you. Can you stay a day or two?'

'No, I'd better get back tonight. I've borrowed a chap's car. Mum, there's somebody I want you to meet. I thought perhaps you and the old man would have dinner with us tonight somewhere, to meet her.'

'Her?' asked Helena.

The colour showed in his fair skin.

'Yes, her. She's Lois Garner and you'll love her. She's a grand person.'

'Not engaged to her, are you, Brian?' asked Helena, feeling that she could not cope with any other crises in her family.

'Well, not officially. Her people are quite agreeable, though, to our being engaged once my job's settled. We don't propose to get married for a year, perhaps two, as we've both got our work and we want to establish something first. She's doing research as well. That's how we met. What about tonight, Mum? Do you feel like it? Or shall I just bring her in to meet you, and make a date for another evening?'

'Would you mind, Brian? I don't really feel up to a dinner date, but I wouldn't like Miss Garner to feel we don't want to meet her.'

'That's all right. She knows you haven't been too well. I'm going to meet her at six, so I'll run her round for a drink or something and then we'll go. Have we got anything?' rummaging

93

in the sideboard. 'Oh, here's a bottle of old Hump's sherry. Just the job. Any more glasses?'

'I—I broke some the night I was silly enough to faint,' she said. 'Can we make do?'

'If I cut along now, I shall be in time to call at Foulsher's and get half a dozen,' he said. 'Now who the dickens is that?' as the door-bell rang. 'All right. I'll go. Probably someone selling brushes or something.'

But a moment later he was back in the room, a tall figure following him.

'Visitor for you, Mother,' he said stiffly. 'Paraway, did you say?' turning for a moment to the man behind him.

Helena rose to her feet. There must be no more fainting or nonsense, she told herself. This thing was for her to face, and for her alone.

'How do you do?' she said, meeting as calmly as she could the eyes of the man whom it seemed she must now know as Giles Paraway. 'This is my son Brian. Mr. Paraway, a—a friend of Alison's.'

The two men took each other's measure, and she saw the kindly animosity in the eyes of the younger as they met the faint but unmistakable amusement in the eyes of the elder.

Neither offered his hand.

'Good afternoon,' said Brian stiffly. 'I don't think we've met.'

'A pleasure too long deferred,' said Giles Paraway. 'I have been looking forward to meeting—Alison's brother, her *elder* brother. The younger one I already know.'

'I'll get the glasses, Mother,' said Brian. 'Good afternoon,' and he gave Giles a curt nod as he went out, closing the door behind him.

'You shouldn't have come,' said Helena at once.

'On the contrary. Do sit down. May I? Will you smoke?' offering her his cigarette-case, an expensive gold one.

Everything about him looked expensive, his very good suit, shoes that had probably been made for him, immaculate linen, a ring with a large solitaire diamond on the little finger of one well-kept hand. It was, she thought wildly, a far cry from the cottage on the Brittany coast.

She shook her head and sat down. He cut and lit a cigar carefully and took a chair near her, one leg crossed comfortably over the other as if he intended to make a long stay.

'You know, you shouldn't have passed out like that the other evening,' he said. 'It might have made things very awkward for you. There's no knowing what I might have said.'

Her eyes widened.

'You didn't—'

'No, no, my dear, I didn't,' he assured her. 'I was discretion itself, showed a proper amount of concern, asked if there was anything I could do, and then took myself off. How did you get on with your explanations afterwards?'

'I didn't do any. What could I have said? You came here as Alison's friend. Why did you? Did you know you were going to meet me, Geoffrey?'

'The name is Giles, my dear. Giles Paraway. Geoffrey Pellet is dead—or at least he will be and can remain so. It depends on you. Yes, I had the advantage of you. I did know I was going to meet you, but I could hardly have prepared you for it, could I? I thought it was the best way, as I imagine you would not have agreed to my coming here had you known.'

'Of course I shouldn't. Why did you come?' she asked bluntly, glad to feel that she was in control of herself through the nightmare horror of the thing. She was not going to faint again.

He carefully removed some of the ash from his cigar before answering her.

'That takes a little consideration,' he said. There were a good many factors. Suppose we take the most obvious one first? I came because Alison wanted me to meet her parents.'

'How dare you bring my daughter into this?' she asked sharply.

'How can we leave her out? She is, after all, the pivot on which the whole thing turns. She considers herself engaged to be married to me.'

'That's impossible! It's horrible! Even if you were not twice her age and in every other way unsuitable, you couldn't possibly marry her, Geoffrey!'

'My dear, do remember that the name is Giles. You really must get used to saying it or it might cause you considerable embarrassment.'

'There is no point in my calling you by any other name since we are not likely to remain in touch with each other,' she said defiantly.

He laughed softly.

'Ah, but that's where you're making a mistake, Helena, a very big mistake. By the way, I think it will be all right for me to continue to call you Helena as the association ripens, as you are, after all, of my own generation and I could scarcely refer to you as Mother, could I?' with another little amused laugh. 'I shall, of course, use the correct form of address and speak to and of you as Mrs. Clurey in the presence of others for the time being, so have no fear. I intend to be most circumspect.'

'Please say what you came to say and go. Your presence here is most distasteful, and no one but you would have forced such a position on me.'

'My dear girl, nobody but I could have, as you call it, *forced* such a position on you. The circumstances are quite unique— and intriguing, if I may say so. Don't you agree?'

'What have you come for?' she demanded again.

If only none of them came in, Alison, Simon, even John! Surely she could get rid of him before Brian came back, bringing this girl with him?

'To see you, of course, and to make the further acquaintance, I hope, of my future wife's family,' he said, unperturbed.

It sickened her to realise that he was actually enjoying it, this cruel baiting of her.

'Whatever is the reason for your—coming back into my life, it can't be for that,' she said. 'You can't seriously mean you intend to marry Alison?'

'Why not? Apart from the difference in age, which I admit is to be regretted but which cannot be helped.'

'It's a vile thought! It's quite out of the question. Why, it's— it's practically—'

She could not finish her sentence, and he finished it for her quite calmly.

'Incest? Is that the word you boggled at? No, it isn't that, my dear. There's no blood tie between your *daughter* and me.'

And then she knew what she had been praying might not be true – that he knew Brian was his own son.

She leaned against the back of the chair, sick with horror.

'You see, my dear, that I do know, about Brian, I mean. I was not quite as bad as you have believed all these years. I did go back to that dreadful little hovel, not for some time afterwards, I admit, but my business affairs took me near there and I just wondered what had happened to you and thought I might as well find out, but the place was shut up. It looked even worse than when we had our miserable existence there, but that woman – what was her name? Dufais? Something like that. She saw me walking round the place and, true to her type, of course she had to come to speak to me, and from the abuse she hurled at me in her more or less unintelligible *patois*, I deduced that you had been unfortunate enough to find yourself with child. Still, as I also gathered from her that your lady mother had appeared and removed you, there was really nothing I could do about it—and of course, I should only have inconvenienced you further by turning up, shouldn't I? Still, I wasn't absolutely certain that you had not succeeded in getting rid of it, until one day a few months ago. Then I knew,' and he was looking not at her but into space, amused reminiscence in his eyes.

'How?' she asked, the question forcing itself from her against her will.

'I'll tell you. It really was a quite extraordinary coincidence, quite extraordinary. My business interests (I have a great many of them nowadays) took me into the city and into the offices of a firm called Galton, Somerley and Co. You know it, of course?'

Helena said nothing. She sat waiting for the net to close around her.

'Your—er—husband's firm, of course. I was asked to wait, and as my business was of a somewhat private nature, I was put into the chief clerk's room rather than the public waiting-room. He was not there at the time—but something else was. A very charming photograph of a family group. You remember it? Taken some years ago, I imagine, but there was no mistaking you, my dear. You haven't changed much, in outward appearance anyway. I was completely fascinated by the sight of you, sitting there so primly with your family about you, such a very different picture from the one that had been in my mind whenever I had thought of you. Then, *then*, Helena, I noticed the boy, and I knew at once.'

'How could you?' she asked sharply. 'He is so exactly like me,' and it was too late to do as she had intended to do, deny strenuously that Brian was his son.

'Like you, yes. But exactly, no. Tell me, Helena. Have you never noticed his ears?' and he turned his face a little so that one of his own was revealed.

The feeling of sickness returned to her and she closed her eyes.

Had she really never noticed those ears? Set close to the head, beautifully proportioned to it – but narrowing at the top into what was almost a point, faun's ears. Giles had them. Brian had them. Had she really never noticed them before? She knew she had, but she had deliberately shut her mind to the thought, refused to admit it, and in all these years she had forgotten what seemed to have so little significance in the life she had made for herself, the closed, safe life of Simon's wife.

She opened her eyes again reluctantly, forced to open them by the knowledge that he was looking at her, waiting for her.

'Well?' he asked. 'Satisfied?'

'You can't suggest that you intend to claim him?' she asked faintly.

He laughed.

'Heavens, no! No, my dear. The last thing I want is to saddle myself with a grown-up son. Why on earth should I? You have done very well for him, you, coupled with the brains I gave him. The worthy Simon has been an excellent substitute for a father, but you can hardly claim that the boy's brilliant record is his doing.'

'Simon *is* his father, in every way.'

'In every way but the one small detail of his conception. I agree. You were lucky there. I take it he doesn't know? or does he? I made it my business to look into things. I went to Somerset House. I found that the boy had been registered in his name at birth, and that you were duly married to Simon Clurey before that event. Did you tell him?'

'No. He has never known,' said Helena in a dull, hopeless voice. 'I suppose now you mean to tell him? It will kill him.'

'Oh, I don't think it would do anything as dramatic as that, but don't be afraid. It is no part of my plan to tell him—if the rest of the plan works out.'

'You're a devil incarnate,' she said.

'No, only a very human man occupied as most of us are in doing the best for myself and getting what I want out of life.'

'And what do you want? Alison, I suppose?'

'Probably. I'm in love with the child, which, seeing that she is very much like what you were twenty years ago, is not to be wondered at.'

'You're surely not going to pretend that you were in love with me?' she asked bitterly.

'There would be no pretence about it. I was in love with you, what you were when I first met you. You were charming, lovely to look at, well born and bred, and with the enchantment of your utter unworldliness and with the fascination of such absorbing love for me that you were not only ready to throw your bonnet over the windmill for me, but actually did so.'

'Are you pleased with yourself for what you did to that child I was?' she flung at him.

'I had no reason to be otherwise, or to blame myself. I doubt whether I should have gone away with you as I did if you had not flung yourself at me and left me no choice. You probably remember, though it is so long ago, the exact circumstances in which we ran away together?'

She could find nothing to say. She did remember. It was a thing she had never been able to forget, that frenzy of love, the fear of being parted from him, the absorption of her whole being in it.

'I see you do remember, and that at least you have the grace not to deny it. Well, it is a long time ago. Let's put it behind us and come back to the present.'

'You can't marry Alison,' she said dully.

'Well, we'll see about that. You know she considers herself engaged to me?'

'Not with our consent.'

'In three months she will not need it, but I have no intention of running away with her as I did with you. This time it is to be done in a proper fashion, a church wedding since that is what she wants, *and* the blessing of her parents. I intend to become an accepted member of your family, Helena.'

'Never!'

'You are on very dangerous ground, you know. Ah, there is someone coming,' as they heard voices in the hall. 'By the way, who is that odd-looking woman who always seems to be dodging about on the stairs when I come? A servant?'

'Mrs. Oliver. They live on the top floor,' she said shortly.

He lifted his eyebrows.

'My dear, I had no idea you had to let rooms! How unpleasant for you. Ah, here is your son,' as Brian came into the room, bringing with him a small, dark, vivacious girl who glanced from one to the other with interested, intelligent eyes.

Brian scowled at Giles Paraway and then ignored him.

'Mother, I've brought Lois,' he said.

She rose and took the girl's hand in hers and looked at her with a feeling of release, as if she had come out of a morass of darkness and filth into the sunshine of a clear sky.

'My dear, I am very glad Brian has brought you,' and then she was obliged to present her other visitor. 'This is Mr. Paraway. Miss Garner.'

He smiled with a little bow of old-fashioned, charming courtesy.

'Delighted,' he said, looking into her clear eyes. 'I'm only sorry I must tear myself away, but I have no doubt we shall be meeting again. You must bring Miss Garner to lunch at my club one day, Brian. Dinner, if that would be more convenient. How about ringing me up there? The New Ocean in Jermyn Street.'

'Thank you,' said Brian stiffly. 'We are both of us very occupied at the moment.'

'Well, any time. Any time. I'm living there at the moment, until I can find the sort of flat I want. The New Ocean will always find me, though. Good-bye, Miss Garner—or shall we say *au revoir*! I shall look forward to getting to know you both better. Good-bye, Mrs. Clurey. Don't bother to show me out,' and they took him at his word, Helena standing motionless, Brian moving so that the departing guest should not even brush against him as he went.

They heard the click of the front door as it shut behind him.

'Detestable blighter,' commented Brian. 'You're sure we can't persuade you to change your mind about dinner, Mum?'

'Not tonight, dear. Do sit down, Lois. Is it all right to call you that? It's such a charming name.'

'I certainly shouldn't like you to call me anything else,' said the girl prettily. 'You'll come another evening, won't you? I know you haven't been very well, but you're feeling better, aren't you, Mrs. Clurey?'

'Much better. It was nothing really. Will you have some tea, or would you rather have sherry?'

'I'd love some tea if we can get it ourselves. You sit down and let us wait on you. Come on, Brian. Show me where the works are.'

'I shouldn't dream—' began Helena, but Brian pushed her down into her chair.

'You do as you're told for once,' he said. 'Lois and I are dabs at doing things. She can even make cakes, but there's not much time for that, so we'll have toast. Any anchovy, Mum?'

'Yes, in the kitchen cupboard, though I really don't like—'

'Well, you do what you don't like for a change. Here's the evening paper. Read all the scandals and be ready to entertain us with them when we come back. Come on, woman. Shake a leg.'

She could hear them talking and laughing as she sat there, the newspaper on her knee, but quite unable to read a word of it.

Oh, God, nothing must happen to him, to them, these young, happy things with their lives in front of them! Nothing must spoil it for them, no shadow cast by her, nothing sordid or mean.

But how could she protect them, always, against everything?

Lois Garner was just what she would have chosen for him, as young as he was, clear-eyed, with truth and candour and sweetness shining from her like a beacon. One could not miss it. It was there for all to see.

And they were in love with each other. One could not mistake that either, though it was the loving of the modern generation with nothing stickily sentimental about it. They were no moony-eyed romantics. They saw life as it was, with no rose-coloured glasses to give it a fictitious value. They had the same interests, too. She would help him, not only with her brain and her scholastic knowledge but also with her personality, that sureness of herself which would keep them separate entities, however deeply they loved. Brian would never demand subjection from her and she would never give it.

Nothing, nothing, must spoil what they had found, each other and their loving.

'I don't believe you've read a word,' said Brian, coming back with a loaded tray, tea and a pile of crisp toast, anchovy for them, buttered for her since she did not like anchovy.

'No, I was just resting,' she said.

'You should do a lot more of that,' he said, setting down the tray.

Lois brought her a little table.

'Is it all right for me to pour out, Mrs. Clurey?' she asked. 'Or am I taking too much on myself?'

'Of course not. It's very nice to be waited on,' said Helena with a smile.

When they had finished, Brian took Lois to his mother's room to 'tidy up', as she put it, though the short dark hair looked perfectly neat and she wore the least possible amount of make-up. Then he returned to the living-room.

'Well?' he asked, smiling.

'She's perfectly charming,' said Helena.

'And how! I knew you'd like her. Tell you all about her some time. What was that blighter Paraway doing here?'

'I—he—he just called to see how I was,' said Helena.

'What does it matter to him? He's nothing to do with us.'

'My dear, he's Alison's friend,' she said weakly.

'Then the sooner he isn't, the better. He's an absolute bounder.'

'But you don't know anything about him, Brian, do you?' she asked, frightened.

'Not really, but it sticks out a mile. Who is he? What is he? Nasty smarmy type, with his clothes, and that flashy ring. He's not our sort at all. What on earth does she see in him? And he's *old*.'

'Much too old for Alison,' she agreed. 'I don't know quite what we can do about it, though. If we refuse to let him come here, it will only drive the affair into something furtive and secret.'

'Well, I shall jolly well make it my business to find out something about him, something that may put her off. It shouldn't be difficult. A man like that, and at his age, chasing a girl like Alison! It's disgusting. He's probably got a wife somewhere, or has had one. He's just that sort. You leave it to me. I'll dig up the blighter's past. You wait.'

'Brian, be—be careful. After all, Alison—she's in love with him, or she thinks she is, and—and she'll be twenty-one so soon and able to do what she likes. Don't drive her into anything.

Promise me you'll stay out of this, Brian. Please, please don't interfere!'

He frowned impatiently.

'Well, if that's the way you feel about it, of course I'll hold my horses for the moment, but we can't possibly let her *marry* him.'

'No. No, of course we can't—but don't try to do anything about it yet, dear. Leave it to your father and me for the present.'

'O.K., if I must. Ready, dear?' as Lois returned. 'Let's get going then. See you soon, Mum, and for heaven's sake take care of yourself.'

VI

SOME two or three weeks later, the telephone bell rang whilst Helena was in the bath-room, polishing the taps. Once again the daily woman whom Simon had insisted she should have had let her down. This time it was one of her children who was ill. Helena, a mother herself, could not but accept the excuse as reasonable, though it was remarkable on how many occasions in a matter of little more than a fortnight one or other of Mrs. Weeks's children, or her husband, had been ill.

She started to leave the bath-room, but someone whisked down the stairs in front of her and, with annoyance, she recognised the tail of the drab overall which was Mrs. Oliver's almost unvaried attire.

She heard the snatch of the receiver off its base, and Mrs. Oliver's honeyed pseudo-B.B.C. voice produced for such occasions.

'Yes? . . . No, this is not Mrs. Clurey. This is Mrs. Oliver, Florence Oliver,' with a little refined giggle. 'Shall I call Mrs. Clurey for you? I think—'

But Helena had run down the stairs by this time and was beside her.

'Thank you, Mrs. Oliver,' she said curtly. There is no need for you to answer the telephone.'

Mrs. Oliver surrendered it with a scowl.

'I'm sure I don't want to—' she began.

'Then please don't,' snapped Helena, and, into the receiver, 'This is Mrs. Clurey.'

Giles Paraway's voice answered her.

'I suppose that was your lodger?'

'What is it?' she asked, and turning to Mrs. Oliver, who still stood at her elbow and could probably hear the other voice, 'Please go back to your own part of the house.'

'Oh, certainly!' said the woman and flounced away, but Helena was aware that she had not gone farther than the staircase.

'What do you want?' she asked Giles, an edge to her voice. 'I wish you would not telephone.'

'It's only a matter of courtesy, my dear, to know if it is convenient for me to call.'

'It is not convenient,' she said, but dare not replace the instrument. He would only ring again.

'I'm sorry you take that attitude, Helena, because I still propose to do so. A little later in the day, perhaps?'

'No,' she said and this time rang off firmly.

As she had surmised, Mrs. Oliver was still there.

'Mrs. Oliver, I must again ask you to be good enough not to come into this part of the house unless it is absolutely necessary, and above all, not to answer the telephone. It was made quite clear to you that it is not for your convenience, so any calls which come through are not for you.'

Mrs. Oliver bridled. There had been a change in her attitude lately, or else Helena, worried and apprehensive, imagined there had been. The woman's tone to her bordered on actual insolence, and she had developed a way of looking at her which sent a little shiver down her spine.

'As you were upstairs, I was only trying to 'elp,' said Mrs. Oliver, her beady eyes full of malice. ' 'Ow was I to know that it was your gentleman friend—or is 'e Alison's? I'm sure it's difficult to know, seeing the times he comes 'ere when she is at the office.'

Helena's head went up.

'You are impertinent, Mrs. Oliver,' she said. 'You have been asked many times to find other accommodation and leave this house. I shall be glad if you will do so at once.'

'You can't play them games with me, Mrs. Clurey, and well you know it. The law's on my side and so long as I pay my rent, you can't turn me out—*and* so long as me and my family be'ave decent, which *we* do. There's nothing against *us* and we can stay 'ere just as long as it suits us. That's the law.'

'The law was never intended to oblige house-owners to put up with insufferable conditions, and, as you know, we need the whole of our house for ourselves and our children.'

'That's as may be, but just you try to get us out. Just you try! We got the law on our side and it's about time people like you was taken down a peg or two. Times 'as changed and it's people like us as 'ave got the w'ip 'and now. England belongs to the people now, and folks like you 'ave 'ad their day, *Lady* Clurey. Lady Clurey!' and with a sniff, she went up the stairs, leaving Helen speechless and helpless.

Mrs. Oliver was right. She had the full force of the law on her side and there was nothing she and Simon could do to get rid of them until they chose to go.

She went draggingly back to her work, but her thoughts were not with it. She reflected miserably about what Mrs. Oliver had said of the increasingly frequent visits of Giles Paraway, not only during the evening when Alison was in (in fact, they were less frequent then), but during the day, when she had to receive him alone. The woman's unveiled suggestion that she was carrying on an intrigue with her daughter's 'gentleman friend' behind Alison's back was revolting. It was just the sort of thing such a woman would think, of course. Indeed, was it not possible that other people might think so, in the circumstances?

She went on mechanically with her hundred and one jobs, prepared the vegetables for the evening meal, sewed some buttons on Simon's shirts, found John's football boots caked with wet mud and put them outside to dry, washed a blouse which Alison would want the next day and was hanging it on the line when she heard her name and turned to find Giles Paraway beside her.

'I came in at the garden gate to save you opening the front

door,' he said.

'I prefer you to ring the bell,' she told him curtly, certain that Mrs. Oliver would be watching from her top window. The back gate squeaked and would have announced his arrival.

'Surely not going to treat me as a visitor, are you?' he asked. 'I feel like one of the family now.'

'Well, you're not,' she snapped and went into the house, followed by him. 'I wish you would stop coming, Giles.'

She had forced herself into the habit of calling him by that name.

'I'm not going to, Helena,' he said pleasantly, too pleasantly. She was always aware of the threat in his voice, his certainty that he held her in the hollow of his hand.

In the living-room, she faced him with the courage of desperation.

'Why do you torment me like this?' she asked. 'You've got what you want. You've forced yourself on us and obliged me to let you come here to see Alison. Why do you come when she is not here?'

'Isn't it obvious? To see you, my dear. You're still a very attractive woman, and I find the situation intriguing and amusing. I feel I never really knew you. If you had shown half the spirit in the old days that you do now, I might never have left you.'

'I am glad that at least you realise I am *not* the girl you deceived and betrayed. I am a woman, and Simon Clurey's wife, and you mean nothing at all to me personally now.'

'I regret that, of course, because I'd like you to be interested in me. In fact, in many ways I am more interested in you than I am in Alison.'

'Then let her alone.'

'Does that mean that if I were willing to do that, you would be a little kinder to me?'

'No. Never. You know all I want from you, that you leave me and my family alone.'

He smiled, and she knew how faint was the hope that she

could get rid of him.

'Now, come, Helena. Should I have taken all the trouble to contact you again just to fade away again? And think how desolated Alison would be if I did! I was really only putting a hypothetical case when I suggested I might transfer my interest from the daughter to the mother. Alison is passionately in love with me, and you know better than most people how it feels to be that. Also how it feels to have *me* for a lover.'

'Love! You don't know the meaning of the word,' she said scornfully.

'You thought I did once.'

'To defile and betray a girl who believed in you? Who gave you the best that was in her?'

'My dear Helena, it was impossible to live up to what you wanted of a man. You didn't see me as a man at all, but as a sort of Sir Galahad, a *preux chevalier*. You expected far more of me than a normal man has to give.'

'I expected decency and kindness and some sort of care for my welfare. Is that too much to ask? Giles, is there nothing I can say, nothing I can do, to keep you from wrecking Alison's life as you did mine?'

'You've got quite the wrong idea. I don't propose to wreck her life. I assure you I shall make her a model husband. I have already told you I don't want any hole-and-corner affair like ours. I've done with all that. I'm prepared to settle down and be, as I say, a model husband.'

'You don't really love her. You're not capable of unselfish love.'

'Perhaps not. I don't suggest that I'm not hoping to get something out of marriage with Alison—quite apart from a young and charming and adoring wife.'

'Then what do you expect? Money? Simon and I haven't two halfpennies to rub together,' she said contemptuously.

'Oh no, my dear, not money. I have plenty of that and I can always make more, as much as I want. You've never known much about me, have you? About my beginnings, I mean? Let me tell you.'

'Must you?' she asked, her lip curling.

She heard the front door close and knew, thankfully, that Mrs. Oliver had gone out, though what might she have been able to hear by listening at the door?

'I think so,' he said. 'Do sit down, my dear. You look like an accusing angel standing there—or a mother hen protecting her chicks. You've nothing to fear from me. Do believe that. You've only to let matters take their course, go on peacefully. I don't want things to be any different, nor need you. But do sit down so that I can do so. You see how my manners have improved? Quite the gentleman now!'

She sat down and he took a chair near hers. Her face was a pale mask, her mouth set, her eyes expressionless.

'I was born in very humble circumstances. You never knew that, but I don't mind telling you now. All our cards on the table, I think. My father was a bricklayer, not one of the lords of the earth as they are now, but just an ordinary working man who had to work for his living with no thought of becoming a trade union leader, and getting into parliament and becoming a peer or anything like that. We had enough to eat, but only just. We lived in a cottage in a village, and I went to the village school and was taught to know my betters when I saw them and to touch my cap and say "sir" when I was spoken to. I hated being subservient even then. Later on I managed to become a clerk. No brick-laying for me, though I could be only a very minor sort of clerk, still having to say "sir" to most people. I left the village and went to London, got a slightly better job through my native wits. I told you Brian got his brains from me, didn't I? Perhaps rather unfortunately, I got in then with a group of students from Oxford who were amusing themselves during the long vacation by doing what I suppose they regarded as slumming. I was about eighteen at the time, and I was rather pleased with myself for linking up with them. We taught them such things as boxing (I was quite good at that) and organised games, billiards and table tennis and darts and so on. The Oxford men also lectured on various subjects, though that left me out, but I joined in the debates and thought myself no end of a dog. Though some of them had titles of a sort, "Honourables" and all that, I wasn't expected to do any "sir-ing", but I called them by their names just as they called me Pellet. Then it came to an end. The vacation was nearly over and we packed up and at once I realised the difference. They all began to call one another by their Christian names, but I was still Pellet to them. They chaffed one another about the next term, about what they were going to do, about their plans for the winter vacation, winter sports and so on, but it was obvious that they did not any longer include me. Except for my fortnight's holiday, I had been going on with my work at the office, of course, spending all my evenings with them at the settlement, but once they started packing up, I saw that they'd never really accepted me as one of themselves. They even ordered me about, got me to carry things for them, their golf bags and their various kit for the week or two that they had kept free for their own holiday in France, or at posh seaside places, or at the homes they called their "places".

'The iron entered into my soul and I hated them, despised them and yet bitterly envied them. Nobody suggested that I should join them, or spoke of seeing me again. They were not interested in me. I had been part of their slumming! I tell you, Helena, that that was what set me on the road I'm on now, the road which would take me into their sort of life and force them to make me one of themselves. I slipped up when we had our little affair, you and I. I was quite madly in love with you, whatever you may choose to believe, but I may not have gone so far with you if you hadn't been who you were, Helena Thorwell, living at least on the fringe of the sort of life I intended to make my own. I was twenty-three then, and I'd gone quite a long way by using my brains and never missing an opportunity. I had done all sorts of things to make money, and I'd made quite a bit and I felt sure that your mother would bow to fate and accept me. Well, as you know, she didn't. She cast you off, though a good deal of that was your own fault. You remember that I tried to get you to communicate with her, but you refused. So there I was. You were a dead loss to me as far as any social advancement was concerned and that was what I was after. It's what I am still after. Now do you understand why I've come back into your life? Not into the life of Simon Clurey, a pettifogging little solicitor's clerk, but into the life of *Sir* Simon Clurey of The Holt. Understand?'

Helena had listened without interruption, without any sign of even hearing him, but every word had sunk in and now she did understand. Had it not been so potent a factor in her own life and that of those she loved, she might have found it in her heart to sympathise with him and be sorry for the proud, frustrated boy who knew he had it within himself, in his brains, to be the equal of those offshoots of the class he despised and yet longed to join. As it was, she had no sympathy, no pity.

'Well?' he asked as she remained silent. 'Do you understand what I want of you? But of course you do. As the friend of the Clureys, as the son-in-law of Sir Simon Clurey, I shall be in that social class at last and meet on terms of equality the sort of people who once sent me scurrying at their bidding, carrying their golf-clubs for them, fetching this and that. If I meet any of them, as I shall do, they are not likely to remember me. Why should they? I doubt if they ever troubled to look at me, a badly dressed lout who often needed a hair-cut and didn't even speak their language. Well, that's my story. Interesting?'

'You mean you intend to go through with this, marry Alison and remain in our circle of friends if and when we go to The Holt, for the rest of your life?' she asked with a dull certainty that that was what he did mean.

'Yes. Can you blame me? I have got where I am by never missing an opportunity, and when I saw your photograph that day in Galton and Somerley's office and realised why the name Clurey rang a bell in my mind (the typist had mentioned it when she showed me into his room), I knew that I was being given another golden opportunity. It is an unusual name, and I have a good memory, and I had read in the papers that when Sir

Curtis Clurey died, he would be succeeded by a man at present working in the offices of a London firm of solicitors. Simon Clurey—and his wife was you, Helena. I didn't lay any very definite plans then, but I made inquiries and they led me to Alison—and that's the whole story.'

'You're ruthless and sadistic as ever, Giles,' she said in a low voice.

'Not really. It's merely that I set myself a goal and I've never wavered from my intention of reaching it. Is that someone at the door? We seem fated to be interrupted, don't we? Perhaps your lodger coming back?'

But it was Alison, an hour before her usual time, Alison looking anxious, and surprised to find Giles with her mother.

Helena got up from her chair, annoyed to find that her face had flushed guiltily.

'Alison dear, you're early. Is anything wrong?' she asked.

'I don't know. Is there? Someone telephoned. Said I was wanted at home. You've not been ill again?'

'No, dear. But who could have telephoned? Who was it?'

'I don't know. The girl on the telephone took the message, just that I was wanted at home. It wasn't you, Giles, playing a trick to get me home?' turning to him for the first time.

'No, darling. It was nothing to do with me, though of course I'm delighted to see you. I was just going, as a matter of fact. I was passing and looked in to see your mother and should have called you later.'

'You're sure nothing's wrong, Mum? You don't look too well, you know, does she, Giles? She's so pale,' now that the colour had receded from Helena's cheeks again.

'I'm quite all right, dear, and I think the message must have been given to you instead of somebody else,' but the horrid thought came to her, almost a certainty, that it had been Mrs. Oliver who had telephoned, Mrs. Oliver bent on Alison's finding her here with Giles Paraway at a time when she herself was not expected.

'Yes, I suppose that must have been it,' agreed the girl. 'Well,

Giles, since I am home, there's no need for you to hurry away, is there? I'll make some tea. Sit down again both of you. I shan't be long. Will John be in?'

'No, he's been asked to the Robinsons'.'

Left alone again with her, Giles turned to Helena.

'Would you rather I went?' he asked.

'Oh, what does it matter what you do now?' she said drearily.

She could see no escape. She had accused him of being ruthless and sadistic and she knew him to be so. He would not hesitate to destroy her by telling the whole story to Simon if she refused to accept him and his plans, and for Simon to know would be worse than death to her.

What she had once told Ruth was true. She had not loved Simon when she married him, and she had never felt for him the wild, passionate abandonment to her emotions which Geoffrey Pellet had called forth in her. But during the years, she had come to something far better, something enduring and indestructible. What she had felt for Geoffrey was not love as she knew it now. She and Simon had drawn ever closer together, the bond their children and Simon's calm, unvarying affection for her, his care of her, the children loved, but Helena always his first thought. Through the years they had become truly one, bearing with each other's foibles and weaknesses, sharing the same problems and finding a solution together, their home the centre and meaning of their lives.

She truly loved Simon, loved him with all her heart, with gratitude for his unfaltering love, for her safety within that love, her knowledge that he would never fail her, that when the children were gone, as go they must to make their own homes and lives, he would still be with her, dependable, unchanging.

But to have him know her for what she really was! To know how she had tricked and trapped him and foisted off on him another man's son, the son of whom he was so proud, for whom he had made many sacrifices, for whose sake, he had confessed to her rather shyly one night, he would be glad to accept the otherwise unacceptable title when it came to him.

And if the truth were ever known, would Brian even be able to have it?

The shame, the disgrace, to Simon! They were unthinkable. To have repaid all his years of heavenly kindness to her like that!

She shrank down in her chair and let the easy flow of the conversation of Alison and Giles pass over her, though she was aware that every now and then the girl looked at her with an odd expression in her eyes, not just anxiety for her but something else, something different and vaguely disquieting.

He was still there when Simon came in.

'Oh—that you, Paraway?' he asked. He seldom called him by his Christian name, setting a gulf between them in his dislike of the man.

Alison was swift to leap to the defence of her beloved.

'You'd better stay to supper now, Giles. Hadn't he, Mother?'

That was another thing she had noticed about Alison lately, the use of the more formal 'Mother' more often than the old, loving 'Mum'.

'I—yes, dear,' she said weakly.

'I don't want to seem inhospitable,' said Simon with the stiffness he could not overcome towards Giles, 'but could you make it another evening? As a matter of fact, something has happened which will make us rather busy this evening and Mrs. Clurey will probably like to be rather free.'

'What's happened, Daddy?' asked Alison, obviously bent on not having Giles excluded from whatever affected her family.

Simon hesitated, then decided to explain.

'Well, as a matter of fact, they have been on to me from The Holt again and they want us to go down tomorrow."

'Us?' asked Helena, surprised.

'Yes. You were specifically mentioned, and Brian and Alison. I said we shouldn't want John to miss any of his schooling just now, even for a few days. I dare say Ruth would have him, wouldn't she? I have spoken to Brian, and he can manage it. You can fix it up, Alison, I suppose?'

She looked excited.

'Oh yes, I think so. We're not very busy, and I've got a few days owing to me anyway. You don't mean that anything's happened? To Sir Curtis?'

'No, but it was his doctor who spoke to me, and it seems that Sir Curtis is worried, and is most anxious to see us, and I am afraid I was obliged to say that we would go. Not that I want to, of course.'

'I can't see why either Alison or I should be needed,' said Helena. 'You, of course, and one can understand he'd like to see Brian—'

'He is most insistent on us all going, except John, of course. Anyway, I have said that we will go and that I will look out the trains and let them know.'

'Why not let me drive you down?" asked Giles. 'I know just about where it is, and though it is not far by road, it will mean a change by train. I could take the Bentley and get you down there much more comfortably—and it would be far less tiring for Mrs. Clurey.'

Helena gave him a defeated look. Whatever arguments they put forward, this was what would happen. She knew it.

'We couldn't put you to that trouble,' said Simon stiffly.

'I assure you that far from being a trouble, it would be a pleasure,' he said. 'Alison, support me,' turning to her with an assured smile.

'But of course I support you,' she said. 'It's a marvellous idea. I know I'd much rather go in the Bentley than dragging there by train, and as you say, it will be much less tiring for Mother.'

Simon was not pleased, but the advantages of the suggestion were too obvious to be brushed aside and he accepted with what grace he could.

'That would be very kind of you then—Giles,' he said. 'What time would you suggest starting? I said we would be there well before lunch.'

'Oh—about eleven then? I'll call for you here, of course. And I quite understand that you won't want to be bothered with an extra one for a meal this evening, so I'll take myself off,' and he did so.

'I should be quite all right by train,' said Helena somewhat ungraciously after he had gone. 'Won't it put us in a difficult position, introducing a perfect stranger there at such a time?'

'Oh, Mummy, Giles isn't exactly a stranger, is he? After all, even though you won't let us be openly engaged, he is my fiancé,' said Alison defiantly.

'You're not to say so to Sir Curtis,' said her father with unwonted severity. 'In fact, if he has any tact, he will not come into the house at all. I shall make it quite clear to him that he does not go there as an invited guest.'

But whether he made it clear in his own view or not, Giles walked calmly into The Holt with them the next day and was received without question by the housekeeper, Mrs. Potter, when Alison took it into her own hands to introduce him as 'Mr. Paraway, who kindly brought us down in his car to save my mother a tiring journey'.

Though The Holt could not be described as one of the stately homes of England, it was large enough and important enough, standing in large gardens and a small expanse of parkland, to be very impressive, at least to the two young Clureys. Built of grey, weathered stone, with long windows opening to a flagged terrace, with its spread of stables and out-buildings behind it, and the roof of a large glass-house, the place had a look of dignity and spaciousness, and when they were inside the wide hall, old Persian rugs on the floor and the walls covered with family portraits, they could see that everything was well kept and designed for comfort.

'Sir Curtis asks you to excuse him from joining you at lunch,' said Mrs. Potter, ushering them into a pleasant sitting-room, 'but he will be with you afterwards. Dr. Mace is with him now and will take luncheon, and Sir Curtis's solicitor, Mr. Earnley, will also join you. I will have the luggage taken up and then I will show you to your rooms. Sir Curtis would like you to make yourselves quite at home. There is whisky and sherry on the side-table here, but I will have coffee brought to you if you prefer it. Luncheon will be served at one-thirty.'

She was a pleasant woman, brisk and business-like and showing no sort of resentment of the new-comers, though she must have known their mission, which was to prepare to take possession in due course.

'Mr. Paraway will be staying?' she asked.

'If it is not encroaching on Sir Curtis's hospitality,' said Giles quickly before anyone else could speak. 'I shall be at anyone's disposal then with my car.'

The housekeeper allowed herself one quick glance at the uninvited guest and Helena felt herself flushing, but Giles was quite unperturbed.

'It can easily be arranged,' she said, and when she had left them, there was a moment's uncomfortable pause, even Alison slightly out of countenance. Brian looked thunderous.

'I didn't think you proposed to stay, Paraway,' he said.

'My dear chap, it's purely for your mother's sake,' said Giles easily. 'How about these drinks? Shall I do the honours?'

'Certainly not,' said Simon curtly, and went towards the table on which they were hospitably set out. 'I think you should have a brandy, Helena. I see there is some here. What about you, Alison?'

'It's something of an adventure for me to have strong drink at this time of day,' said Alison, forcing lightness into her tone, 'but may I have sherry? The dark one?'

'You, Brian?' asked his father.

'Whisky and soda for me, Dad. This is a very pleasant room, isn't it?'

'A good house altogether,' agreed his father, pouring out the drinks. 'Whisky for you, Paraway?'

'Thanks. Yes. Getting a bit chilly for the time of year, isn't it? Or perhaps it's the atmosphere of the ancestral hall. Jolly view from this window, isn't it? It must cost a packet to keep these gardens up, but I imagine money's no object here.'

He was the only one of them completely at his ease, so completely that of necessity the atmosphere thawed. The

Clureys could not do otherwise than accept the situation forced upon them, and they were chatting more or less amicably by the time Mrs. Potter returned to take them to their rooms.

The bedrooms were large and comfortable and the bathrooms adequate.

'I have put you in the West Wing, Mr. Paraway,' said the housekeeper. 'We have only three guest rooms in the main part, but I think you will be quite comfortable. Will you come with me?'

'This will be very jolly,' he said imperturbably, but it was obvious to him that he was being regarded as outside the family to whom she wished to show every honour. The room was, as she had said, comfortable, but it had no view of the gardens and he had to go down a corridor to a bath-room.

'I hope Sir Curtis will not feel I am intruding,' he said, 'but as I am engaged to Miss Alison Clurey, I can almost be regarded as family.'

'Indeed?' was the housekeeper's only comment.

His lips tightened when she had left him. An outsider, was he? Well, time would change all that.

Lunch was a pleasant affair. The doctor and Mr. Earnley were obviously *habitués* of the house and could talk of its history, and though they, too, showed a little surprise at the presence of the uninvited guest, Giles could talk well and was so much at his ease that the slight stiffness passed off. To the surprise and somewhat to the chagrin of her family, Alison had appeared with a beautiful diamond ring on her engagement finger, without giving them an opportunity of commenting on it, and she had openly introduced Giles as her fiancé to explain his presence.

Afterwards Simon went alone to meet his cousin, but after he had had a short, formal talk with him, Sir Curtis appeared in the sitting-room and made the acquaintance of his other guests.

It was obvious that he was a very sick man, his tall form thin to emaciation, his aristocratic face, so unlike Simon's, chalk white, but he insisted on accompanying them on a tour of the main rooms of the house and, well wrapped up and leaning on a stick, to the gardens and stables. He excused himself from going as far as the dairy in which, by modern methods, the output from the small home farm was dealt with.

Giles Paraway, to the surprise and slight discomfort of the family, showed himself in a new light as intelligent and knowledgeable about the workings of the estate, small but complete, and Sir Curtis warmed to him, walking ahead with him and discussing what was clearly a passion with him. He loved his home and had spent large sums on it, and showed his anxiety about it passing into the hands of a man who, as a solicitor's clerk with a small London home, could not be expected to know anything about running such an estate. Simon, looking harassed and out of his depth, did his best to make intelligent comments, but there could be no doubt of Giles Paraway's superior knowledge and ability.

Brian was gloomy and Helena felt the whole thing was a nightmare, but Alison was plainly delighted with her fiancé's success.

'Isn't Giles marvellous?' she asked them happily whilst Paraway and Sir Curtis discussed the comparative merits of hand- and machine-milking and the yield of the small Jersey herd which was Sir Curtis's pride and joy. 'I'd no idea he knew about such things. He's certainly a dark horse, isn't he? I wonder how he got all this knowledge? Nobody could have guessed it, could they?'

The acquisition of such knowledge had cost him rapid, intensive study during the past few weeks, learning from books, agricultural records and farming papers, but his quick brain had assimilated it so that he could use his superficial knowledge impressively and by the time they returned to the house, he had become 'my dear fellow' and his host's hand was thrust through his arm to give him added support, for he was very tired.

'You should rest now. Sir Curtis,' said the doctor anxiously, but he was waved aside.

'A chair, and something to rest my feet on,' he said. 'I'm far too much interested in this scheme of yours for cross-breeding to let the subject drop yet. I'm against cross-breeding, Paraway, especially with the Jerseys, but what you tell me is very thought-provoking, very. You say you can give me chapter and verse?'

'Well, I haven't got the exact data with me, of course,' said Giles, 'but I can easily get it for you and send it down.'

'Can you write for it?'

'Certainly, though it will take a few days. I could run up to town for it.'

'Do that, will you? You're going to stay a while, I hope? And you, Simon?' though this was something of an afterthought. It was clear that for him, Giles Paraway had become the most interesting of his guests.

'A day or two if you wish,' said Simon stiffly. 'I have arranged to be away from my office for as long as you think desirable.'

'Quite. There are a few things I want to discuss with you, of course. I'll leave over that matter of the new Will, Earnley, for a day or two. Now that other thing you were saying, Paraway—?'

'About the recent experiments in afforestation, you mean? As a matter of fact, I did pick up just before I left the article I was referring to. It's in my bag. I'll fetch it.'

Giles, the opportunist, went up to London the next morning, returning in good time for dinner.

During his absence, the family saw little of their host, who kept to his room until word was brought to him that Mr. Paraway had returned.

'I must say Paraway sprang a surprise on me,' said Simon as the four of them sat at lunch alone that day. 'Did you know he was so knowledgeable about estate work, Alison?'

'I hadn't any idea,' she said happily; 'but then, he's a man of so many parts that I shouldn't really be surprised, I suppose. What a good thing he came down with us. Without him, it would have been awkward for all of us, wouldn't it? You and Brian couldn't have put up much of a show, Daddy, could you? What a lot there is to know, and I suppose this isn't what you'd call a big estate, is it?'

'Bigger than I thought,' said her father gloomily. 'I didn't know there was all this farming and intensive cultivation. I understand Curtis has had a good bailiff, or agent, or whatever you call them, but he's left recently, too old for the job or something, and I can only hope Curtis will find another before any of this devolves on me. What do you say, Brian?'

'It isn't in my line,' said Brian in the same gloomy tone. 'Never will be, either—though thank goodness it won't have to be, not for a good many years anyway. I'm no farmer.'

With the exception of Alison, they were all vaguely apprehensive of Giles's return. The visit had turned out to be quite different from anything they had anticipated and far from their being obliged to explain and apologise for bringing an outsider into what was to have been a family conclave, it was they who felt themselves outsiders and Giles to whom Sir Curtis turned and on whose opinion he showed himself inclined to rely.

Yet Giles's manner to his fellow-guests was beyond reproach. In their presence he was modestly retiring, except when Sir Curtis singled him out, as he frequently did. His manners were irreproachable, and he showed no sign of elation at his success. On the contrary, he tried in every way to draw Simon into the discussions he had with Sir Curtis, deferring to him and even treating him as an older man in a recognisably superior position in the house.

'Damn it, Helena,' said Simon irritably as they prepared for bed on the fourth evening of their stay, 'the fellow's as old as I am, if not older, and he actually called me "sir" once or twice. Did you notice it?'

'Of course,' she said quietly. 'I suppose it's all part of his plan."

She had given up the struggle against Giles. It was all too much for her, and she was sunk in a lethargy of resignation to the inevitable even though her mind constantly seethed with the horror of what had now become Alison's open engagement to her former lover. She neither sought nor wanted any private conversation with him. What could she say or do? Nothing, whilst they remained at The Holt and Giles was the most acceptable guest.

And at the end of the week, an uncomfortable week for most of them, the solicitor asked them to have a conference with him.

'We'll just wait for Mr. Paraway,' he said, and there was a tenseness in his look and tone which told them that he, at least, had not fallen under the spell of the man whom he actually disliked and distrusted. 'He is with Sir Curtis at the moment and will be with us shortly, but in the meantime I have Sir Curtis's authority to tell you of a new arrangement he has made. He has appointed Mr. Paraway as his agent in place of Mr. Fanshaw, who, as you know, had to give up the post through ill health some weeks ago.'

The Clureys were stunned. It was the last thing any of them, except Alison, had expected or desired. It meant that, whatever their private wishes or views, Giles Paraway had established himself as an integral part of their lives.

No one spoke, and Mr. Earnley's quiet, precise voice added a few details.

'Sir Curtis wishes Mr. Paraway to take over his duties at once, and I understand he has agreed to that, so he will be returning to The Holt as soon as he can clear up his present affairs, which I understand will be in about a fortnight. Meantime, there is the matter of Sir Curtis's new Will. Ah, here is Mr. Paraway,' as Giles joined them, his manner genial, his face expressive of the lively satisfaction he felt.

He looked round as he took the seat left vacant for him.

'I see that Mr. Earnley has told you of my surprising good fortune,' he said. 'More than surprising to me, of course, but very much to my delight. It's the sort of job I've always thought I'd like, but it never entered my head that I could ever achieve it.'

They kept their own counsel, though to Simon and Brian and Helena it was beyond doubt that he had planned the whole thing, and would have accomplished it even if he had not had the supreme luck of this early and unexpected chance of arriving at The Holt under the aegis of the family.

'You've been very lucky then,' said Brian, his lip curling.

'I think it's marvellous, darling,' said Alison, giving them a withering look, 'but of course it's absolutely right for you.'

'Thank you, dear,' he said, with a flashing smile. 'Is there some other business, Mr. Earnley?'

'Er—yes. Sir Curtis wishes me to make you acquainted with the provisions of a new Will which he signed this morning. The estate, being entailed, comes to you, of course, Mr. Clurey, together with sufficient additional funds to keep it up in its present style, a thing which Sir Curtis greatly desires. In fact, he has made special provisions to ensure that. So long as Mr. Paraway continues to act as the bailiff of the estate, a large sum is to be appropriated to its upkeep in addition to the provisions I have already indicated, and—er—on the marriage of Miss Alison Clurey to Mr. Paraway, a further sum is left to her for her personal use, together with the house known as Frant House situated at the north corner of the estate and at present occupied by Sir Hugh Brasset, who will be willing to vacate it when required.'

Alison drew a sharp breath. She understood now why she had been specially invited by Sir Curtis to go over the house, and Sir Hugh Brasset's interest in her. It was a substantial house, standing in its own grounds, an important place for a young bride, far exceeding any home she might otherwise have attained.

'There are bequests to you, Mr. Brian Clurey,' went on the lawyer's unemotional voice, his eyes on the notes from which he was reading, 'and a Trust Fund for your younger brother, John, and Sir Curtis wishes you, Mrs. Clurey, to have, for your lifetime, a valuable collection of jewellery and silver, these going after your death to Mr. Brian Clurey's wife or, failing any such wife, to Miss Alison Clurey. Those are the main provisions. There are bequests to servants, and a few to charities, and Sir Curtis has made separate provision for the payment of the bulk of the death duties, which will of course be considerable. If there are any questions you would like to ask me, please do so.'

After a few moments' silence, Helena surprised them all by speaking jerkily, the words forced from her almost against her will.

'Does this mean that if my daughter does not marry Mr. Paraway, she will not benefit at all?' she asked.

'Well, not to the same extent, I am afraid. I advised Sir Curtis against this line, advised him very strongly,' said Mr. Earnley, shooting a glance at Giles whose meaning was unmistakably hostile, 'but he insisted on it. There is, of course, a clause covering the possible death of Mr. Paraway before the Will becomes operative, or before such a marriage can reasonably take place, but that is the main idea. Sir Curtis is anxious, most anxious, that the marriage shall take place and that Mr. Paraway's—er—connection with the estate shall be as far as possible—er—consolidated.'

They were dumbfounded, all of them except Giles himself, who appeared entirely at his ease and in no way intimidated by the formidable plans set out for him.

Apart from paying a formal visit to Sir Curtis, who after the exertions of the week, was very tired and had taken to his bed again, there was nothing to keep them there any longer.

'I'll run you back to town, of course,' said Giles genially. 'I may have to come back in a day or two to discuss a few matters with Sir Curtis when he is able to see me, but it will take at least a fortnight for me to clear up my most pressing affairs in London before coming back to The Holt to begin my work in earnest. How soon can you be ready, Mrs. Clurey? Shall we say half-past two? That will give us comfortable time for lunch and to get back before dark. I'll pop in to have a final word with Sir Curtis when you have all said good-bye to him, but he is a very tired man so we won't exhaust him any further.'

It was clear that he had already accepted his new position.

Whilst they waited, sitting in his car with the luggage already loaded on, Brian looked about him and resolutely broke the silence which lay like a leaden weight on them all.

'It's a lovely place,' he said. 'I never imagined it anything like this, did you. Mum? You've seen it before, of course, Dad.'

'Once, a good many years ago. Curtis has improved it a lot since then. I suppose, having lost his wife and then so tragically his sons, he made it the main interest in his life, but it's we who are really going to reap his harvest, though not yet, I hope.'

'It's pretty obvious that it can't be long,' said Brian. 'A pity. I quite like the old boy, even though he's a bit—well, queer about the place. Who'd have thought Paraway would step into the picture like this? All right, all right, Allie! Don't get your hackles up. We've got to accept the situation and make the best of it, and after all, the old boy must think he's a capable bloke or he wouldn't have done it, and you and I don't know anything about it. We should have to have a capable man in any case. I'd hate to see the place go to rack and ruin, or in fact, to be anything but what it is now. Look at that line of trees! Put there to break the wind, I suppose, but aren't they just right? Everything seems to me just right. I don't want old Curtis to rub out, of course, but—well, all this does something to me. Have you got an odd feeling of—of belonging, Dad?'

'No, I can't say I have,' said his father rather grimly. 'I don't feel as though I should fit into it all, so perhaps it's a good thing you do, as the eventual owner.'

'Well, that will be a good many years off, we hope, but—when it's yours, Dad, I'd like to bring Lois here. You know the old part of it, that they don't use now? Mrs. Potter was telling me that it was intended for the use of Curtis's eldest son, before he inherited the lot. It's complete in itself, kitchens and all, and Curtis was going to modernise it like the rest of the place when young Curtis married. I've got my eye on it for Lois and me, if that would fit into your schemes, Dad? If I get my new job, this won't be too far away for us to live.'

Helena roused herself. She found the whole subject horrible, now that Giles Paraway had secured such a stake in it for himself. She would never want to live there. If only Simon could be persuaded not to do so!

'I suggest you drop the subject, Brian,' she said, an unusual note of acerbity in her voice. 'Do you realise you are already making plans for Curtis Clurey's death? It's—it's indecent.'

Brian laughed. Even Simon smiled, indulgently.

'Your mother's quite right, of course,' he said. 'It *is* indecent. Still, I'm glad you feel like that about it, son. I don't want it, or the title, for myself, and I could very well do without it, but it gives me a lot of pleasure to feel that I shall have something to pass on to you which you really do want and will value. You'll make a much better lord of the manor than I ever shall! There's Paraway,' his tone changing as he saw Giles approaching the car.

VII

HELENA had reached a conclusion, reached it painfully, inevitably, knowing that in doing so she was about to lay her life and her happiness in ruins. Still greater pain was it to know that she would wreck Simon's happiness as well.

But she could not let Alison marry Giles Paraway. Apart from her natural revulsion at the thought of her daughter marrying the man who had been her own lover, and was Brian's father, she knew the man himself too well to believe for an instant that Alison could find any happiness with him. Alison was at heart a romantic, as her mother had been, and for all the veneer of modern ways of thought and conduct and speech, she was a dreamer living in a world of her own imagination. Giles had said that she, Helena, had invented her own image of him, a *preux chevalier*, and had been cruelly disillusioned when he failed to live up to it. Alison was living in the same unreal world, seeing him just as Helena had seen him, and she would be as cruelly disillusioned, as bitterly hurt.

Though it pleased him to be, or to pretend to be, passionately in love with the girl, it would not last. Alison would no more be able to hold his interest or his so-called 'love' than she had been, for they were too much alike. And it was just because they were so much alike that Helena knew only the most drastic ripping away of the veil of glamour in which she had robed Giles could possibly make the girl see him as he really was.

So, white-faced, stony-eyed, not attempting to defend herself, she took the first steps by deliberately fostering Alison's suspicions about the frequent visits of her intended husband to her mother, suspicions which Mrs. Oliver was only too glad to support.

'Your young man's in there with your mum,' she would say, having watched for the girl's return so as to catch her in the hall.

'Bin in there hours, 'e 'as too. I must say it's nice that 'e and your mum are so friendly. 'Ere yesterday too! Well, well.'

Alison never replied to such comments, but her colour would rise and there would be an ominous flash in her eyes and an edge to her voice when she interrupted what Helena had made to look like an intimate *tête-à-tête*.

And when she felt she had prepared the ground sufficiently for the step she intended to take, Helena rang up Giles's club to ask him to call. Her time was running short, for it would soon be time for him to take up his residence at The Holt and she must act before that happened.

He came in in his usual breezy fashion, rubbing his hands and going to warm them at the fire which the chilly September day made acceptable.

'You always manage to create a homely atmosphere, my dear,' he said. 'I shall miss these cosy afternoons and this room when I go to The Holt, though I'm to have very comfortable quarters there—until Alison and I go to Frant House, of course.'

'That's what I wanted to see you about, Giles,' said Helena steadily, having steeled herself all day for this moment. 'You will not be living at Frant House, nor will you marry Alison nor go to The Holt as Sir Curtis Clurey's bailiff.'

He turned to her in surprise, but with an indulgent smile.

'Really? And who is going to prevent me from doing these things?' he asked.

'I am, Geoffrey.' She had not called him by that name for a long time. Now it came from her lips deliberately. 'I have made up my mind. I am going to tell Simon the truth, and Alison, and if you force me to do so, Sir Curtis Clurey as well. When I have done so, each and all of them will realise that it is impossible for the present plans to be put into effect, any of them.'

She had looked straight at him, eyes and voice unfaltering,

whilst she spoke. He could not doubt her absolute determination.

He was silent for a few moments. Then he spoke with a deliberation which matched her own.

'The truth. What exactly do you mean by that, Helena?'

'That I was once your mistress,' she said steadily.

Again he appeared to be considering his words carefully before he spoke them.

'That will not be the truth, Helena. You were not my mistress,' he said. 'You were, and are, my wife.'

'No!'

Her lips framed the word but no sound came. She stood still, staring at him, her eyes wide, her mind trying to grapple with the meaning of the unspeakable thing he had said.

'You're lying, of course,' she said at last, her voice shaking.

'No. In this instance, and at whatever cost, I am not,' he said. 'Our marriage was legal.'

'But you said—you told me—oh no, no! I don't believe you. I don't!'

'I'm sorry, my dear, but I'm afraid you will have to,' he said calmly. 'Do you mind if I smoke? It's almost as much of a shock to me to have to tell you as for you to hear it, but you've forced the position on both of us.'

She watched him with the fascinated gaze of a bird hypnotised by a snake, as he took out a cigarette and lit it.

'I still—don't—believe you,' she repeated slowly, mechanically, but she did. He could not have made such a statement, damning to them both, had it not been the truth.

Then she dropped weakly into a chair and put her hand over her eyes.

'You—fiend,' she whispered.

'I see that you do believe it, my dear. Why should I say such a thing, in all the circumstances, if it were not true? It is easily proved, of course. I know I told you when we parted that it was not a legal marriage, that I had engineered a fake one, but it suited my purpose then, just as it suits me now to tell you, but only you. *Only you*, Helena.'

She uncovered her eyes and looked at him.

'What do you mean by that?' she asked.

'Exactly what I say, that there is no need for anyone else to know. It need not change the situation at all, except that, of course, you will no longer oppose my marriage to Alison or my other plans. If you did, you would not be stopping at the ruin of your own personal life. You would bring down with you everything and everybody. It would make you Simon Clurey's mistress instead of his wife, it would make your two younger children bastards, and it would make Brian my legitimate son and *not* the heir to the Clurey title and estates. And think of the publicity it would bring on you all, the notoriety, I should say. Can you picture the headlines in the newspapers, especially as there has already been some publicity over what the newsmongers called the "romance" of Simon's inheritance? No, my dear, I don't think you will want to say or do anything *now*!'

'You don't mean—you can't mean—that you intend to marry Alison?' she gasped. 'It would make you a—bigamist!'

'Well, my dear, you're one, you know.'

He let it sink in, not looking at her but standing there before the fire, leisurely flicking off the ash from his cigarette, stooping to push farther in a piece of coal which was sending smoke into the room.

She felt like death. If only that could happen, if only she could die here and now, escape this awful thing which had come to her! But people do not die just because they want to. If they did, the world would not have survived.

Round and round ran her thoughts in the squirrel's cage of a mind which could find no way out. Any solution was unthinkable. It was just as he had said. None of them could escape utter disaster if she spoke; if she kept silent, Alison would marry a bigamist and her own mother's husband!

'You'd better go,' she said at last, speaking with difficulty. 'I—I must be alone—think—decide—'

'Yes, I realise I've given you something to think about. I'm truly sorry it had to come to this. I never intended that it should.

I was content to leave things as they were, to let the past bury its own dead and never exhume it. But you know, you really did force my hand, Helena. You were unwise ever to cross swords with me. You should have known that you could not hope for victory, that I should never allow you or anyone to divert me from my purpose. I am truly sorry for the position you are in, but, after all, why not accept the easier solution? I'm not such a bad chap at heart, though I know I gave you a raw deal. I was young then, and trapped into a situation I had never intended. I would have made you a good husband, and nothing need have happened to our marriage if your mother had not taken up the indefensible attitude she did. She forced us into a position that was tenable for neither of us, living that wretched existence which ended in the filthy hovel in Brittany. In my own justification, I will say that I didn't know you were with child. That might have made a difference. I don't know. We were heartily sick of each other. We had used each other up, mentally and physically. I was young and healthy, but you know, my sweet, you made inordinate demands on me without perhaps realising that a man uses himself up where a hot-blooded woman does not—'

She put her hands over her ears.

'Oh stop, stop! Need you go into all that? Need you try to push me any farther down?' she cried wildly.

'No, perhaps I'm not being quite fair—though surely I am entitled to a little fairness myself? Let's leave it for the moment. As you say, you need a little time to think, but don't take too long. You can't, you know, as I shall be going down to The Holt in a few days. I haven't really any doubt as to the conclusion you will come to. It would be such arrant folly to come to any other. There's someone at your door. Shall I let them in as I go out?'

'I can't see anyone,' said Helena, crouching down in her chair, and she took no notice of the voices which reached her faintly through the closed door after he had left her.

The caller was Ruth Mallow.

From one circumstance and another, Ruth had not yet met

the man who was known to her only as Giles Paraway, and when she saw who had opened the door to her, she stood still in amazement, recognising him at once.

'You—good heavens, *you*!' she said, staring at him. 'You're Geoffrey Pellet, aren't you? What on earth are you doing here? You *are* Geoffrey Pellet, aren't you?'

He made her a little mocking bow and stood aside for her to enter.

'I was,' he said. 'That was a long time ago, though. I have been someone else for quite a few years now. The name is Paraway, Giles Paraway, at your service.'

'You are Giles Paraway? *You?*' she asked blankly.

'Surprised, I expect. You'd better go in to Helena. She's a bit upset. She'll tell you—well, some of it, anyway,' and he smiled, gave another little bow and went out.

He had often wondered what would be Ruth's reaction when, as was inevitable, they met, whether she would even recognise him after all these years. Helena would possibly tell her sister the whole story, since Ruth's arrival had happened to coincide with such a moment in her affairs. He thought it would be as well if she did confide in Ruth, who was made more after her mother's pattern than after Helena's. The older sister would bring her hard common sense to bear on the situation, would urge her to the most convenient rather than the most ethical solution. He could not see Ruth advising her to throw everything up for the sake of having a clear conscience. Ruth would be as much an opportunist as he was himself, as Mrs. Thorwell had been when she seized on the chance of marrying her pregnant daughter to Simon Clurey, as of course she must have done. Helena alone would never have engineered so convenient a marriage. She would have sunk down in the pit and let herself be engulfed in its miry waters without even trying to get out.

Yes, definitely Ruth was the proper person to handle this affair.

Ruth exclaimed anxiously as she went into the living-room to find Helena sitting bolt upright in her chair, her face drained of colour, her eyes staring with a wild light in them, her hands tearing to shreds the handkerchief they held.

'Good heavens, my dear. What's happened?' she asked. 'Is it that man? Giles Paraway indeed! I recognised him at once, but what on earth's going on? Why didn't you tell me he's Geoffrey Pellet?'

'I couldn't. It was too awful. Oh, Ruth, I haven't known what to do! I don't know. Everything's simply ghastly,' and she gave way to her overwrought feelings by flinging herself into her sister's arms and bursting into tears.

Ruth let her cry for a bit, and then pulled her up by her shoulders determinedly, giving her a little, friendly shake.

'Now come on,' she said. 'You've had your cry. Now tell me what it's all about and bow on earth Geoffrey Pellet came on the scene again. He's not really engaged to Alison, is he? Why, he's old enough to be her father.'

But until, haltingly and always having to feel for her words, Helena told the whole story, omitting nothing, Ruth had no idea of the real enormity of what the reappearance of Geoffrey Pellet in Helena's life signified.

When the full tale was told, she sat for a few moments in stunned silence. It was incredible, and had she not heard it from Helena's own lips, she would not have believed it. Of course, Helena was just the sort of person who *would* get into a mess of that sort!

'I always knew there was something fishy about your sudden marriage to Simon,' she said at last, 'but never in my wildest dreams would I have thought of that! Do you suppose Mother had any idea? That your marriage to Geoffrey was legal, I mean?'

'Oh, she *couldn't* have,' said Helena. 'It was—it was bigamy, Ruth!'

'I know, but I wouldn't put it past Mother. She'd never have thought it possible that he would turn up again like this, after all this time, and propose to marry your own daughter. Still, there's no sense in speculating about that, and thank heaven she's not alive. She'd have ten thousand fits, especially with the Clurey title about to descend on you. Of course you're not going to own up, are you? I suppose he's blackmailing you?'

'Not for money. He's got much more than we have, probably more than we shall have after Curtis Clurey dies. No, it's not that. He's determined to marry Alison! Oh, Ruth, what shall I do? What shall I do?' and the tears started again.

'Well, stop crying for one thing,' said Ruth firmly. 'That won't get us anywhere. And you haven't answered my question. Are you or are you not going to admit this other marriage? Think what it would mean!'

'That's just it. I do know what it would mean. It would simply kill Simon,'

'And you too, from the look of you. I wonder why things like Geoffrey Pellet are allowed to live?'

'You'd better not call him that, Ruth. Nobody but us knows that's his real name. He's Giles Paraway to everybody else.'

'All right. Giles Paraway, then. A muck heap by any other name would smell as foul. You say he wants to marry Alison, so evidently *he* doesn't want his first marriage to come out. What exactly does he threaten?'

'That's the awful part. He doesn't threaten anything. He doesn't have to. He won't say a word if I don't. He'll just go on being Giles Paraway—and marry Alison—and take this job at The Holt—and live there—oh, Ruth!'

'H'm. Sticky. Very. You're in a spot, whatever you do, but on the face of it, I should leave things as they are. Make yourself bear it, and grin if you can. It's the only way. Anything else would do just as much damage and raise a most unholy stink into the bargain. And what will you have gained by it? Only the satisfaction of preventing Alison from marrying a man she's crazy about.'

'But he can't marry her! He's married already—to me.'

'Well, my dear, so were you married, though you didn't know it, when you married Simon, and that's turned out all right.'

'But I didn't know, and now I shall do. I can't let him marry her, Ruth. I can't! Even if he weren't the sort of man he is, I couldn't.'

'Then face the alternative. Tell Simon you're not his wife, that Brian's not his son, that the other two are illegitimate, that Brian won't get the title, probably not get this job either. In that sort of job, they won't choose anyone with anything murky in their family, and this is rather more murky than most, his father an adventurer and a complete rotter and with all the publicity there'll be. If that's what you want, then tell them, tell them all.'

'I'm miserable enough without your being so beastly about it.'

'I'm not being beastly. I'm endowed with a bit more sense than you are, and if anybody's got to be sacrificed, better Alison than the lot of you and she won't feel herself sacrificed at all. After all, she wants to marry the man and he's got everything to gain by turning over a new leaf with her.'

'She couldn't be happy with him. No woman could.'

'Well, no sensible woman expects to be happy after the honeymoon's over,' said Ruth. 'You didn't expect it yourself, but by the mercy of heaven, you somehow achieved it. And you're prepared to throw all that overboard just to prevent Alison from marrying the man she wants to marry. Don't be such an idiot, Helena. If you can't think of yourself for a change, then think of Simon and Brian and John.'

The talk and the arguments went on to the point of exhaustion, and at last Helena dried and bathed her eyes, let Ruth apply a little powder, and went into the kitchen to start preparing the meal. She still had not made up her mind what to do, but at least she had promised Ruth that she would do nothing that night.

'I believe in sleeping on a thing, whatever it is,' Ruth told her.

'Sleep? I feel as if I shall never sleep again,' said Helena.

'Nonsense. I'll give you a couple of my pills and you'll go out like a light. I've got some in my bag. Ugh! Fancy having to mess about with that spinach, or whatever it is. That's one thing you won't have to do any more when you're milady. I'm going now, but mind, no more tears, and not a word to any of them until tomorrow, or until I've seen you again. If I can't give you some sense in any other way, I'll move in on you and stick your mouth up with plaster.'

Helena managed a smile. Though the burden had not lightened, it did not press on her quite so heavily now that she could share it with Ruth.

'I wish to God he'd die,' she said in a fierce whisper.

'That would certainly be a get-out, but his sort don't die. They don't even fade away. Good-bye for the moment, ducky, and keep your chin up.'

Left alone, Helena tried to do as she had been told, and to occupy her mind as well as her hands with the preparations for supper, grilled steak, roast potatoes, spinach, and treacle tart, and John, coming in from school, sniffed with great satisfaction.

'I only hope when we have to live at The Holt that their cook will be as good as you, Mum,' he said.

Even John could not let it alone, she thought!

Simon looked at her with some concern when he came home, but she was conscious of Alison's aloof attitude, which hurt her bitterly. What, she asked herself wildly, would be that attitude if she told the truth about Giles Paraway and made it impossible for the girl to marry him? Was Ruth right when she counselled her, from her worldly wisdom, to let things take their course? Was that what she must do, stand by and let Alison entrust her happiness to a man whom she herself knew to be incapable of holding anything in trust? She searched her heart and mind to know the truth about herself. Was it for her dear ones that she feared, if she decided to take Ruth's advice, or was it for herself, for the sake of her own security and happiness?

As they were finishing supper, Brian telephoned.

'That you, Mum darling? I wanted it to be you. Lois and I have done the deed. She's let me buy her a ring and we're officially engaged, parental blessing and all. I want to bring her round, just for a few minutes. May I? In about an hour's time?'

'Of course, dear. I'm so happy for you. Tell Lois so, will you?

Dad will say the same, I know. Do you want to speak to him?'

'No. I must buzz off. I left her in a tea-shop whilst I came to ring you up. We're going to her place to show them the ring, and then to you. Good-bye, Mum, bless you.'

'And you, my darling boy,' said Helena tremulously, rang off and told the others the news.

She saw the look that flashed across Alison's face. There had been no jubilant celebrations for her own engagement, though she now wore Giles's ring all the time.

Simon saw the look too, and his kind heart felt for her. After all, they all seemed to have accepted him now, and it was her right to have him included in the family party.

'Would you like to ring up Giles and ask him to come in, Allie?' he asked.

'Oh, Daddy, may I?' she asked gratefully. 'I know he'll like to come,' and there was nothing that Helena could say or do about it.

Only John demurred.

'Oh, Mum, I was going round to Stinky's. We're making a new lay-out for his trains. Do I have to stop in for all this lovey-dovey stuff? We've had enough of it with Allie and Giles mooning about the place.'

His mother smiled. How blessedly simple if all of them were John's age still!

'All right, dear. I don't think Brian and Lois will mind. Don't be late, though.'

'Right ho! Thanks a lot, Mum. See you presently,' and he barged out, whistling.

Simon was upstairs shaving, and Alison in the kitchen hastily making some of the little cocktail snacks to go with whatever drinks they could find, when Giles came in, using the garden gate and the kitchen door as John and Alison usually did.

He kissed her, but was pushed away laughingly and told to go and make himself useful in the other room.

'Mother's raking out what she can find in the drinking line,' she said. 'It won't be much though. You know what our cellar's like!'

He remembered the occasion when John had been sent down to get a bottle of sherry, and that the boy had said there were some other bottles of some sort down there.

He mentioned it to Helena.

'If I'd thought of it, I would have brought something in with me,' he said. 'Shall I go out and buy something now, or do you think I could find some in the cellar? I don't mind going out, of course.'

Helena never knew whether the idea had been born then, or if it had even been born at all, if it had not been rather the sudden impulse of a moment, but when she had refused Giles's offer to go out and buy a bottle or two, and had gone with him to the door in the hall which opened on the cellar steps, she suddenly closed the door on him as he felt with his foot for the spar of the broken step.

He fell with a cry and a heavy crash, and instantly she pulled the door open again and screamed, the scream of fear and horror and of an over-wrought mind which could bear no more.

She did not know who came first at her cry, Simon from the landing above, Mrs. Oliver or Alison, but they were all there, all talking at once, whilst she stood leaning against the wall, white as death, making vague gestures with her hand towards the feebly lit pit of the cellar.

Then Alison screamed.

'Giles! Where's Giles? Did he go down there? Has he fallen— oh no!' ending on another scream as she leaned forward and caught sight of him, crumpled up and motionless on the stone floor below.

Simon pushed them aside but Helena tried to hold him back.

'Don't go, Simon. Get someone. Don't go. You'll fall—too,' she cried hysterically.

'I'll be careful, dear,' he said, 'but of course I must go,' and they stood watching him, Helena with a hand gripping her throat, as he went carefully down, holding John's rope 'ladder' to steady himself as he negotiated the broken treads.

They could see him bending over the still form of Giles. Then he looked up at them.

'I'm afraid he may be hurt,' he said. 'He's unconscious. Get Dr. Hewlett on the phone, Alison, will you? I daren't move him without knowing how he's hurt. Throw me down a rug or something, Helena, and a cushion. It's very cold on this stone floor.'

Mechanically she did as she was bidden, whilst Alison rushed to the telephone and Mrs. Oliver 'dear-deared' and 'my-myed' and stood as close to the top of the steps as she could, peering down with the ghoulish enjoyment of her type.

'Enough to kill 'im, big man like that fallin' right down them steps,' she said. 'I always said as there'd be an accident one o' these days and now it's 'appened. Is that enough, Mr. Clurey, or shall I fetch one of me own cushions?' she called down, when Helena had dropped the light rug and cushion from the sofa into Simon's outstretched arms.

'This will be enough, thank you, Mrs. Oliver,' he said. 'I think we can manage.'

But she stood her ground. It was not often she had the pleasure of being involved in a real accident, and Helena, catching the malevolent look in her beady eyes, had a moment of panic. Did that look signify only the woman's enjoyable curiosity, or was there something else behind it, something threatening and knowledgeable? Had she seen? What had she seen? Where had she been when—when —

Not even to herself would she let that ghastly thought form itself in words.

Dr. Hewlett lived only in the next street, and at Alison's urgent call, he had left his surgery patients and walked round. He made a careful descent under Simon's instructions, but needed only a cursory examination to know that life was extinct.

He straightened himself slowly and extinguished the torch which he had carried in his pocket. He spoke in a low voice to Simon, too low for the women at the top to hear.

'I'm afraid the poor chap's gone,' he said.

'Gone?' echoed Simon, shocked unspeakably. 'You mean he's—dead?'

'Afraid so. Broken neck, I should say. Fell down those wretched steps, I suppose?'

'Yes. He came down to get a bottle of wine. I ought to have had them mended.'

He had said it so often.

'I must get those steps seen to. I'll do it tomorrow,' he had said, but that was one of the tomorrows that had never come – and now Giles Paraway lay dead.

'What—had we better do, Hewlett ?' he asked shakily, still in a whisper.

'The police will have to know, so perhaps the best way would be to get them in right away, and they can move him. No point in staying down here, Clurey. Only catch your own death of cold.'

Alison had caught the word 'death' and she cried out to them.

'Daddy—Dr. Hewlett—what is it? He isn't—he can't be—'

The doctor climbed up to the hall again, catching the note of hysteria in her voice. He was remembering that he had heard something about Alison Clurey being engaged. To this man? If so, poor child.

He put a hand on her shoulder to steady her.

'I'm afraid so, my dear,' he said gently.

'But he can't be! He can't be—dead!' she cried. 'Do something for him. Somebody must do something—'

'I'm so sorry, Alison, my dear but there's nothing anyone can do,' he said in the same gentle voice. 'Mrs. Clurey—?'

Helena, the calmest of the three women after that first wild cry, came mechanically forward and put her arm about her daughter.

'Come into the room, darling,' she said. 'If there's nothing any of us can do, we're better out of the men's way.'

'But we can't leave him there! There must be something— how do you know there's nothing that can be done?' she demanded of the doctor, but his face gave her the answer, the grave shake of his head, the compassion in his eyes, and she burst into wild sobbing and let her mother lead her into the living-room and close the door.

As she did so, they could hear Mrs. Oliver's excited voice.

'I can get the p'lice for you. I'll dial 999.'

The police!

Helena's eyes widened.

'What do they want the police for?' she asked sharply.

Alison lifted her head for a moment.

'I suppose they always do when there's an accident,' she said. 'Oh, Mummy, Mummy, isn't it awful? I can't bear it. I can't live without him. I love him so. I love him so!'

Helena soothed her with the same feeling of being detached from it all, of playing a part written for her by someone else, and all the time her real mind was telling her: 'You did it. You killed him. You closed that door on him knowing that it would make him fall. You meant to do it. That's why you wouldn't let him go out and buy the wine. You wanted him to go down the cellar. You meant it to happen. You meant to kill him. You did kill him. You did it, you, Helena Clurey.'

But aloud she only spoke calming words to Alison until presently there was a tramping of feet in the hall, and fresh voices, and then Simon came in to stand silently beside them, his hand seeking Helena's and holding it firmly in his own.

'The inspector says they may be some time, dear,' he said. 'They've got to get the camera man here. They've sent for him.'

'Camera man? What for?' she asked sharply.

They do, when there's been an accident, in case there's anyone to blame for it. I'm afraid I shall get it.'

'Get what?' she asked in the same sharp tone.

'The blame for keeping the steps in that condition, knowing they were dangerous. I ought to have done something about them long ago, of course. I've kept saying I would, and I didn't, and now this has happened. It—it might have been—Brian, or John,' he added in a whisper, a shamed whisper that caught

Alison's ear.

'You say that as if you don't mind since it's only Giles!' she accused him wildly.

'I'm sorry, Allie dear. I didn't mean it that way,' he said. 'I ought not to have said that, of course. Is that a taxi drawing up? If so, it's probably Brian and Lois. I'd better meet them and explain to them. They've come for a celebration, too!'

They came in, grave-faced, giving Alison sympathetic glances and kissing her.

'Very bad luck, old girl,' said Brian gently, and 'I'm so terribly sorry, Alison dear!' said Lois.

She was. Suppose it had been Brian? She shivered and kept close to him.

Those damned steps,' said Brian. 'I always knew something would happen.'

'Yes. I'm very much to blame,' said Simon.

They waited uncomfortably, saying very little, until the police inspector came in to tell them that the body had been removed to the mortuary and that he was now free to ask them a few questions. Mrs. Oliver came in with them.

'I s'pose it's O.K. for me to come in 'ere?' she asked of them all. 'Seein' as I saw wot 'appened, the inspector says as I'd better stay down 'ere.'

Helena gave a half-suppressed cry, and Simon held her hand again.

'Yes, of course, wait in here, Mrs. Oliver,' he said quietly. 'I also saw what happened as I was about to come down the stairs at the time.'

Helena clung to his hand. What did he mean? What had they seen, both of them? She felt sick with fear, but she must not, would not, faint again. She must hear what any of them said, know what any of them had seen or thought they had seen.

'I understand that you were with the deceased man when he fell down the cellar steps, Mrs. Clurey,' said the inspector. 'You are Mrs. Clurey?'

'Yes. I—I was in the hall when he – Mr. Paraway – opened the door to the cellar, but—I didn't see what happened. He—he—must have slipped—fallen—he screamed out something and I—I opened the door—'

'You opened the door, Mrs. Clurey? But I thought you said the deceased opened the door himself?'

'He did, but—he must have pulled it—or it swung to behind him—'

'Yes,' put in Simon. 'That is what did happen, Inspector. He caught at the edge of the door with his hand when he found himself falling, and it closed on him and I suppose pushed him so that he really did fall.'

'*I* didn't see 'im put out no 'and,' said Mrs. Oliver, 'nor I didn't see the door swing on its own neither. It ain't a door wot does swing on its own.'

It was not what the inspector had anticipated, any divergence of opinion or story, and he looked from one to another and then rose to his feet.

'I think perhaps it would be best if I saw you all separately,' he said. 'Is there another room, Mrs. Clurey, which I could use for that purpose?'

'The other room on this floor is a bedroom,' she said. 'We could go in there and wait and you can use this room, if that will do.'

She looked very tired and strained, but she was in complete control of herself. It was as if with the culmination of Giles Paraway's death, her shattered nerves of the past weeks had been suddenly made whole again.

The inspector glanced at the fire.

'It will probably be cold in there,' he said. 'It will be more comfortable for you to stay in here if I may use the bedroom myself. I think perhaps I had better start with you, Mrs. Clurey. Would you come?'

Detective Inspector Cuver had happened to be in the station, with his car outside, when the call had come, and he took the sergeant and a police officer to the Clureys' house and had remained. It seemed it might be a matter for him, and he had taken over.

Helena went with him like an automaton, her mind floating in a space peopled with bodiless, nameless phantoms. Through them only one real and tangible picture emerged, that of the man who had lain in an untidy sprawl at the foot of the cellar steps.

He was dead.

He could not threaten her life or the happiness of her loved ones any more. He was dead, and with him fear was dead and she was filled with this strange, unreal calm.

Seated in a chair in her bedroom with Inspector Cuver seated opposite her, she heard his questions through the haze of that calm, answered them as if the mind of someone else framed the words for her.

Mr. Paraway had offered to go down into the cellar for a bottle of wine. They were going to celebrate the engagement of her son.

Yes, he knew that the steps were unsafe.

No, he had not been down there before.

She went with him into the hall and unlocked the door but she did not remember opening it. He must have done that himself.

She could not say what had actually happened, but the door must have been opened, mustn't it? Otherwise he could not have gone inside. Then it had closed again behind him. She did not know what had caused it to do so. She heard him cry out and fall. No, she did not think she opened the door again herself but she might have done. It had opened anyway, and she had seen that he was not there, not at the top of the steps any more. Yes, the light was on but she did not remember turning it on. Yes, Mr. Paraway could have done so as he opened the door. The switch was just inside. She had called out, and then her husband was there, and Mrs. Oliver. No, she did not know whether they had been there when she cried out or whether they came because she cried out.

It was all quite simple, quite logical. It had happened so

quickly that she could not say exactly what had happened.

'Well, thank you, Mrs. Clurey. I am sorry to have to distress you with questions, but of course we have to know exactly what happened to cause this tragic affair.'

Exactly what happened.

The phrase kept coming up. Yes, that was the important thing, the thing nobody must know and could not know if she did not tell them.

The rest was soon over. Alison, still weeping inconsolably, had nothing to say as she had been in the kitchen. She returned from the bedroom after a few minutes' absence only, to sit again at the table, Brian's arm about her, her head resting against him, Lois at her other side holding her hand.

Helena did not go to her. Alison and Brian had always been very close in any emergency, though they might spar and squabble as all brothers and sisters do about things that don't really matter.

Simon came back, looking care-worn, worried, old in a way that would have caught at her heart; but she had no heart. She was just a bodiless mind swimming about in that space with other bodiless and unrecognisable things.

He came to her, sat on the arm of the old chair and put his arm about her.

'Not much longer now, dear,' he said, and she nodded – or the head that did not belong to her nodded.

Mrs. Oliver was the last to be called. She went trippingly, her beady eyes throwing a comprehensive glance at them, this high-and-mighty Clurey family to whom she was an unwanted interloper – an interloper in her own home, furnished and paid for out of what Joe earned by his honest sweat, working for the Council. She always referred to his job like that. It sounded better than saying he worked on the sewerage.

Simon's arm tightened its hold a little.

'Of course she would have to be in on it,' said Brian disgustedly. 'What was she doing on the stairs, anyway? Snooping as usual, I suppose.'

'She was coming downstairs,' said Simon, his voice shaking a little.

'Probably knew we were coming,' said Brian. 'Nothing that happens in this house ever seems to escape her.'

Nothing that happens. There was that word again – exactly what happened.

A faint stirring in Helena's mind warned her that it was going to belong to her again. What if Mrs. Oliver knew 'exactly what happened'?

She made a little, strangled sound and Simon's hand pressed her shoulder.

'Don't worry, dear,' he said. 'It will soon be over.'

But it was not over. Not quite.

In the bedroom, Mrs. Oliver was being verbose, thoroughly enjoying herself.

Yes, she had been coming down the stairs when it happened. She had to use the stairs, though anybody would think she was expected to get in and out of the window, the way they always looked at her if they saw her on the stairs or in their precious hall, or going through their kitchen, as she had to if she wanted to put anything in the dust-bin – her own dust-bin, though she wouldn't put it past them to use it if their own was full up. Only the other day she found an empty asparagus tin in it. Asparagus, and they were supposed to be hard up! She couldn't afford asparagus, on Joe's money. Not she. But then, Joe did honest work, not the sort that lawyers do – if you can call a clerk in a solicitor's office a lawyer!

Oh, coming down the stairs? Yes, she was coming down to put something in the dust-bin. (They found it afterwards, a screw of dirty paper with a few potato peelings in it, something that could have waited till the next day.)

Did she see Mr. Paraway fall?

Fall? Well, of course you might call it that, but he wouldn't have fallen, poor gentleman, if *she* hadn't been there, right behind him.

'She?' inquired Inspector Cuver, frowning as he picked out

the significant facts from Mrs. Oliver's verbosity, his trained mind trying to get a clear picture without all the trimmings with which the woman confused it.

'Mrs. Clurey—*Lady* Clurey wot's going to be,' said Mrs. Oliver venomously.

Patiently the inspector drew out the story Mrs. Oliver had to tell. He went with her to the staircase and stood at the spot on which she said she had been standing when she saw the accident. Yes, she could have seen the cellar door from there, if she leaned over the banister rail.

He went down again and opened the cellar door and left it to swing back, but it remained open. It was a door of light match-boarding, and it hung in such a manner that it would remain open rather than close with its own weight.

'She pushed it. Musta done,' repeated Mrs. Oliver truculently.

'Must have done? Then you did not actually *see* Mrs. Clurey touch it?' persisted the inspector.

'Well, wot else could 'ave 'appened to it? Tell me that. There was 'im and there was 'er and there was the door, open. An' the next minute there it was, shut an' 'er screaming 'er 'ead orf and 'im coming outa the bath-room and pushin' by me without so much as a by-yer-leave. Mighta bin knocked down meself and then there would be two of us, an' good riddance to both they'd say!'

'You say Mr. Clurey did not come out of the bath-room until after Mrs. Clurey had screamed? I want to get a clear picture, Mrs. Oliver.'

'Well, 'e couldn'ta come out, seein' as 'e was in there w'en I come down the top stairs and I didn't pass 'im an' it on'y took me a jiffy to nip down the stairs. I move fast w'en I'm in an 'urry, for all I shan't see forty again and eleven stone.'

'And why were you in such a hurry to get to the dust-bin, Mrs. Oliver?' asked the inspector blandly.

She coloured a little, then became truculent again.

'Well, I ain't got all the time in the world to spare like some folks. I wanted to git back to see to Joe's supper. Joe's my 'usband,' as if she might be suspected of having an illicit lover up there waiting for her.

'Well, thank you, Mrs. Oliver. You have been very helpful,' he said, suggesting that the interview was over.

They were back in the bedroom, a room she had never been inside before – well, not as *they* knew – her mind added.

'Anythink else I can do, Inspector,' she began hopefully.

'Thank you. I will ask you,' he said.

'Goin' to be a big case, I wouldn't wonder?* she asked. He could almost see her licking her lips. A viperish woman.

'Oh, no, not necessarily. When an accident case is clear—'

'Accident?' Mrs. Oliver sniffed. 'Oh well, o' course, if *you* say so, Inspector—'

'Thank you, Mrs. Oliver,' he said firmly, opened the door for her and closed it behind her.

An accident. That was definitely what he thought it was, what it seemed to be – and yet—

He sat down again and pulled his little sheaf of notes towards him. The young police officer who had remained at the other side of the room watched him with interest. What was going on in that mind, behind the concealment of the spectacled grey eyes? With the inspector, you never could tell.

Accident.

Well, why not?

Mr. Clurey had said that he could see the door of the cellar swing back as he came out of the bath-room, which was at the top of the stairs, on the hand-rail side. He opened the door in question and went up to stand where Mr. Clurey had said he was, where he would be if he had just left the bath-room. Yes, from there he could see the door, but only the top of it. If Giles Paraway had caught at its edge in an attempt to save himself from falling, his hand would not have been visible. Neither would any other hand which might have closed the door been visible.

And why did Simon Clurey happen to come out of the bathroom at that moment? He came out before his wife screamed. He was quite definite about that. But what had brought him out, if not that scream? He said he had just finished shaving. But he had not quite finished, not, that is, at the stage at which a man like Simon Clurey would have finished. There had been traces of soap still on his face, near the ears. Why should Simon Clurey leave the bath-room before he had taken all the soap off his face?

The inspector went up to the bath-room again. Yes, there was the shaving brush, just thrown down in the soap rack above the basin, the soap still in it. And on the shelf over the basin, a tin of after-shaving powder. Who else would use such powder in this house? The son, Brian Clurey?

Inspector Cuver went into the other rooms on the same floor as the bath-room in the old-fashioned, tall house. One was a girl's room, one obviously belonged to the boy John who had not yet come home. No doubt about that, thought the inspector with a smile. The third room, also a bedroom, must be Brian's, but it had a fitted wash-basin and the toilet articles suggested that he used his own basin and did not shave in the general bathroom. In any case, *he* used after-shaving lotion in a bottle, not the older style of powder.

It looked very much as if Simon Clurey had been surprised out of the bath-room before he had quite finished, and what would have surprised him if it had not been his wife's scream from the hall below?

But he had been quite definite about his movements, and that he had been at the top of the stairs when the door of the cellar had closed – 'swung to' had been his expression.

And Simon Clurey was a lawyer – or at least, he held a responsible position in a lawyer's office and would be a reliable witness.

Mrs. Oliver had said something about 'good riddance to them both' if she, too, had fallen down the stairs and been killed.

Good riddance to *both*. He could well believe that the Clurey family would feel it was a good riddance to be rid of Mrs. Oliver. But why of Giles Paraway, the accepted suitor of the daughter, and a man who might well be considered acceptable, in spite of the considerable difference in age?

He sent for the finger-print man and got him to examine the door for prints. Of course, they would tell him nothing, but it was a thing he could not neglect. If Mrs. Clurey's prints were on it – well, why not? It was her home, and her finger-prints could be reasonably supposed to be on anything. And if Giles Paraway's were on it, well, hadn't he on Mrs. Clurey's own showing probably opened the door himself?

Still, he would get the story of the prints for what it might be worth. Wonderful what could be deduced, what could be reconstructed, from finger-prints even when it was reasonable that they should be there.

VIII

THE verdict at the inquest on Giles Paraway was 'Accidental death', with a rider censuring Simon Clurey for gross negligence in allowing the steps to his cellar to remain in their unsafe condition, knowing that they were in such a condition.

John, who had not been allowed to attend the inquest, was loud in his condemnation of whoever had caused that rider to be added.

'It wasn't Dad's fault,' he argued. 'The steps were perfectly safe for me. I've been down them dozens of times. It was Giles's own silly fault. A man of his age going down there!'

'No, son. It was my fault,' said Simon. 'I did know the steps were unsafe and I should never have allowed even you to go down there. It might have been you.'

Helena gave a little shiver. It would not have been John.

'You're cold, dearest,' said her husband. 'All this had been too much for you, but thank heaven it's over now. I wish I could persuade you to take Alison away somewhere. Have a rest and a change of scene.'

But she would not go, and Alison agreed with her.

'There's nowhere to go at this time of year,' she said, 'and if you're thinking of me, I'm better at work. I don't want more time to think. If Mother changes her mind, you take her, Daddy. You need a holiday if anyone does. You look like a ghost.'

Simon did look ill, and Helena knew he was not sleeping, though she had never before known him not able to drop off to sleep the moment he wanted to do so. She herself was under the care of the doctor, who gave her the drugs which at least produced unconsciousness, long hours of heavy, restless sleep in which she sometimes muttered things to which her husband, lying awake beside her, tried not to listen.

It was not that she said anything which should have disturbed him. Her words seldom made sense. But there was always the strain, the strain and the fear.

What was she afraid of? On the face of it, there was nothing which should make her afraid. Yet the fear was there, inescapable, unmistakable.

She was persuaded not to go to the funeral, but Alison went, standing stiff and pale and composed through the service which seemed to her such a mockery. Giles had not believed in any after-life.

'This one's good enough for me,' he had told her once, 'and I'm going to live it to the full, squeeze everything out of it—and there's plenty to squeeze,' sweeping her into his arms and lifting her in spirit to the threshold of a world hitherto undreamed of, a world of magic and enchantment – the world she would never now reach, never even stand at its threshold again.

Simon wanted to get her away from the house, to get them all away from the place where, whenever they came or went, they had to pass that door. Too late, he had had the steps repaired, though none of them, not even John, would ever want to go down there again.

Then relief came in the sudden death of Curtis Clurey, and their removal, after yet another funeral, to The Holt. Ironically enough, the Olivers were allotted a Council flat at the same time, and the only advantage to the Clureys of the thing they had so long hoped for was that the house would fetch a better selling price.

There had been time after Giles Paraway's death for Sir Curtis to make another new Will, in which he made a substantial bequest to Alison, but there had not been time to appoint another estate bailiff, so that Simon was immediately faced with that difficult task. To his surprise and thankfulness, Alison showed an interest in this.

'I shall feel that in a way I am helping to carry on the work Giles would have loved to do,' she said, and when the new man was found, a capable and experienced middle-aged man with a wife and small family, she continued to give her help and to learn everything she could about the management of the estate. She had grown up during those few weeks, grown up and into herself and away from the family life which she had loved.

The thing that distressed her father by his inability to do anything about it was that there was no longer the close relationship between her and Helena which had once been so sweet a thing.

'Don't trouble, Mother,' she would say when Helena offered to do some of the little things for her which she had always done. 'Mrs. Potter will see to it.'

Mrs. Potter saw to everything, relieved when she found that she was expected to stay on, in spite of the coming of a mistress of the house again, and as a result, Helena had nothing to do.

Receiving and paying visits, arranging the flowers, agreeing with Mrs. Potter about the meals, ordering from the list submitted for her approval, which was a foregone conclusion – and after that, nothing.

Nothing to do.

Ruth came down to stay, charmed with everything, delighted that her sister should at last be in surroundings which should have befitted her, Ruth felt, far better than the inconvenient old house, with the ubiquitous Olivers, where she had always been at the sink.

'Nothing to do?' she cried, echoing Helena's words. 'Give me this sort of nothing for a change! My dear, it's a heavenly place and you're just right for it—*Lady* Clurey. What does it feel like? I should adore to be Lady Mallow! Buck up, old darling. There's surely nothing to worry about *now*! Perhaps I ought not to say it, but of course I feel it. We both do. It really was a miraculous release from a ghastly position when Geof—Giles fell down those steps. Fate doesn't often give a helping hand to females in distress, but she certainly did so there.'

'Ruth, don't! I mean—it seems so—awful.'

'Not a bit of it. Of course Alison feels bad about it, but she's young and she'll get over it. Come on. Put on your bonnet and shawl and let's go and have a look round. I saw someone, the housekeeper is she? carrying a basket of the most luscious-looking grapes which she told me had come from your own hothouse. Let's go and have a look. I want to go everywhere and see everything.'

But when Ruth had gone back, Helena sank into the same state of listless indifference. She could not shake her mind free from the past and from the burden of her secret knowledge, the knowledge that but for her, Giles Paraway would still be alive. She did not want him alive again, but she bore as a heavy weight on her spirit the knowledge that she had killed him.

She was a murderess. A murderess.

It had seemed impossible at first that they did not all know, Simon, Brian, Alison with her pale face and averted eyes, the inspector who had come to the house again and again, even after the inquest and the funeral, poking about, opening and shutting that cellar door until she wanted to scream the truth aloud at him, taking measurements, always looking – looking.

What for? Was not the thing over and done with? Had it not been agreed at the inquest that Giles Paraway's death had been the result of an accident, with Simon, poor worried Simon, blamed for not having the steps mended?

Finally Inspector Cuver had appeared satisfied and had stopped coming to the house, which was hanging fire because of its gruesome associations with accident, death, and a public inquest.

What was there for her to worry about?

She would have worried even more had she known that the inspector had not yet put the case of Giles Paraway's 'accidental death' into his file of 'matters finished'.

His mind still worried at one or two details which seemed to him to lead to unfinished trials.

Why had Simon Clurey been so positive that he had finished

shaving when he hadn't?

What had Mrs Oliver really meant when she said the Clureys would have felt it would be good riddance to *both* if she, too, had fallen to her death?

And what was Mrs. Clurey afraid of? Upset, worried about her daughter's grief, horror-stricken that the accident should have occurred in her house and in her actual presence – but why *afraid*?

He decided to go back into the past of Giles Paraway. Who was he and where had he come from?

It was not easy. Giles Paraway seemed to have been a wanderer, with no settled home. He had appeared almost out of the blue, or rather out of various parts of South America, traced back to there by his passport and through some of the many concerns in which he had an interest, firms for which he had acted as agent for almost every conceivable thing, pulling in a good deal of money in the process.

Before the earliest records of his various addresses in South America, however, there seemed to be no trace of him and none of the London representatives of any of these firms could tell him much about him, less indeed than by that time he knew himself.

He had drawn a blank. Two curious facts emerged, however. One was that, although the birthplace and date of birth showed on his passport, he could not substantiate that Giles Paraway had ever been born at all; the other was that in his Will, which he had made recently, he left all his possessions to be divided equally between Alison Clurey and 'Helena, who was married to Simon Erdington Clurey in the year 1930'.

He pondered over the somewhat unusual wording of that bequest a long time. Why had he not merely put 'Helena, the wife of Simon Erdington Clurey'? Was there something different from the usual in that marriage?

The firm of solicitors who seemed to have conducted most of Giles Paraway's business affairs had not drawn up the Will and knew nothing about it, and the executors were Simon Clurey and the Trustee and Executor Department of a London Bank. Probate was in process of being established. There was nothing out of order about it.

Unable to let the case drop, in spite of the findings of the coroner's court, he looked into the record of the marriage of Helena Thorwell and Simon Clurey, but could find nothing unusual about it. Then a chance remark of Tony Joyce, his young assistant, made him prick up his ears.

'Did you say Helena Clurey was married at Bickford? That rings a bell. I've come across that somewhere before. Bickford. Bickford. Where have I heard that recently?'

'In connection with the Paraway case?' asked the inspector quickly.

'Let me think. Yes. Yes, I'm pretty sure it's whilst we've been on this. A note-book. A bit of paper perhaps. There wasn't much, was there?'

Cuver left him alone to think. Tony Joyce had that invaluable asset, a good memory. He stored it with a wealth of seemingly irrelevant details, and at the right moment, up it would come, something no one else had even noticed.

'I've got it,' he said. 'You remember that old leather case we found among his things? Nothing of any importance in it, but there was a note scribbled on the inside, on the leather lining. Looked like the time of a train: 2.23 Bickford. I'm almost certain it was Bickford.'

'We'd better get hold of it and have another look,' said Cuver, 'though goodness knows what good it will be to us. Can you get the wallet or whatever it was?'

'I expect so. Nothing will have been done about his personal things until Probate is granted.'

They were able to verify, for what it was worth, that the faded, almost indecipherable word was Bickford.

'Where do we go from there?' asked Tony.

'I don't know. Probably nowhere, but it's a link, or it may be. Bickford's a small place, only a village, but Helena Clurey was married there, and Giles Paraway referred rather oddly to that marriage, and he caught a train either to Bickford or from it a good many years ago. And Helena Clurey is afraid of something. And according to Mrs. Oliver, the Clureys might have felt that Giles Paraway's death was a good riddance. Does it amount to anything, or doesn't it? And there's also the odd fact that Giles Paraway doesn't seem to have been born.'

'Not as Giles Paraway,' observed Tony.

'Quite. Not as Giles Paraway. As who, then?'

'Or should it be "whom"?' murmured Tony, a question which his chief very properly ignored.

'We've been through the records with a fine tooth-comb," he said. 'I'm pretty certain that at one time or another he must have had a record because we haven't found the origin of his money, and I've always felt there might be something fishy about it. He made his money in so many ways and so many places and so damned easily! Look, Tony. Here's a job that will keep you quiet for a very long time. Get busy on the records for—when was that marriage? Nineteen-thirty. Before that. Start at this place Bickford, not that it will probably be much good, but go into everything, look at everything you can get hold of, specially photographs. Here, take this one of Giles Paraway.'

Tony rubbed his head.

'Given me some job, haven't you, chief?' he asked.

'I told you it would keep you out of mischief for a long time. Whilst you do that, I'm going back on the case of the Hassard diamonds and I don't want to hear the name Paraway, or Clurey, until you've got something to tell me.'

The search kept Tony Joyce out of mischief for, as his chief had rightly said, a long time, but there came a day, three months later, when he turned up in Cuver's office with a grin on his face.

'Well, what do you want?' asked Cuver. 'Eaten the canary, or what?'

'Probably what, but take a dekko at that,' and he put down on the table an old photograph and beside it the portrait of Giles Paraway.

'What do you think about this?' he asked.

Cuver looked at them, polished his glasses and looked again, and then read the short police dossier attached to the photograph.

'Geoffrey Pellet,' he read. 'Wanted in connection with the case of Richard Jewell. Fraud,' and there was nothing added to the effect that anything further had transpired.

He compared the photographs again.

'Might be. Might be,' he admitted cautiously. 'Changed a lot, of course. When was this? Nineteen-thirty-four. Twenty years ago. Twenty years. A long time,' and he went over the two photographs, feature by feature.

'See the ears, guv?' asked Tony. 'Come to points. Unusual.'

'Yes, I hadn't missed them,' said Cuver drily. 'I think you may have got something, young Joyce, but don't get high hat about it. Twenty years is a long time. Better bring me the file of this Richard Jewell case.'

But there was nothing to learn from it except the almost certain fact that 'Geoffrey Pellet' had been a wrong 'un. Richard Jewell, the absconding solicitor, had been apprehended in Bermuda and shipped home for trial, but had eluded his captors when the ship was in sight of Liverpool, jumped over the side and subsequently been picked up dead. He had left no trace of the money he had acquired by defrauding a wealthy client, an elderly, credulous woman, and no trace of his clerk, Geoffrey Pellet, who had disappeared with him but against whom there was strong suspicion rather than actual proof of complicity.

Largely because, even if they caught him, there was no proof, the police had abandoned their search for Geoffrey Pellet and the file had been put away as 'concluded'.

But there remained the faded photograph which Ronald Cuver felt quite sure was that of Giles Paraway.

'Doesn't get us far, does it?' he asked Tony.

'Only the name. Where do we go from here?'

'Lord knows. Why was I ever a policeman? Get back to this Geoffrey Pellet. Do we know where he lived at the time? When was it—oh, nineteen-thirty-four. It's all such a damned long time ago, but he must have left *some* traces whilst he was Geoffrey

Pellet. We should have gone into all that when we were trying to find him for the Jewell case.'

A day or two later, Tony appeared with his notes and an odd look of reluctance about him, as if he had found something he did not want to find.

'I've got this, guv,' he said.

'I wish you wouldn't address me in that singularly unpleasant fashion,' said Cuver irritably.

Tony Joyce grinned. He was on excellent terms with the man to whose service he had been specially consigned. He had done his two years 'on the beat' and had been singled out as likely to go far in his chosen profession, which was why he had been sent to Inspector Cuver, from whom he would learn many of the intricate workings of the police service with a view to finally getting him where he wanted to get, which was on the C.I.D. staff of Scotland Yard. It was a far cry, but he meant to get there.

'Sorry, Inspector,' he said cheerfully, and then the grin faded again and he watched his superior's reactions to the information he had brought.

Ronald Cuver gave a low whistle and it seemed that he, too, was receiving the information with little pleasure in its startling purport.

'H'm. Married in January, nineteen-thirty to—Helena Thorwell,' he said, and added nothing to the comment, fiddling with a pencil and reading the slip of paper again and again.

'Rather tears things apart, doesn't it?' asked Tony after a long pause.

'And how! Anything about a divorce?'

'No. Nothing.'

'All right. You can go. I've got to sort this out,' said Cuver, but when he was alone he still sat there, fiddling with the pencil, looking at the slip of paper but no longer seeing the words.

Married to Geoffrey Pellet in January, 1930. Married to Simon Clurey in November, 1930, ten months later – and no sign of a divorce.

He pulled the Paraway file towards him. No detail was too

small in such a case not to be recorded, and there it was – Brian Clurey born in May, 1931, six months after Helena Thorwell had married Simon Clurey.

He suddenly knew that he hated the whole thing, that he had hated it all the time and yet had felt obliged to go on with it, even after the death of Giles Paraway seemed to be one of the things about which no further questions need be asked. He had not been able to let it rest, feeling with the sixth sense essential to success in his chosen profession that there was something behind it all, something which with care and time he ought to uncover.

He searched his conscience. Would he have pursued the case in which Helena Clurey was so much implicated had her personal association with him come before the death of Giles Paraway instead of after it? An association so deeply concerned with his own happiness that he would never forget her?

It had happened during the weeks that followed his entry into the case, before the death of Curtis Clurey had caused the new owner of The Holt to move away from London.

Never a deeply religious woman but looking desperately for comfort and guidance, Helena had gone one day into the little Roman Catholic church which kept its doors always open. She had never been in it before, and though the statues, the flickering candles before a small shrine and the smell of incense conveyed nothing to her, the whole atmosphere of the place seemed to offer her a momentary feeling of peace, of suspension whilst she remained in it of the tormented unrest of her mind, and almost unconsciously she had gone down on her knees before the calm effigy of the Mother with the Baby in her arms.

She was not actively thinking; her mind seemed detached; kneeling there in the quietness, she was nothing any more, not Helena Clurey, not Helena Pellet – nothing.

And then a persistent little sound penetrated her consciousness and she resented it but could not ignore it. It was the sound of a woman sobbing, kneeling near her, the sobs low and hopeless and unchecked.

The woman, little more than a girl she looked, was sitting in a chair close by, not kneeling or making any attempt to find the sort of consolation Helena was trying to find in the peace of the little chapel, but rather as if she had gone in there so that she might weep unseen and undisturbed.

Helena, to whom even in her own trouble all women's troubles were her own, hesitated and finally rose quietly and went to sit beside the only other occupant of the church.

'You're in trouble,' she whispered gently. 'Is there anything anyone can do for you?'

The girl took her handkerchief from her eyes and looked, startled, in the direction of the quiet voice.

Helena was right. She was little more than a girl, years younger than she herself was, not much older than her own Alison, quietly dressed, pretty in a somewhat doll-like way, a shopping basket beside her, some of its contents spilling over on to the tessellated floor.

'No,' said the girl. 'No, there's nothing anybody can do,' and she struggled with her sobs now that she was not quite alone.

'I suppose you wouldn't like to tell me, would you?' asked Helena diffidently. 'I'm a lot older than you, and—I came in here because I'm troubled and unhappy too. It sometimes helps to tell somebody who doesn't even know you.'

The girl looked at her doubtfully, looked at the calm, untroubled face of the Mother, and back to Helena's.

'I can't—here,' she said chokingly.

'Let's go somewhere else. There's a seat outside, and if it is raining, we shan't get wet there.'

The girl nodded, and Helena helped her repack her basket and carried it for her as they tiptoed out of the church and to the seat in the porch.

There Milly Cuver told her something of her story, of the folly which had broken up her marriage to the man for whom she still cared deeply, of her longing to return and her miserable certainty that she could not do so.

'I didn't even care for Bill really, not the way it used to be with Ron,' she said, 'only I was left alone a lot. Ron couldn't help it. It's his job. I knew that, but I was lonely, and when Bill took to coming round, and sometimes we went to the pictures, or out on the back of his motor-bike, it was a change for me, somebody to talk to. He made me laugh and—and when he started to kiss me, I—I never thought it would matter. Then Ron stayed away for a night. He was on a case, and I let Bill stay late, and after he'd gone, and I'd gone to bed, he came back again because the bike had gone wrong and I—I let him stay, and Ron came back before he'd gone, and—there was nothing I could say about it. There was I and there was Bill and I just—cleared off with Bill. It seemed the only thing to do. I felt so—*ashamed*. It finished me with Bill really, but—I had to go with him. I'm still with him, living in rooms—but I'm so miserable, and I don't love Bill and sometimes I think he hates me. He's not kind the way Ron is. Ron's the best man in the world and I'd give anything if I could be back with him again, anything. I'd even have a baby. Ron wanted me to but I wouldn't. Now I would, if I could only be back with him.'

'Have you had any breakfast?' asked Helena practically. The girl looked worn out and ill and was neglecting herself, though she struck her as being careful of herself in the ordinary way, careful over her appearance. Her clothes were becoming and chosen with care for detail, but now her shoes needed to be cleaned and her stockings had the seams running sideways and there was an unmended hole in her glove.

Milly Cuver looked startled at the abrupt change in the conversation.

'No, I didn't bother,' she said. 'Bill went out early without having anything. We had a row. We're always having them,' she ended drearily.

'Well,' said Helena, 'I always have a cup of coffee about this time and if I'm hungry, some toast or something. Why not come back with me and share it with me, and we can go talking if you like? There won't be anybody else at home—except the Olivers, who have part of our house, but they don't matter.'

She purposely made her domestic setting as near to what she felt the Cuvers' would be as possible, sensing quite rightly that she would be of no use to the girl if she regarded her as in any sense a superior, and Milly even looked round with a slightly disparaging air when she was brought into the Clureys' living-room, obviously one room for all sorts of purposes. Milly herself had a dining-room *and* a sitting-room, and she and Ron had the place to themselves without having to have lodgers.

Ron!

The tears flowed again, but gradually ceased as Helena brought coffee and buttered toast and sat talking whilst she shared it with her, though she had not wanted it and every mouthful was difficult. She had not had breakfast either. She had only pretended to eat whilst Simon and Alison and John breakfasted.

Helena talked gently and wisely, wise with the knowledge of her own sorrow and her fears, with the memory of her years with Simon – Simon who was also the best man in the world, Simon who, if all the truth were ever known, might be lost to her as Milly's Ron was lost, for what would be left to her if Simon's trust and faith in her was gone, even though she might still be living in his house?

'Go back,' was the burden of her advice. 'Go back and give your husband and yourself a chance to start afresh.'

'What if he won't take me back?' quavered Milly. 'I've never seen him since, but he wrote and told me he would divorce me so that I could marry Bill—and I don't want to! I don't want to! I only want Ron.'

But in the end she had agreed to do as Helena urged her. Nothing worse could happen to her than had already happened, and Ron had never been unkind, just couldn't be unkind.

The little drama had played itself out. Ron had been very much more than just 'not unkind' and now, though it was still too early to be sure, Milly was going to have a baby and Bill was as if he had never been.

And that had been due to Helena Clurey – Helena Clurey

whom Ronald Cuver was trying to hunt down because his duty had made that obligatory on him.

Duty.

Sitting with the appalling likelihood in his mind that Helena Clurey was not Helena Clurey at all, that she had been Giles Paraway's wife and a bigamist and that her children, Alison and John at any rate, were illegitimate, that Brian Clurey was not in actual fact the heir to an honoured title and the eventual owner of Simon's new estate, Ronald Cuver had for the first time a distaste that amounted to an actual loathing of his job.

To hound people down. That had been the job he had chosen to do, had taken pride and satisfaction in its doing.

And now he was hounding down Helena Clurey, the woman whom Milly had told him frankly had been the sole instrument in sending her back to him, in remaking his broken life, in rebuilding it on such sure and safe grounds that Milly, his adored young wife, had come back to him to be as she had never been, loving him as she had never loved him before trouble had touched her and shown her all that she had to lose.

And now there was to be the child he longed for, the child she had always denied him, the child that would set the seal on their new, deep happiness and make an unbreakable link between them for ever.

And in return for the gift she had given him, he was to break up Helena Clurey's own life and tear her happiness apart, for there could be no possible doubt of her happy married life with Simon Clurey and with her children.

He could leave things as they were. The file was, to everyone else but Tony Joyce, completed and put away. Giles Paraway had died an accidental death. Simon Clurey had become Sir Simon, and Helena was his 'wife', secure, happy, infinitely blest by providence and circumstance.

He sighed and put the file aside – aside, but not away.

What was his duty? How far did it reach when human lives and happiness were at stake?

Giles Paraway was dead, and with him had died Geoffrey

Pellet. What possible gain was there to anyone still living if he, Ronald Cuver, raked over the dead ashes and brought out into the light of day the vile refuse that they had hidden?

Tony Joyce, given some other job to do, came back into his office some days later with the job completed.

'Well, that's all tuckered up,' he said. 'There's your evidence.'

'Yes,' agreed Cuver and pushed it aside for consideration later. 'Thanks, Tony. Good work.'

The boy hesitated.

'Anything else?' asked his chief.

'Er—about the Paraway case. Are we letting it ride?'

Cuver shot a glance at him, with the rather unexpected thought that Tony, no more than he, wanted it reopened.

'I don't know,' he said slowly. 'There's a lot to it, isn't there?'

The boy nodded.

'Mm,' he agreed. 'Quite a lot—especially with Clurey a baronet, and all of them at that place, and Brian Clurey—'

'Did you see that he's got that appointment confirmed and his engagement to General Garner's daughter announced? Put the cat amongst the pigeons there all right, won't it?'

'Yes.'

'Bit rough on all of them. Bad job for Alison Clurey, of course, seeing that she was engaged to Paraway, but—well, she's a jolly nice girl and—'

Cuver shot another look at him. Tony's face had reddened and he was shuffling his feet and looking down at them.

'Interested?' asked Cuver.

The boy hesitated, examined his well-polished shoes again, and then looked up, the flush deepened.

'Well—yes. Since you ask me, I am,' he said. 'She wouldn't look at me, of course, as things are. I mean, with this chap only just dead and all that, her father with a title and so on—but I shan't always be a glorified bobby running about doing your dirty work—or shall I?' with a disarming look at his chief.

Cuver did not restrain a smile.

'No, I don't expect you will,' he agreed, 'but it'll be a long time.'

'Well, I can wait—and I don't think Alison's the sort to rush into anything else yet awhile—and there's old Patterley for what he's worth,' with another grin.

'Old Patterley' was Tony's uncle, an offshoot of a very reputable old family whom up to the present his nephew had referred to with some derision, disclaiming any pride in the connection or use for it. The possession of 'old Patterley' in the background, however, seemed to have assumed a new importance now that Alison Clurey had come into the picture.

Cuver smiled again, absently, and dismissed him from the conversation.

'You know,' he said, the smile fading again, 'there are times when I'd rather be anything but a policeman. Well now, what about this Clarke business?' picking up the papers which he had pushed aside. 'Better have him picked up.'

IX

WHEN the Clureys moved down to The Holt, the council flat which had been promised to the Olivers was not ready for their occupation, and it had been a matter of indifference to Simon and Helena whether they went at once or stayed on in the house after it was put up for sale. It was, in fact, a convenience to have them there, to forward letters and to admit people who were sent by the agents to view the house. In the event of its being sold (as had actually happened), the Olivers agreed to move in time to give vacant possession since it was now only a matter of weeks before the new flat would be ready.

So Mrs. Oliver was still there, though packed up ready to move, when a ring at the front door-bell brought her downstairs.

The caller was a woman, her middle age only partly concealed by the bright gold of her hair and the youthful cut of her smart, somewhat flashy attire.

'I've come—' she began in a high, affected voice, but Mrs. Oliver cut her short.

'The 'ouse is sold,' she said. 'I've told the agents but they keep on sendin' people.'

'I haven't come about the house,' said the woman. 'I've come to make inquiries about some people called Clurey, Sir Something he is now. They used to live here,' her glance round the hall now cluttered up with the Olivers' possessions suggesting that she did not think much of it.

Mrs. Oliver became interested. This was not at all the sort of person usually known to the Clureys.

'Yes, that's right,' she said. 'They're not 'ere now, but I'm a

168

friend o' theirs, just lookin' after the 'ouse for them until the new people get 'ere. Come in, won't you? I'm afraid it's in a bit of a muddle, but we're on'y just stayin' 'ere, pigging it as you might say,' with a little affected laugh. 'Still, as I said to Lady Clurey, wot does it matter w'en you're doin' a good turn for a friend?' ushering the visitor into what had been Helena's bedroom, but into which Mrs. Oliver had moved her 'lounge suite', a hideous affair upholstered in bright green plush of a different shade from the square of carpet.

'Nice room, isn't it?' she asked. 'Me and Lady Clurey always liked this room. Like sisters we were. "I shan't 'arf miss you, Flo," she said w'en they went. Me name's Florence reely, but it's such a mouthful between friends. We're leavin' 'ere soon, o' course, and she wants me to go down an' 'ave a bit of an 'oliday with them at The 'Olt. That's the name o' their place, you know.'

Much of this would greatly have surprised Helena, of course, but it was not every day that Mrs. Oliver could roll the name of a 'reel lady' off her tongue.

'Very nice, I'm sure,' said the visitor. 'It wasn't really the Clureys I wanted to see. At least, only this Sir Somebody Clurey. It was really about the man who died here, a man called Paraway,' shooting out the name with a venom which did not escape Mrs. Oliver.

'Oh,' she said. 'Oh yes. That's right. Giles was the name, Giles Paraway. Shockin' thing. Fell down them cellar steps. Engaged to the daughter 'e was, Alison.'

'Oh, was he?' asked the other woman ominously. 'Well, I've got something to say about that, not that it's much good now he's dead. But if I'd found out before he was dead, I'd have had a lot more to say,' with a derisive laugh.

'Oh?' prompted Mrs. Oliver hopefully.

She had never liked that Alison. Not that she had liked any of them, nasty, stuck-up lot, but Alison least of all, giving herself airs as if she was the queen of England, and what was she? A typist. One of the sort as called theirselves *seckertaries*.

Mrs. Oliver sniffed at her thoughts.

'Engaged, was he?' pursued the visitor. 'I'd have seen to that all right!'

'Why?' asked Mrs. Oliver, her curiosity now thoroughly aroused. Pity Mr. Paraway was dead. It would have taken that young madam down a peg or two for someone to put a spoke in that engagement of hers!

'Why? Because he couldn't have married her, seeing as he's got a wife already.'

'No!' exclaimed the delighted listener.

'Yes. Me,' said the visitor, taking a cigarette-case out of her imitation leather hand-bag and pulling out a cigarette. 'Have one with me?' offering the case to Mrs. Oliver.

'I don't mind if I do,' Mrs. Oliver said obligingly. 'P'raps you'd like a little drop o' something? I don't as a rule, but we keep a drop in the 'ouse, just in case, you know. I'll fetch it.'

Over a gin and orange squash, the friendship grew apace. Mrs. Oliver slipped off her shoes ('Me feet 'urt me something cruel. I bet it's goin' to rain,' she explained to her visitor) and presently pattered out on her stockinged feet to bring in the bottle of gin for a refill.

'That was the end of the orange,' she said, 'but p'raps you'll 'ave a drop o' water, Mrs. Paraway. Or do you like it neat? Sometimes I think, w'en you're down, it puts a bit more life in you neat.'

The visitor agreed.

'It sounds queer to hear you call me that,' she said. 'It wasn't 'is name when 'e was married to me, though.'

Under the influence of the gin and Mrs. Oliver's pleasant company, some of her careful aspirates got lost.

'No. It was Pellet,' she said. 'Geoffrey Pellet. Still, it don't matter what you call me. My name's Gertrude—Gertie, you know. What I really wanted to see this Sir Clurey about was my money, my money what's my rights as Geoff's true and lawful wife. He never had any when we lived together. Leastways, if he did, I never saw the colour of it, give you my word! Tight as a wad, 'e was and no mistake! When he left me, it was good riddance to bad rubbish, I thought, and I was better orf without 'im. I went back to the stage. I was on the stage before I married him, not big parts but reg'lar. Gertie della Cross. You might've heard of me. Spelt little d e, little l a and then C r o i x-della Cross. My name was really Pragg, but Gertie della Cross sounds better on the bills. I didn't miss Geoff. Not much to miss! But you coulda knocked me down with a feather when I was looking at a paper the other day whilst the kettle boiled, an old one it was, matter of fact the fish was wrapped in it. What did I see but my old man's photo, not a good one, mark you, but it wasn't likely I shouldn't know him, for all they called him Giles Paraway. Didn't think too much about it at the time. After all, when you haven't seen a man for more'n twenty years, you don't cry your eyes out because 'e's dead, do you? Still, I was interested, and I kept me eyes open for anything else they might have to say about him, and blowed if there wasn't something a day or two ago about his Will and that he'd left whatever he had to this Alison Clurey and her mother! 'Ere, 'ere, I said to meself, if there's anything to leave, it ought to be mine, as his lawful wedded wife. What do you think, Mrs. Collier?'

'Oliver's the name, but call me Flo, dear. I quite agree with you. Us wives 'ave quite enough to put up with w'ilst they're alive without bein' done out of our bounden rights after they're dead—not that Oliver'll 'ave much to leave, if I know 'im.'

'Well, I thought I'd go and see this Sir Somebody Clurey.'

'Simon, 'is name is,' interpolated Mrs. Oliver, her mind working at top speed.

How could she turn this unexpected gift of the gods to her own advantage?

'Now look 'ere, dear,' she said after a lightning-like flash of thought, 'I'll tell you wot. I got to go down and see Lady Clurey tomorrer. Keeps at me, she does, to slip down for a cup o' tea with 'er. Don't you do nothink until I've bin down and spied out the land, like. You see, Sir Simon's a lawyer and you know wot *they* are. If there's a chance for them to put their 'ands in yer pocket and keep 'em there till you got nothink left, they'll do it, and there isn't one of 'em as would let anyone else get away with wot they *'ave* got their 'ands on, and this money of yer late 'usband's is as good as in 'is pocket already, seein' as 'ow it was left to 'er ladyship and young Alison—though wot 'er ladyship's got to do with it, I *don't* know, Mrs.—er—Gertie. If you ask me, there was some funny goin's on *before* the accident,' added Mrs. Oliver darkly, stepping out of character in an unguarded moment from the bosom friend of Lady Clurey. 'Wot I'd like to know is wot call 'e 'ad to leave *'er* money, and equal with Alison, 'is intended, mark you!'

Gertie's eyes grew rounder.

'Wy, whatever do you mean, Flo?' she demanded.

Mrs. Oliver recollected herself.

'Oh well—p'raps I was makin' too much of it, and o' course she *was* Alison's mother, and if they were sort of friendly, wot matter? Anyway, 'e must've thought a lot of 'er, to leave 'er 'arf the money like that.'

'How much?' asked Gertie.

'Well, that I don't know, dear. I reely don't know. 'E was always dressed up to the nines, and with a big car and all that, and Alison 'ad a ring with diamonds as big as peas, but then you never know, do you? As I was sayin', dear, as I 'appen to be goin' down to see 'Elena – that's Lady Clurey, you know – tomorrer, wot about letting me 'ave a dekko at things, sound 'em out, so to speak? Wot I mean to say is, if it was all show and there was nothing but a pound or two all said and done, is it worth yer w'ile throwin' good money after bad to try and get it out of Simon Clurey, a lawyer mark you, once 'e's got 'is mitts on it?'

'Well, whatever it is, it's mine,' protested Gertie, though she was ready to be convinced that her new friend's plan was the better one. She did not really relish the thought of going to this grand place, wherever it was, and facing this Sir Somebody Clurey, especially now she knew that he was a lawyer, a professional class of which she stood in considerable awe. Mrs. Oliver was right. If he *had* got his hands on Geoff's money, it might be something of a job to get them off it again, and if there *was* only a pound or two – well, was it worth the struggle to get it? She wasn't that hard up, and she had a gentleman friend who – well, anyway, she wasn't so hard up that she would have to use a corkscrew to get a measly ten pounds or so out of these Clureys.

Still, if it was more than ten pounds or so . . .

' 'Course the money's yours, Gertie,' agreed Flo, 'an' I'm the one to see you get it. After all, I can talk to 'Elena as a friend like, put it to 'er as one woman to another, an' she can't *want* your 'usband's money now, can she? No, you leave it to me, dear, and pop in to see me—say—Friday?"

'Well—I don't know. I think perhaps I'd better go down to this place myself,' decided Gertie, after all. 'Tell you what, though. You come with me. I mean, you knowing them so well and everything, it might make it easier for me. But I think I'd better go.'

'All right, if that's the way you feel about it,' said Mrs. Oliver, disappointed that she was not to be the bearer of the news herself, and chagrined at the prospect of having to reconcile her boast of being Helena Clurey's intimate friend with the reception she would quite certainly get at that lady's hands. Still, she intended to go, if only to see how they took the news, which would be sure to be made public, that their precious daughter had got herself engaged to a married man. That would be a flea in their ears all right! 'Well, if that's the way you feel about it, dear,' she said, 'we'll go together. 'E'll want some proof, o' course. Got any?'

It would be just her luck if it was discovered that her new friend was pulling a fast one on them.

'Proof?' asked Gertie, tossing her head. 'I got me lines. Got 'em here in my bag,' patting it protectively.

'Oh well, that's all right then. No one can say fairer than that! I always say, if a woman 'angs on to 'er marriage lines, she's always got *something* to tie 'em down, the devils. Well, ta ta, dear. See you tomorrer? You look up the trains and let me know. Or tell you wot, I'll just slip on me coat and walk with you to the telephone box at the corner an' you can telephone to the railway an' ask. You could've telephoned from 'ere, but they 'ad it cut orf w'en they left, mean devils.'

'Thought you were such friends,' said Gertie warily.

'Oh well—yes, but it was 'im. You know what these lawyer blokes are, after every penny,' said Mrs. Oliver quickly, recovering ground.

Simon was in the library going through the mass of papers connected with his new affairs when the parlourmaid came in to announce visitors.

'Two ladies you say, Annie?' he asked.

'Well, in a manner of speaking, yes, sir,' said the girl. 'One of them said you'd know her. Mrs. Oliver.'

'Mrs. Oliver? Oh dear. You say they asked for me? Where is your mistress?'

'I think Her Ladyship is in the hot-house, sir. Drew wanted to talk to her about the vines.'

Helena was trying to create an interest for herself in the gardens.

'Well, don't disturb her. I'll see the two ladies in here.'

'Very good, sir.'

Mrs. Oliver sailed in with outstretched hand and a beaming smile.

' 'Ow do you do, Sir Simon?' she said affably. 'My friend 'ere wanted to see you on a little matter of business, so I thought as it was such a nice day, I'd just run down to see 'ow you're all gettin' on.'

'Thank you, Mrs. Oliver. We shall be very comfortable, I think,' said Simon with his usual grave courtesy, though he wondered what business he could possibly have with the brassy-haired, over-dressed female she had brought with her. 'Is it some business in connection with the house?'

'Oh no, somethink quite private, not the 'ouse at all,' said Mrs. Oliver.

'I see. Well, if it is a business matter, perhaps your friend would prefer to discuss it with me alone?' asked Simon, and rang the bell.

'Oh, I'm sure Gertie wouldn't mind me 'earing wot she's got to say, would you, Gertie? As a matter of fact, it's somethink about the gentleman as was killed down the cellar steps, that Mr. Paraway, isn't it, Gertie?"

'Er—I think perhaps it would be better—oh, Annie, Mrs. Oliver will wait a little while,' as the maid came in. 'Show her into the morning-room, will you? Perhaps you would like some tea, Mrs. Oliver, whilst you're waiting? Annie will bring you some.'

'Oh, I'll wait till you and 'Er Ladyship 'ave yer own, Sir Simon,' said Mrs. Oliver, still managing to be bright in spite of being practically turned out of the room.

'Oh, we should not like to keep you waiting for us,' said Simon. 'Will you see to it, Annie?' and she had no option but to go out of the room leaving Gertie in possession.

'Now,' said Simon. 'Do sit down, won't you? I—er—I don't think you gave me your name7'

'It's della Cross. At least, that'll do. I've got a card here,' she said, not feeling entirely at ease in this solid-looking room with its walls lined with books, a thick carpet on the floor, and behind the huge carved desk the quiet-faced man who did not look at all what she expected.

He took the card which she produced from her overfilled hand-bag, and looked at it with growing surprise.

GERTIE DE LA CROIX
Speciality Songs And Dances

'Well, Miss de la Croix, how can I help you?' he asked. 'I gather from Mrs. Oliver that it is in connection with the late Mr. Giles Paraway?'

'Yes, though he wasn't that to me, Sir Simon. No, when I knew him he called himself Pellet, Geoffrey Pellet.'

'Indeed? Was that recently, or some time ago?' asked Simon.

He had hoped that with the final settlement of the Probate of the Will, he would have heard the last of that gentleman. This, however, threatened to get him embroiled in something quite new.

'Oh, a long time ago. It's more than twenty years since I saw him. That was when he left me, the skunk. You may wonder why I've turned up after all that time, but I only found out about him a few days ago, which is why I haven't been sooner.'

'I see. And you had some connection with Mr. Paraway? I knew him as Mr. Paraway, of course.'

'Connection? I'll say I had. He was my husband,' said Gertie with a toss of her head.

It was adorned today with a hat of white feathers, out of which protruded a large red bird of uncertain species.

Simon gave her a look of startled interest.

'Really? You can, I presume, substantiate that, Miss—er—Miss de la Croix, I suppose that is what you prefer me to call you?'

'Well, it's the name I'm used to. Haven't been Mrs. Geoffrey Pellet for a long time and my public know me as Gertie della Cross. Stage, you know. You may have heard of me?' hopefully.

'Well, no. No, I'm afraid I—er—I am not very well up in the modern theatre,' said Simon with an apologetic smile. 'You say you have proof that you were this man's wife?'

'I got me lines,' and she produced from her bag an envelope containing a soiled and discoloured slip of grey paper, which she handed to him.

He read it slowly.

It seemed authentic. It was a certificate of marriage between Geoffrey Arthur Pellet, bachelor, and Gertrude Pragg, spinster, and the date was the tenth of June, One thousand nine hundred and twenty-seven.

He refolded it and handed it back to her after making a few notes on a pad of paper on his desk.

'That certainly looks like substantial proof, Miss de la Croix,' he said. 'Proof, that is, that you were married in nineteen-twenty-seven to a man known as Geoffrey Pellet. What makes you connect him with Giles Paraway, however?'

'Saw his photo in the paper and reckernized him. Knew him at once,' said Gertie.

'I see. And so you came to see me about—'

'About the Will,' she said. 'How much did he leave?'

'Er—at the moment I am not really in a position to—er—disclose that,' said Simon, shocked at the discovery of the duplicity of the man who had asked Alison to marry him – if, indeed, this was the man, and he felt that this woman was telling the truth, though that would have to be established, of course.

'There was something, though? There must be or he wouldn't have split it up between your wife and your daughter. I mean, you don't go to the trouble of splitting up nothing, do you?'

'No. No, you don't,' said Simon with a faint smile.

'You see, he hadn't got any right to leave it to anybody else, not when he has a lawful wife living, had he?'

'No,' said Simon, 'not on the face of it, though of course you quite understand, Miss de la Croix, that these things have to be proved? That the identity of Mr. Giles Paraway with that of your husband, Geoffrey—er—Pellet,' consulting his notes, 'will have to be fully established?'

'But I reckernized him. Know him anywhere, even after all this time. And I've got me lines,' argued Gertie.

'Yes. Quite. But you see, I am Mr. Paraway's executor, and as such it is my duty to see that the law is in every way satisfied. No doubt there will be ways and means of establishing what you say. You understand that I cannot commit myself until the case has been looked into?'

'Yes, I suppose that's fair enough,' agreed Gertie reluctantly. 'But when you find out that it's right, and that he *was* Geoffrey Pellet, my husband, I suppose you can hand over the money?'

'Er—as a widow, you would of course be entitled to—put forward a claim,' said Simon.

He was thinking what a good thing it would be if he could hand over Giles Paraway's money to someone else. Alison, with the bequest from Curtis Clurey, did not need it, and Helena had already refused emphatically to take any of it. How much simpler if he could hand it over, intact, to this woman who certainly needed it far more than they did. He did not think it necessary to tell her that, in actual law, she could claim only that portion of her husband's estate to which, as his widow, she would be entitled in spite of his having made a Will excluding her. Thank heaven that if she did prove that she was Giles Paraway's widow, there would be no lawsuit about it. Alison would not want a penny from a man who had so grossly deceived her. Miss de la Croix, or whatever her name really was, could have the lot.

'Well,' he said, rising, 'I think that is all we can do for today. I have taken down the details of your marriage certificate, and I will have some inquiries instituted. Meantime, if you have any other papers in your possession, some old photographs perhaps, would you let me have them? They would be quite safe with me,' with a little smile.

He had not missed the way she had watched him whilst he examined the marriage certificate and the relief with which she had received it from him again.

'Well, I dare say I can turn out some snaps, old ones, of course—and I expect you'll think I looked a bit different then,' with an arch smile at him which suggested that he would think her far more attractive now. 'Such funny clothes we wore then, didn't we? And the hats! A proper scream.'

He kept his eyes resolutely from the red bird and agreed gravely.

'You send me anything you can find which may help to establish your husband's identity,' he said. 'In the meantime I shall, of course, do nothing more about the provisions of Mr. Paraway's Will.'

'I'm glad I came to you, Sir Simon, though I don't mind telling you I was scared out of my wits, you being a titled man *and* a lawyer, and coming to this place and everything.'

He gave her his nice smile and held out his hand.

'Well, you see you need not have been frightened, need you? I assure you solicitors are not nearly such bad people as they are made out to be. Good-bye, Miss de la Croix. Oh, would you like some tea before you go? They can easily make some fresh for you.'

'Oh no. I shouldn't think of troubling anybody,' said Gertie, her awe of the place overcoming her again now that she was to be sent out of this room and away from this kind man who was so easy to talk to after all, and who she was sure wouldn't try to rob her of her rights as that Flo Oliver had said he might.

Meanwhile, Mrs. Oliver had not been inactive.

She was shown into a small room, comfortably furnished and with a good fire burning, but clearly only a minor room, and when tea was brought to her she gave a mental sniff. The folding-table which came with it was not set with the massive silver and crested equipment which her reading of lurid paper-backed novels had assured her was used in 'big houses'. The china, too, was pretty rather than valuable.

'Don't treat me to their Severs,' she thought, picking up a plate when the maid had gone and examining the manufacturer's mark underneath it. 'Don't think I'm good enough, I s'pose, *nor* good enough to 'ave tea with 'Er Ladyship. 'Er Ladyship!' with another sniff. 'Don't buy decent cakes neither. Rotten little 'ome-made things. Oh well, if *this* comes out, it'll take 'er 'igh-and- mighty Ladyship down a peg or two.'

She finished her tea quickly, leaving one of the little cakes 'for manners', and decided to take a look round, but she had got no farther than the dining-room, which had a door leading to the passage from which the hot-houses were reached, when that door opened to admit Helena.

She stopped in amazement and annoyance.

'Why—Mrs. Oliver! I didn't expect to find you here,' she said.

'No, I didn't expect to find meself 'ere since I never bin invited,' replied Mrs. Oliver spitefully. 'I come down with a friend w'o wanted to see yer 'usband on business. You got a nice place 'ere,' looking round condescendingly, though secretly impressed with the dimensions of the room and the ancestral portraits, the effect being to increase her outward show of feeling quite at home.

'Have you had tea, Mrs. Oliver?' asked Helena, not knowing quite how to receive this highly undesirable guest, but with the Englishwoman's usual thought about four o'clock in the afternoon.

'Oh yes, they brought me a snack,' said Mrs. Oliver disparagingly.

'Well—er—won't you sit down?' asked Helena.

'Thanks. That little room w'ere I 'ad the tea was a bit warmer,' said Mrs. Oliver, ostentatiously drawing her coat with its imitation leopard-skin collar more closely about her. 'I suppose you *got* a droin-room?'

'Oh, yes, but we find it difficult to keep the big rooms warm,' said Helena, leading the way back to the morning-room, which the family used as a sitting-room when they were not specifically entertaining.

Annie appeared.

'Will you have tea, my Lady?' she asked.

'Thank you, Annie. I'll wait until Sir Simon is free,' said Helena, and the maid withdrew.

('Wait an' 'ave crumpets and some decent cakes, I s'pose,' thought Mrs. Oliver.)

Aloud she said, 'Somethink of a change for you, isn't it?'

Helena felt her resentment grow and she sat very upright in her chair. Whatever Mrs. Oliver had come for, she was not going to be encouraged to make a second visit.

'Mrs. Oliver, I may as well speak quite plainly,' she said. 'It *is* a change for us to be here, in a home which is exclusively our own, and it would be preferable to both me and Sir Simon if you are able to conduct any further business you may have with us by writing rather than calling.'

She amazed herself by stepping so far out of character as to be actually impolite to even an uninvited and unwelcome guest, but the appearance of anyone who could thrust her back into the horror of her last days in her London home was petrifying.

What had the woman come for? She had been the root of her greatest fear.

Mrs. Oliver's face turned scarlet.

'You're very 'igh and mighty with me, Mrs. Clurey,' she said, 'but p'raps you'd like to know wot my friend 'as come about? P'raps it'll surprise you, and p'raps it won't, to 'ear that my friend 'as come to see yer 'usband about that Mr. Paraway, or the man wot *called* 'imself Mr. Paraway.'

'Well. Go on,' said Helena, feeling for the support of the chair.

'P'raps it will surprise you, and p'raps it won't, to 'ear that 'is real name was Geoffrey Pellet *and* that 'e 'as a lawful, wedded wife *and* that she isn't your daughter Alison.'

It was the last thing Helena had expected. She sat staring with a lost feeling into the woman's venomous little eyes. How could she possibly have found out?

'Ah, I thought that would make you sit up,' added Mrs. Oliver, though that was not the actual physical effect. Helena was leaning against the high back of her chair, her eyes filled with horror.

'*An'* we got proof,' said Mrs. Oliver as her enemy remained silent. 'You don't like that, *Mrs.* Clurey, do you? Make a proper stink it will, after all the talk there's bin in the papers about 'is death and you comin' into all this. I wouldn't like to be in your shoes, you and and your family—not that I'd ever be likely to.

'We may be 'umble people to your way o' thinkin', but we 'ave respectable friends wot don't get themselves in the papers.'

Helena struggled to find her voice.

'I cannot discuss my—private affairs with you, Mrs. Oliver,' she began, and was saved by the appearance of the maid again.

'Excuse me, my Lady,' she said, 'but the other lady is ready to leave now.'

Helena rose precipitately.

'Thank you, Annie. Please take Mrs. Oliver to her and show

them out,' she said.

Mrs. Oliver looked annoyed. She would have been glad to present Gertie to her, show her the sort of wife Giles Paraway really had, but she was frustrated. Helena stood without offering her hand and the maid waited by the open door, and after a moment's uncertain pause, Mrs. Oliver flounced out.

'You'll be 'earin' more of this,' she said ominously, and a few moments later the front door closed on them.

Helena went blindly out of the room and up to her bedroom, the big, airy room at which she and Simon had had a private chuckle the first time they were alone in it, and where, on the first night they had spent in it, something seemed to have caught them back to the earlier years of their marriage, the earlier years with something added to them and infused into them which brought them nearer to each other, closer in love, than they had ever been in those years.

Simon had been her lover that night.

'This is the sort of place to which you were born, my darling,' he said. 'This is what I've always in my heart wanted for you. At last I've got something to give you.'

'Oh, Simon, you've already given me everything I' she said. 'It's wonderful here, but material things don't really matter, do they, so long as we've got each other.'

He held her closely.

'I always find words difficult when it's a case of my own feelings,' he said. 'I've never been able to tell you what you are to me, all the happiness you've given me. I wish I knew how to tell you, my dearest.'

'That's all I need you to tell me, that I am your dearest,' she whispered. 'Thank you, Simon, for all the years.'

'Do you love me?' he asked, and he had never asked it before.

'Don't you know that?' she asked chokingly.

And because there were no words, because of the surging need they had of each other, body and spirit, he made love to her as he had never done even in their youth, and afterwards, relaxed and spent, even the heavy burden of her fear for the moment forgotten, she lay with his arm about her and slept with her head on his breast.

That had been in this room with its soft, beautiful bed and the massive furniture made in the days before machine-filled factories had made men forget the loving craftsmanship which had created beauty to outlast the short span of its creator's life.

Now the peace had fled again, the altar despoiled – despoiled by the greedy hands of the past, her own hands.

The truth had never occurred to her. She had at once assumed that it was her own marriage to Geoffrey Pellet which had somehow come to light, and come through Mrs. Oliver, how she could not imagine nor did she try to imagine it. It was enough that Mrs. Oliver knew, that that unknown woman had known, and that now Simon must know.

What was he going through now? What bitterness and disillusionment? Thinking of all the years through which she had lied to him, of the children she had borne him, and of Brian. Would he know about Brian too? Know that the child of whom he had been proudest, for whose sake he had welcomed his inheritance, was not of his own at all, but the son of Geoffrey Pellet?

What difference would it make if she protested to him that she had not known herself to be Geoffrey's wife all these years? Would he even believe her? Looking back to that time of misery and utter domination by her mother, hazy with the years, she wondered how she could have been so witless, so credulous, as to believe Geoffrey when he had told her she was not his wife. In her frantic haste to repair as best she could the irreparable damage done to her, a girl of eighteen, Mrs. Thorwell had thrust her at Simon, rushed her into marriage with him to cover up that disaster with Geoffrey Pellet, apparently had not even tried to find out the truth about that first 'marriage'.

Or had she known? Helena would never know that, but her mother's ruthless determination would have stopped at nothing. And she, Helena, had to reap the terrible harvest, she and those she loved better than life, her children and Simon – Simon—

He did not come to her. Did she really expect he would? He would be sitting there, his hands still, his face expressionless, his eyes staring – staring at the ruin she had worked for them all, his children illegitimate, and Brian not his son.

Years ago, the worry about Brian filling her mind again (it was when the death of the last of Curtis Clurey's sons had left Simon as the heir), she had written under an assumed name to one of the magazines which offer advice on every subject from how to grow mushrooms to how to win back an erring lover.

Was a child, born after marriage but not conceived by the husband, legitimate? she had asked.

The answer was at that time reassuring.

A child born in wedlock is, in law, the legitimate offspring of the husband and wife; a child born before the marriage of the parents is legitimised by such marriage provided that neither party was married to a third person at the time of the birth. If either party had had a husband or wife living, however, the subsequent marriage of the parents of the child would not render it legitimate.

That had been a relief to her. Though Brian was not Simon's son, even if he had not been born in wedlock, he would be legitimised by her marriage to Simon.

But she realised, when Giles Paraway told her that she was actually his wife, that nothing could make Brian legitimate, even if at some time or other she married Simon legally.

Who had that woman been who had brought to Simon proofs of her, Helena's, marriage to Geoffrey Pellet? And also presumably proofs that Geoffrey Pellet and Giles Paraway were one and the same man? How had she obtained such proofs? What were they?

She herself had had no record of the marriage. It had not occurred to her to ask for or to keep a certificate. Why should she have done? She was little more than a child, and deliriously happy, supremely confident in her world of dreams.

Suppose somebody, somehow, had found that certificate after all these years? Had also found out that Giles Paraway had been

Geoffrey Pellet?

She could conceive of no way in which it might have been done, and yet it had been done. She could still hear Mrs. Oliver's taunting voice, see her evil, spiteful eyes.

Somehow Mrs. Oliver had found out, Mrs. Oliver who had not been able to destroy her by her story of having seen her kill Giles Paraway, and who had pursued her fiendish and inexplicable vengeance by digging all this out of her past. What satisfaction could it possibly be to any woman to destroy another? What had Mrs. Oliver against her, other than the resentment of the whole Clurey family at her presence in their home?

It was utterly disproportionate revenge. The woman must be a devil incarnate.

But of what use was it to think thoughts like that? The thing was done, never mind who did it or why.

Down in the library, Simon was sitting much as Helena had pictured him, though not with the expressionless face, the staring eyes, of her imagination. Rather was he puzzled how best to tackle the problem set him by the highly coloured Gertie de la Croix. He had no real doubt of her ability to prove her contention that she was the wife of Geoffrey Pellet and that Geoffrey Pellet and Giles Paraway had been one and the same. Nor had he the least objection to handing over to the widow, intact, all the money and other possessions which he had left. Alison, who was already well provided for, had shown no interest in it and would certainly not want any of it once she knew (poor child) the truth about the man she had hoped to marry, and Helena would not have touched a penny of it in any case.

The thing that tormented his mind, if this Gertie person could prove her case, was that he could not see how he could avoid letting Helena and the children know about it. It was very improbable, since their family affairs had twice, and recently, made newspaper headlines, that this new turn of events would escape the notice of the news hounds. The Gertie person herself would almost certainly spread it, coming as she would into some ten or twelve thousand pounds.

Then there was that poisonous woman, Mrs. Oliver. The Gertie person had explained her association with the business, and that Mrs. Oliver, knowing the family, had 'very kindly' offered to go with her, though it was obvious that Geoffrey Pellet's widow, or Giles Paraway's widow, did not need the advice or support of another woman. Mrs. Oliver had come for her own satisfaction, to gloat, if she were given an opportunity, over what she would consider the 'downfall' of the Clureys in their new and high estate!

Confound the woman.

Well, there was no need to tell the family about it until he had made quite sure that the Gertie person really was what she represented herself to be, and not an adventuress trying to get hold of Giles Paraway's money. Giles Paraway, or Geoffrey Pellet. Simon found that he was not really surprised at the turn of events. Without being able to put his finger on anything, he had felt there was something fishy about him, never liked the man, quite apart from his obvious unsuitability from the point of view of age to be Alison's husband.

Helena had felt that too. Yes, definitely Helena had felt it, though she had never mentioned it specifically, had merely based her objections to him on his age. Helena had been different, unhappy, restless, ever since Giles Paraway had made his appearance amongst them, though until this moment he had never pinpointed the time of the change in her.

His thoughts were arrested at that. His mind went back to the first time they had seen the man. That had been the time Helena had fainted, and she was not given to fainting. In fact, as far as Simon knew, she never had fainted before. There had been no reason for it either, no discoverable reason anyway.

Or had there?

Was it possible that in any way Helena had become possessed of the knowledge of Giles Paraway's marriage? If so, how? His thoughts went back to Mrs. Oliver. Had she been the one to know? Had she been able to ferret it out through some underground channels and *told* Helena so that the sight of him, in the flesh, had made her actually faint? It was Mrs. Oliver who had brought the woman here – and Mrs. Oliver who had seen, or said she had seen, what really happened when Giles Paraway fell to his death!

His thoughts went round and round, terrifyingly. Coming out of the bath-room at the sound of Helena's wild scream and looking down into the hall, he had seen – what on her face? Just the horror of that fall?

He knew that it had not been only that. Something in her face had called to him, had made him do something quite out of keeping with his whole character, his legal training, his unwavering regard for the truth. In that instant he had seen at once what could have happened, seen it in that look in Helena's face, seen it even before Mrs. Oliver had made her allegations that Helena had herself closed the door on Paraway, allegations which he had at once, and quite calmly, refuted, his word accepted before that of the spiteful, venomous woman whose every word and look showed her as Helena's enemy, bent on doing her harm.

In the face of his own statement that he had himself seen what happened, seen the door close without Helena's touching it, Mrs. Oliver had ceased to make her assertion and he was pretty sure that she had not seen what she had at first said she had seen.

But what if her allegation had been true, even though she made it from spite and not from knowledge? He knew that his own lies had been told instinctively to protect Helena if she were in need of protection.

But if Helena had known that Giles Paraway was a married man, might she not, on the spur of the moment, have taken that way out for Alison? She had always been a tigress for her children when anything threatened them. Had she been capable of even that? Not with any preconceived intention or plan, but snatching the opportunity without thought except for her daughter's safety and happiness?

His blood ran cold, not from any thought of Helena's crime, but because of the danger which had faced her, though that danger, thank God, was now over.

He forced his thoughts away from that horror, back to the present.

The best thing he could do would be to see Cuver, with whom he had been on friendly speaking terms for a long time before Paraway's death brought them into closer contact. He would need the help of the police in verifying or disproving the claim of the Gertie person to be Giles Paraway's widow, and Cuver was the obvious referee. No point in saying anything to anyone until that was established, certainly not to Helena. If it were proved to be a false claim, she need never know anything about it or hear the name of Paraway again.

He looked up the trains to town and went to find Helena and give her the reasonable excuse he had invented for the sudden journey, but on inquiry, he was told that Her Ladyship had gone out taking the little car. She had not driven for years, but she had taken out a provisional driving licence since her own had been out of date for so many years, and though Simon did not like her going out alone in the car, she was proving herself a capable driver.

'You don't know where she has gone, Annie?' he asked.

'I think only to the farm, sir. She said she would not be long.'

'Oh, very well. Please tell her when she comes in that I have had an urgent call to town on business, and that I may stay the night if there is any fog. I shall not be in to dinner in any case. Tell Drew he had better come to the station with me to bring the car back. He can bring the Humber round if he is dressed.'

'Yes, sir.'

Simon took a somewhat boyish pleasure in the possession of two cars, the little Hillman he had bought for Helena and Alison, and the big old Humber which had been his cousin's. He had not kept on Curtis's chauffeur, but Drew was a capable driver and served such purposes as this.

Helena had gone towards the farm, a mile or so away from

the house, but she had driven farther, to the A.A. telephone box at the cross-roads. She wanted desperately to talk to someone. She had always wanted this, to lean on some stronger personality and draw from it the strength she could not find within herself. She envied passionately the people, Simon, Alison, even John, who were able to draw from their reserves that power to stand alone. She knew she would never have it. Only once in her life had she ever taken a plunge entirely of her own volition, and that was when she had made that fatal error of throwing herself into Geoffrey's arms, abandoning everything that had made up her life apart from him and turning the whole course of her life; and she knew in bitterness of spirit where that had landed her.

Now there was no one to whom she could turn but Ruth.

She had not dared to use any of the telephone lines to the house for fear of being overheard. It was possible to listen at any of the extensions to what was being said at any other.

But Ruth was not there, and by the time she had been obliged to talk to Humphrey, who treated most women like pleasant children to be humoured, especially if they were attractive, she returned to the house to find that Simon had gone. Annie gave her his message.

She interpreted it at once as being his reaction to the story which this woman brought by Mrs. Oliver had told him. He had not been able to face her. He always took time to think. He had gone away to do that, without giving her any chance to explain – if indeed any explanation were possible.

She went listlessly to bed, pleading a headache, and presently Alison came up to find her.

Already there was a subtle change in Alison. In the four months they had been at The Holt, she had lost much of the strained, exhausted look and the spiritless acceptance of life as something to be borne.

At first she had thrown herself into the work of the home farm because it offered her the hard physical labour which might give her sleep and make her at least temporarily forget.

Gough, an elderly and very capable man who was in charge

of the farm, had protested at the sort of jobs she chose.

'That bain't no sorta job for a young lady to do, Miss Alison,' he said, when she wanted to clean out the pigsties and the cow byre and cart the muck in a heavy barrow to the midden. 'Young Joe'll do all that. Now you take a basket and collect the eggs, and presently you can take a measure o' com to 'em.'

'Let Joe do that if he wants a job,' said Alison. 'I want to *work*,' and though it went against the grain with him, she had her way.

But it was not all cleaning out and carting muck. She wanted to know how things were done. Even at The Holt, where wages were good and conditions beyond the customary, there was a shortage of labour as men drifted into the towns where easier money was to be earned and cinemas and dance halls available, and Alison soon proved herself quick and adaptable, her superb young strength and quick-thinking brain, coupled with her will to work, making her far more than the purely ornamental 'young lady' looking for a passing hobby which Gough had at first taken her to be.

The home farm was a small one, most things in miniature since it was designed rather to supply the needs of 'the house' than as a commercial proposition. The only big-scale development was in the prize breed of cattle which had been Sir Curtis Clurey's pride and which bid fair to make a contribution to the national feeding economy.

Alison, secretly afraid of cows and terrified of the thousand-guinea bull which glowered at her out of his luxurious quarters whenever she had to pass them, confined her activities in that direction to the care and feeding of the lolloping, moony-eyed calves which came charging towards her in their small field and which she called by fantastic names which Gough derided but allowed them to keep so that subsequent show winners were to be known as Fairyfoot, Laguna Lily, Allie's Love and even Moira Shearer.

She conquered fear and initial distaste in going into the pig-breeding pens, the two great saddle-backed sows proving to have no malevolent intentions behind their little eyes as they lay on their sides, panting and paying no attention at all to their numerous, clamorous progeny scampering over them and frantically pushing one another away from the most desirable points of supply.

She was in one of the modern, scrupulously clean sties, with its concrete floor and brick-built walls, trying to sort out the squalling piglets, when she became aware that a young man was watching her with amused interest.

As it had been impossible to retain for her farm-work the sombre black in which she had outwardly mourned Giles Paraway, she had adopted a workmanlike uniform of breeches, woollen sweater open-necked and short-sleeved, and rubber Wellingtons. Her corn-gold hair, cut very short, curled close to her head, and she wore no make-up, not even the lipstick without which she would never have been seen in London. Face and bare arms were weather-tanned, and she laughed as she tried in vain to see fair play amongst the scrambling piglets.

'I wish you'd acquire a few manners,' she told them, trying to find a place for the smallest one. 'You want the best places; we have them. Move over, you greedy little wretch. You've already taken two away from him—oh!' as the sound of a chuckle brought her upright, the small pig who always got left out held in her arms.

Tony Joyce, bare-headed, grinned at her.

'You might as well give it up,' he said. There are probably not enough to go round.'

'There are,' she said. 'I've—'

She stopped, realising what part of the sow's anatomy they were discussing and that she had been about to tell him that she had counted them.

'I'll have to feed this one on the bottle,' she said. 'Poor little thing. He's the runt, you know. There's always one in a litter, and the others are absolute *pigs* to him,' laughing at her apt choice of words. 'Who are you, by the way?'

She liked the look of him, a big masculine-looking young

man, brown-haired, grey-eyed, easy in country tweeds with a pipe just removed from his mouth. She had not seen him before – or she thought she had not. Actually he had been in the background on the ghastly day when Giles was killed, but her recollections of that day held only chaotic unhappiness in which her mind had noted nothing but the fact that the man she loved was dead.

Tony decided not to recall that to her mind. This was a very different version of the girl he had seen that day, and if he had lost his heart in pity for her then, he lost it all over again and finally when he saw her as she was now, and was laughing.

'My name is Joyce, Tony Joyce,' he told her, 'and if you are going to tell me that I'm a trespasser and have no right to be here, I shan't be able to contradict you. As a matter of fact, I'm lost. I've been having a tramp in the country. I came down on my motor-bike and left it in the village as it always seems rather a desecration to go roaring and spluttering along lanes like these, but I've lost all track of the village so I turned in at your gate to ask the way.'

'You've really got on to the estate, which is private property,' she said, trying to put a note of reproof into her voice. 'Still, I know it's easy to do that. If you want to get back to Fraybury, your best way now is through the farm and across the fields. I'll show you and put you on your way. I've got to go back with this fellow,' tucking the struggling little pig more securely into her arms.

'He only wants a bonnet and a bib to have come out of *Alice in Wonderland*,' he observed. 'In spite of your short hair, you look rather like Alice.'

'I don't know whether that's meant for a compliment,' she said.

'Definitely,' he said. 'Alice has been the love of my long life. You're sure you wouldn't like me to carry him?' looking doubtfully at the now resigned creature.

'All right. Here,' she said mischievously, and transferred it to his unwilling arms. 'Not like that! You'll poke his eyes out with your pipe. Oh, better give him back. Now, that's better,' she said, settling the protesting piglet. 'Don't make a fuss. You're going to have a bottle to yourself from now on. They haven't any sense, you know, though they're not as bad as chickens.'

'Are you by way of being a land girl?' he asked, though he knew perfectly well who she was.

She laughed.

'Possibly by way of it, but still a long way off it,' she said. 'No, I live there,' with a nod towards the house just visible in the distance. 'I just work here. It's our own farm.'

'Rather jolly having a farm,' said Tony, who knew nothing about farms and very little about the country, and whose tweeds he had bought some time ago as a fitting preparation for the golf he had never succeeded in playing. He had had neither the time nor the money.

'Yes, I think so,' agreed Alison, 'though I'm still scared of cows, and the bull terrifies me. Would you like to see him? He has a horrid fascination for me. I know he can't get out (or I hope he can't!) but there is always the terror of imagining what would happen if he could.'

'I know, like hanging over the parapet of a bridge as far as you can when an express is going by underneath it.'

'Was that your particular dare? It sounds more like my young brother John, though what he seems to like doing best is making fireworks which might explode at any minute.'

'Did I see him as I came in? He and another ruffian were doing a sort of rodeo in a field of young bullocks.'

'Yes, that would be John—and his bosom friend Stinky who is staying with us. Funny. I've never known what his real name is, Stinky is so appropriate. Wait till Gough catches them! Gough's the real farmer. He's over there now, I see,' and Gough entered one of the fields which led to the house.

It would have been quite simple, and sensible, to call to him and hand over the lost visitor to him, but somehow it did not occur to her, and they walked companionably in the other direction, to the neatly arranged collection of low buildings with their surrounding wall which housed the farmyard, the dairy, and the milking-sheds.

Tony looked about him with interest. He had always imagined a farm to be an untidy sort of place, with tumbledown sheds and barns that needed repair and tracks in which one sank to the ankles in mud.

He said something of the sort to Alison, who greeted it with scorn.

'That's not our sort of farm,' she said. 'Of course everything is very small, miniature almost, and there's always been money to spend on it. That sounds very superior, doesn't it? As a matter of fact, it hasn't been ours very long, so we don't take credit for any of this. We're simply trying to carry on in the same way. Our name is Clurey, by the way, I'm Alison,' glancing sideways at him with some suspicion, to see how he reacted to it. 'You're not the newspapers, by any chance, are you?' she added, the thought only just striking her unpleasantly.

'Good heavens, no! Nothing like that,' said Tony cheerfully, though he refrained from telling her just what he was. That, he felt, would finish him with her. Poor kid, she must have had quite enough of that. Some day, of course, he would have to tell her, for it was beyond question with him that there would be another day, many of them. On the face of it, the position was obscure, of course – he was not far removed from his days as a humble bobby and she the daughter of Sir Simon Clurey of The Holt, but his secret knowledge being what it was, who could say what would happen to them all?

Time would tell, but he was not going to put a spanner in the works until it fell in of its own accord – or was insinuated into it by the guv.

'Then you don't know anything about us?' asked Alison, still suspicious.

'Not much. Only what I suppose a lot of people know who— who read the newspapers. Your father has just come into a title, hasn't he?'

'Yes,' she said, and was silent for a few moments, until she turned her face again to look at him, defiantly.

'You knew what happened before? About the—about Mr. Paraway being killed in our house in London?'

He nodded. No sense in denying that.

'Yes. Yes, I heard about it,' he said. 'Bad luck.'

'We were engaged,' said Alison, looking straight before her again.

'I'm sorry,' he said gently.

'Well, we needn't talk about it, need we?' she said with a sharp note in her voice, as if she were running away from something she hated to see but knew all the time was there, lying in wait for her. 'This is the dairy. There's a place the other side of it where we do all sorts of jobs. I'd better put this chap down where he can't come to any harm whilst I get a bottle. Light the gas in that ring, will you? It's calor gas, but I expect there's some there.'

She moved about briskly and deftly, heated the carefully measured milk and water and picked up the little pig, seating herself on a box with the thing in her arms. After some initial doubt about the size of the rubber teat, it sucked at it greedily, quickly overcoming its surprise at having such a plentiful supply of food which it could imbibe without interruption and assault.

Tony stood watching her with an odd and quite unprecedented emotion. He would have scorned to interpret it as a feeling that he was looking at the eternal mother, or at a girl in her right setting, the piglet transformed into a human creature, but that was what, in effect, it was. Her head was bent, watching absorbedly the little creature's successful attempt to adapt itself to the strange method of feeding, but when it was satisfied that food was actually here and peacefully attainable and had settled down to it, she lifted her face and there was a shining, peaceful look in the blue eyes which a few moments ago had been darkened with pain.

'Well, that's that,' she said when the bottle had been drained. 'Let it go, you little pig. Your tummy's bulging and you will probably be sick, but I don't fancy holding you over my shoulder and patting up the wind, so back you go to your mother till next time, or until you can fight for your rights. Would you like to have a look round? I'll restore him to the bosom of his family first We're rather proud of the farm, you know, though I don't suppose you could run a big one on these lines.'

She showed him the hen-runs where an accurate egg-laying record could be kept, and the open runs where the merely farmyard variety of egg-producers lived a communal life, the dairy with its butter-and cheese-making plant, a sick, weedy-looking calf which, now able to stagger towards her on weak legs, was her pride and joy, since she had saved him from early death and Gough was beginning to think he might turn into a winner, and finally they stood as near as they dare to where the prize bull stood snorting and pawing at his strong, protective wall.

She indicated with pride, but at a distance, the rosettes which were his proud possession and spoke with the utmost unconcern of the scheme for artificial insemination which would enable them to produce a larger herd of well-bred cattle than would be possible under natural conditions.

He wondered whether she would ever be happy away from all this, and speculated with very little optimism on the possibility, at some future time, of Cuver offering him a job which would enable him to become one of the big noises at Scotland Yard whilst living in the heart of the country.

But Alison, discreetly sounded on the subject, hesitated.

'I don't know,' she said about permanently living in the country. 'Of course I do love it here. It's all so different and in a way so much more worthwhile. Life's a lot simpler, hardworking but in a leisurely way. Everything takes so much time that no one rushes to get a job done the same day, or even the same week or month. But—oh well, I like other things as well. I don't know that I always want to look like this,' glancing down with a smile at her breeches and boots, 'and sometimes I make a frantic onslaught on my hands and try to do something about my face—and when I tried to get into one of my town frocks the other day, I couldn't! It would be too awful if I got fat, though you'd think all this work would keep me down. I suppose I get hungry and eat too much. By the way, hadn't you better have some tea or something before you go?'

'That would be very nice of you,' said Tony.

But when they reached the house and met Annie in the hall, it was to be told that Helena had gone to bed with a bad headache.

'Oh, Annie! Is she ill, do you think?' asked Alison anxiously.

One of the signs of recovery from the shock of Giles's death was that the girl was beginning to break down the barrier, intangible but real, which she had erected between herself and her mother. Not all, but part of the old loving comradeship between them was replacing the hard self-sufficiency which had been so grievous a thing for Helena to bear.

'Do you mind if I leave you whilst I just run up to her?' she asked Tony.

'Look here, I won't wait. It'll only take me a few minutes to get to the village from here, and I can have something at the "local". Please don't bother about me.'

'I don't like to turn you out like this, without even a cup of tea,' she said, but he saw that she was concerned about her mother and did not really want to have to entertain a visitor.

'Really I would rather go,' he said, 'but may I come again? Just to see how the pig is getting on, you know?' with his nice grin.

She coloured a little and smiled.

'I should like you to,' she said, 'and so would the pig—only come to the house next time, won't you? I'm not *always* a land girl.'

'Thank you. I definitely will. Good-bye—Alison.'

She held out her hand to him rather shyly, a brown, not quite clean hand that had held pigs and stroked calves and been washed perfunctorily under the tap in the dairy.

'Good-bye, Tony,' she said, and when he had gone, turned slowly before running up the stairs.

Helena was lying in her darkened room, wide awake, very pale, with shadowed eyes, and Alison regarded her anxiously.

'I wish I could get something for you, Mummy dear,' she said. 'You look as if you want something more than just aspirin.'

'There's nothing the matter, darling,' said Helena. 'It's just a bad headache. I was a long time with Drew discussing the vines, and it's very hot and stuffy in there.'

'Drew should have known better than to bother you with them. Why couldn't he have asked me?'

'My dear, I must do *something* for my keep,' said Helena, managing a smile.

Dear Alison. What joy to see life flowing back into her veins I It was a long time since she had seemed so vital – happy even.

'Well, something that doesn't mean standing for hours in a Turkish bath,' said Alison wrathfully. 'Mummy—you do like it here, don't you?'

'But of course. Don't you?'

Alison stretched her arms above her head in a gesture of freedom.

'I think I love it,' she said. 'I'm not sure that I would like it for always, never being in town or doing all the things I used to do, and I'd like to dress up again and go gay for once, but after the monotonous grind of the office, with nothing to show for it but dull letters and masses of figures, it's marvellous to be doing something that actually *produces* something – the "end product" they're always talking about in that television programme they've done to death. Do you know, Gough thinks we're going to beat the egg-laying record with those cross-bred hens he bought as a spec? I always feel the poor things are a bit lonely, each with her own house and back yard, but at least we don't keep them in batteries. And they're silly things, after all. Fancy producing eggs and sitting on them and waiting for them to hatch when they *know* they're still virgins! Well, I suppose I'd better go and clean up. Where's Daddy?'

Helena's eyes clouded again.

'He's had to go up to town, dear. He may not be back tonight, not to dinner anyway.'

'What can I send up to you, dear, I wonder?*

But Helena refused.

'I couldn't eat, dear,' she said. 'Besides, I had a huge lunch.'

'That was hours ago. Well, try to sleep, won't you? If Daddy's late, I'll leave a note for him not to disturb you. Good night, Mummy.'

For some reason which she did not attempt to explain to herself, she said nothing about Tony Joyce. She was feeling faintly ashamed of the laughter she had shared with him and the general pleasantness of that hour or two during which she had scarcely once thought of Giles.

Helena clung to the girl for a moment. She might have so short a time now before they would turn from her. She had not been able to make any clear picture of the future, but whether the children would have to know or not, how could life go on as it had done with the heart of it, the perfect unity between herself and Simon, no longer beating?

X

SIMON found Ronald Cuver still at his office but preparing to leave.

'Never mind,' he said cheerfully when his late visitor offered to come back the next day. 'I'll just ring up my wife. Why not come back and have a bit of dinner with us afterwards? Unless, of course, you've other plans?'

'No, I'd like to do that,' said Simon, who had a genuine liking for the inspector, once he had ceased to be a danger to Helena. Helena had told him of her association with Milly Cuver and its happy outcome, and he felt he had a proprietary interest in them.

'It's about Paraway,' he said, coming straight to the point when Cuver had made his telephone call and laughingly told Milly to prepare the fatted calf, even if it turned out to be a haddock. 'A remarkable thing seems to have come to light, and I want you to investigate it before I go any farther. Would it surprise you to be told that he had not always been known as Giles Paraway, but that in his young days his name was Geoffrey Pellet?'

The inspector gave a start of surprise. It was the last thing he had expected Simon Clurey to know, and its implications astonished him by the attitude and tone in which the statement was made. How could any man be so – well, almost jocular about the discovery that his wife was not his wife after all?

He kept his speculations out of his careful reply.

'Yes, as a matter of fact, I did know,' he said.

'You did? Then you know about his marriage under that

name?'

Still there was no sign of great perturbation and Cuver's astonishment increased.

'Er—well—something about it,' he said cautiously.

'It makes a good deal of difference to the Will, of course, seeing that the wife is still alive, and what I want you to do is to go into the matter, discreetly so as not to court too much publicity of course, and if the marriage was valid, and if you can establish the fact that the man we knew as Paraway was then known as Pellet, as his executor I must of course do the right thing by her. My daughter would have to know, I am afraid, and I feel quite sure that in the very unpleasant circumstances she would not wish to have any share at all in what the man left.'

'No. Quite,' said the inspector, wondering if he could possibly be hearing aright.

'I haven't got the actual marriage certificate,' went on Simon, 'but I took the details down from it, and have them here, and of course they can easily be verified. Here they are. The man's name, and the woman's, and the date. The tenth of June, 1927,' and he handed his note across the table.

Cuver's head swam. The figures danced before his eyes. Then, as they cleared, he read the name again, Gertrude Pragg, and the date, the date in 1927.

He reached for some private notes he had kept about the Paraway case, notes which he had so far not been able to bring himself to put into the file, and holding them so that his visitor could not see them, he looked at the date on which Geoffrey Pellet had been married to Helena Thorwell.

November 1930.

Then if this other marriage had taken place in 1927, Helena Clurey had never been legally married to Geoffrey Pellet and she was Simon Clurey's wife. He thanked his lucky stars that he had not been betrayed into revealing to the obviously unsuspecting Simon that he had believed Helena to be the woman to whom Simon was referring.

His head cleared and he put his own notes back in his drawer and turned the key and put it in his pocket. They were dynamite.

'It shouldn't be too difficult to verify this, Sir Simon,' he said, indicating the page torn off Simon's pad. 'We did discover, rather by chance, that Giles Paraway had at one time been known as Geoffrey Pellet and that he had—er—contracted a marriage under that name. You know the woman concerned?'

'Yes. She came to see me this afternoon, the sort of person who would belong to Geoffrey Pellet rather than to Giles Paraway,' said Simon. 'I must say it was a bit of a shock at the time, seeing that the rascal had actually asked my daughter to marry him and would possibly have actually committed bigamy with her had he lived. However, his death was somewhat fortuitous on that account,' looking with a straight and composed glance at the inspector, 'and now my only concern is to see that his widow, if she is his widow, gets what he left.'

'The Will was valid, you know,' said Cuver, 'so she can only claim what is legally the widow's share.'

'I can assure you, Inspector, that if she is his widow, she will get it all. My wife has already said she will not accept the legacy to herself, and my daughter will not want to touch it either once she knows, as unfortunately I suppose she must know. As the executor, I can hardly make her legacy over to someone else without informing her, and my co-executors at the bank will have to be told what we propose to do and they will require both her and my wife to make a legal handing-over of their legacies to the widow.

'Well, Inspector, I think that's all. It's a nasty business, and we can hardly hope to escape all publicity, but you'll do your best to keep it quiet?'

'Of course. Of course. Have you told Lady Clurey about it?'

'Not yet. I thought I would get it proven first.'

'Yes, perhaps so. I'll get someone on to it right away. Might even do it myself. And as soon as we find out that the story of this marriage is true, and that there was no divorce or anything, I should tell Lady Clurey if I were you.'

'And Alison, yes. Yes, I'll do that, of course, since it can't be helped. How long is it likely to take you?'

'Oh, a few days, I expect. Not much more. Now what about that haddock of Milly's? Though I wouldn't mind betting that by this time it's turned itself into something a bit more succulent. I'll give her a ring to tell her we're starting. Foggy, isn't it?'

'Yes. Good job I left word that I should probably stay in town for the night.'

The next day, Ronald Cuver sat for a long time in his office, idle and motionless, and it was in that state that presently Tony Joyce found him.

'Hullo, Guv, gone on strike?' he asked with his engaging impudence.

'More than that, Tony,' said Cuver, not looking at him. 'I'm packing up. Sent in my resignation this morning.'

The boy looked thunderstruck.

'But—but—good Lord, Guv, whatever for? Not ill or anything, are you?' for he knew that, in spite of his many grunts and complaints, the inspector really loved his work and also that he was due for a very appreciable promotion.

'No. Nothing like that. Never felt better. It's only that—oh well, I want a change. Had enough of other people's troubles, poor devils. Thinking of taking a little pub, somewhere in the country. London's no good for living in any more, specially in these fogs—the smog! Bad for Milly and won't be good for the youngster when it arrives.'

'Has she persuaded you into this?' asked Tony suspiciously.

'No, it was my own idea entirely, though she's with me in it, you know. Likes the country and the idea of a little pub. You must come and have a drink on the house when we get it. I'm clearing up outstanding matters before I go. Oh, there's this I'd like you to do, today if you can. A previous marriage of the man Giles Paraway, alias Geoffrey Pellet. Here it is. Name of Gertrude Pragg. June 1927,' handing him Simon's note. 'Somewhere in Portsmouth. Shouldn't be difficult to trace. And find out if there was any subsequent divorce.'

Tony took the note and whistled.

'Phew! Bit of a go-er, our Geoffrey. This means—'

'Yes, I know what it means,' the inspector interrupted. 'It means that he never was married to Helena Thorwell, since that took place three years later—if there was no divorce, of course, and I have no reason to suppose there was. Wire into it at once like a good chap, will you? It's rather urgent The widow's claiming the money.'

'Right ho. But at least tell me this, Guv. Where did you get this?'

The inspector lifted steady eyes.

'Sir Simon Clurey brought it in last evening. The woman had been to see him. Naturally, as the executor of the man's Will, he wants to know whether the claim is true. If it is, his wife and daughter will want, he says, to hand over to the woman *all* the money, not just her legal widow's share.'

Tony digested the information silently. For one thing, if it were true and Alison's mother never had been legally married to the blighter, then Alison was Simon Clurey's legitimate daughter, and though he personally did not care two hoots whether she was or not, he would not want a piece of knowledge like that to lie in secret between him and the girl whom he had determined, on sight, to marry. But the main thing was that, once she knew what an absolute rotter Paraway had been, it would inevitably lessen the time it would take her to recover from his loss.

'And this is all Sir Simon Clurey knows?' he asked at last.

'All,' said Cuver emphatically. 'Since the man is dead, there is no question of prosecution for any bigamous marriage he might have contracted. You understand?'

Tony nodded. He resisted the impulse to grin at his superior, but there was a twinkle in his eye which conveyed to Ronald Cuver that he did not quite definitely understand. Their knowledge of the bigamous marriage which Geoffrey Pellet had contracted all those years ago was to remain in their own keeping.

Good for the guv.

But it was not that which had convinced Inspector Cuver that he had outlived his usefulness to the force which he revered and had served so faithfully – until now.

Even if he revealed to any of his superiors the fact of that bigamous marriage, they would not want to do anything about it. There are times when even the police are content to let the dead bury its dead.

No, it was not that.

It was his certainty that Helena Clurey had killed Giles Paraway, and the knowledge that he intended to keep her secret.

He could not do that and remain in his present occupation. He had always regarded himself as incorruptible. No money could have bought him. He had sworn loyalty to the laws of his country and sworn to uphold the Queen's Justice. Seeing that he had now determined to avert the course of that justice, he had no option but to resign his appointment.

He was convinced in his own mind of her guilt, and knew that she was the type of woman, no hardened or calculating criminal, who could by questioning be worn down into a confession. No one knew of that firm conviction of his, not even Tony Joyce. No one would raise the matter again. With nothing to fear from him, Helena Clurey would be safe.

He could only suppose that she knew who Giles Paraway was, and that she believed herself to be legally his wife and not the wife of Simon Clurey. How such a woman could have brought herself to contract a bigamous marriage, and so soon after her first marriage, he would never know. He had only the supposition of what was the actual truth, that the father of her unborn child had deserted her and that she had rushed into another 'marriage' with the first available man to escape from her desperate plight. After all, she must have been little more than a child, not many years younger than his own Milly.

And what, after all was said and done, was Helena Clurey's crime? He knew that it was a crime against the law of God and the law of man, but what about the law of humanity? She had rid herself, and the world, of a man who had brought untold suffering to her in her youth, and almost certainly brought suffering to this other woman whom he had married and deserted, had reappeared to threaten the whole fabric of the life Helena Clurey had managed to build up in spite of that early disaster, and not only her own life but also that of the husband whose love he, Cuver, could not possibly doubt, and of the children they had brought up in love to honour and distinction.

Who was worse off through Giles Paraway's death?

And the woman who had caused it was the woman to whom he himself owed so great a personal debt, who had sent Milly back to him, to love him as she had never yet done, and to bear him the child for whom he longed.

He had weighed Helena Clurey's life and happiness against his sworn duty, and he had inflexibly decided to give her that life and happiness, whatever the cost.

He returned to the files of papers on his desk. This matter must be settled, and that; this one must be passed over to his successor; Tony Joyce would bring him the verification of the marriage of Geoffrey Pellet to Gertrude Pragg, as he did not for a moment doubt he would do.

Then it was finished.

But for Helena Clurey it was not finished.

She spent that night in uneasy dozing shot with frightening dreams in which she ran from some intangible terror from which she escaped only to find herself awake with the terror still pursuing her, and, awake, she could not escape it.

When Simon came back, she must turn and meet it.

What would he do? What would any of them do? If by leaving him, though the thought of that was worse than death, she could gain safety for the rest of them, she would go. But it would not make them safe. Nothing she or anyone could do would make them safe. Apart from the shock and horror they must all feel if they knew (and how could they not know, once Simon knew?), there was Brian – Brian whom in all these years she had never thought of as other than Simon's own son, Brian who had done so well, his career assured and now believing himself to be heir to the Clurey baronetcy and to The Holt, proud of the name he bore, proud to offer it with all its potentialities to the girl he loved.

And there was Lois herself, born of a distinguished father, as proud in her way as Brian was in his. Would it mean his losing Lois as well as everything else?

She knew Simon's rectitude. If he still wanted her to stay with him, he would make her legally his wife. She would still be Lady Clurey – but what of Brian? She remembered what she had been told long ago, that since she had had a husband living at the time of Brian's birth, her subsequent marriage to the man who might still think himself his father would not make Brian legitimate, would not make him the Clurey heir. Simon would not foist on the Clureys a son who was not entitled to be the heir.

She had her breakfast sent up to her, but made only a pretence of eating it, and Alison came up to find it practically untasted.

'Dearest, are you sure you ought not to have the doctor?' she asked again. 'You look so terribly pale. Have you slept at all?'

'Oh yes, quite a lot—and I never have much colour, you know,' said Helena, falsely bright.

'Well, you'd better put a bit on before Daddy sees you or he'll have Dr. Mace here in two shakes. By the way, he rang up to say that he would be down on the eleven-fifteen. I didn't disturb you, and I've told Drew to meet him at the station. I should stay in bed if I were you.'

'No, I'll get up. Did he—did he sound all right?'

'Of course. Why shouldn't he? I didn't tell him you were ill, of course, or he'd have chartered an aeroplane! If you're sure you want to get up, I'll turn on your bath. I still haven't got over the joy of having a bath whenever I want one, and without any Olivers rattling at the door-handle, have you? What sort of bath salts do you want in it, you extravagant person?'

'Anything you like, dear. I don't mind,' said Helena wearily.

Bath salts when your heart was breaking!

But when she had had her bath and dressed, with a little colour on her cheeks and the becoming shade of lipstick which Alison had chosen for her, she felt better able to face what had to be faced, but she remained in her room when she heard the car drive up. She would not risk being interrupted in what she and Simon would have to say to each other.

She heard his voice in the hall, asking Annie where she was, and the next moment his step was on the stairs, and then he was in the room.

'Helena—'

The look on her face, her instinctive step from him, stopped him.

Whatever he had made up his mind to say, she must speak first, let him know that the long deception was over, save him from the shame of having to tell her that he knew.

'Simon, I want to tell you that I know,' she said, her voice sounding oddly in her ears.

He knitted his brows.

'Know what?' he asked.

'That *you* know. That at long last, you *know*. I saw Mrs. Oliver yesterday. She told me what that woman had come to say, what she had found out. It's true, Simon. You need not have gone up to London to find out. I would have told you—then. I ought to have told you years ago. I ought never to have married you. But I can only ask you to believe that when I married you, I didn't know. I thought Geoffrey had told me the truth, and that I had never been his wife. I have never known all these years. It was only when I met him again that he told me the truth.'

'The truth? What truth?' asked Simon, all at sea.

'Why, that I was his wife and not yours at all,' and she turned from him blindly, groped her way to the bed and threw herself down on it, her face in the pillow. She could not bear him to see her shame, could not bear to read his own in his eyes.

He stood for a moment looking down at her in complete perplexity, trying to make sense of what she said.

She had been married to Geoffrey Pellet? She was Geoffrey

Pellet's wife and not his, Simon Clurey's?

When he spoke, there was more concern than perplexity in his tone.

'I'm afraid you're very ill, my dearest,' he said. 'Annie told me you went to bed early last night and had had your breakfast sent up, but not that you were really ill. Go back to bed, darling. Let me help you, and I think I'd better get Mace in to have a look at you.'

She sat up, rubbing her hand across her eyes.

'Don't be nice to me, Simon. Don't try to treat me as a child. Don't try to pretend to me. Don't let's have any pretence any more, even if you've come back with the idea of putting things right by making believe they've never happened.'

He sat down beside her and tried to take her hand, but she pushed it away.

'Helena dear, I don't understand, unless you're really very ill,' he said.

'I'm not ill, not in body. It's only in my mind that I'm sick— sick so that I want to die. I'd rather have died than that you should know.'

He got up and walked to the window, trying to make sense of what she had said, of this terrible distress in which he had found her.

She had told him that she had never been married to him, but that she had been married to Geoffrey Pellet – Giles Paraway! The thing was utterly fantastic, incredible – and yet—

He came back to her slowly. She was still sitting there, upright, her eyes wide and tearless, her face, under its now garish make-up, white and strained.

'Look, my dear, hadn't you better tell me the whole story?' he asked gently, though his mind felt shattered.

'Don't you know it? Isn't that what that woman came down to tell you yesterday? Isn't that what you rushed up to town for after she had gone? What else is there for me to tell? I've told you. I was already married to Geoffrey Pellet when I married you. I've never been your wife. I'm your mistress and the children are illegitimate.'

'I must believe you,' he said at last, after a long pause, 'though it's fantastic, incredible. When did all this happen?'

'Oh—I don't know. Years ago. Before Brian was born,' she said wearily.

Now that she had told him, she was exhausted in body and spirit. It scarcely registered with her that she *had* told him, and that until she had done so, he had not known.

'Brian,' he repeated, and there was a strange note of regret, of longing, in his voice. 'Helena, will it help you at all if I tell you that I know about Brian? That I have always known?'

That startled her into attention again.

'Known? Known—what, Simon?'

'That he was not my son, dear.'

'You've known that? All the time?'

'From the beginning, yes.'

'Mother—'

He shook his head.

'No, your mother didn't tell me. That was the reason why she persuaded you to marry me, wasn't it? I think I knew even then. After Brian was born, I was sure. You see, I knew he was full time, dear. I was fairly ignorant of such things, but no one could mistake it, and the nurse did not deny it though she would not admit it. I suppose they had been well primed by your mother! So you see, dear, if you are thinking it is a shock to me to know about him—it isn't. But he's been my son in every respect but that, loved like the others, perhaps loved even more because of what he cost you in tears and anguish throughout the years. I have never told you. I should never have told you. But this—this makes such a difference, such a terrible unbelievable difference. I can scarcely believe it, Helena. Are you sure that what you're telling me is the truth? That you married this man, Geoffrey Pellet – Giles Paraway!'

'Do you think it is a thing one would make up?' she asked bitterly.

'No,' he said and he was silent again, his mind grappling with all the implications, the potentialities, of what she had told him.

Then, as his mind cleared, he turned to her again.

'Helena, when was all this? When did it happen?' he asked her urgently.

'I've told you. Years and years ago,' she said in that weary, defeated voice, her hands making a helpless gesture.

'Yes, but when? I must know. *When* did you marry this man? What year?'

'I can't remember. Yes, it was—how old is Brian? When was he born? Nineteen-thirty-one, was it? Yes, it must have been. Then it was nineteen-thirty when I married Geoffrey. Does it matter?'

'Yes, it does,' he said, a new note of eagerness and of hope in his voice. 'It matters very much. This man Pellet, or Paraway, was an unmitigated scoundrel, and as it turns out, he's going to prove himself an even worse scoundrel than I had believed. The woman who came to see me yesterday, Helena, did not come to tell me that *you* had been married to him, but that *she* had. She showed me a marriage certificate. I have no doubt at all but that it is an authentic one, and it proves beyond doubt that you were never married to Geoffrey Pellet because he had a wife living at the time. That marriage was in nineteen-twenty-seven, and it must have been before he went through the same performance with you because, come to think about it, in nineteen-twenty-seven you could only have been fifteen, and not even that sort of man would marry a girl of fifteen. The scoundrel!'

She was staring at him, trying to take in what he was saying, trying to believe that it held her release from the ghastly burden she had borne ever since Giles Paraway had thrust it on her shoulders and laughed as he did so.

'You mean—is it true? Was he really married before? Does it mean that—that I never was really his wife? Oh, Simon, does it?' tragic pleading in her voice, pleading but no gladness. How could she be glad ever again, now that Simon knew what she had done to him?

But he had known. During these years of their happiness, he

211

had known, known that Brian was not his son, that she had rushed into marriage with him to hide her shame and to foist off on him another man's child! He had known, and never by word or look had he betrayed his knowledge, never varied in his loving care of her, in his pride and affection in Brian.

He took her hands in his.

'Yes, my dear, it does mean that – if the claim of this woman to have married him in nineteen-twenty-seven is substantiated, as I am sure it will be, you have never been his wife but only mine, always mine, Helena.'

She looked into his plain face with the lines of kindness which the years had etched around his eyes, with his goodness, his patience, his clear purpose in life written there for all to see, not a handsome man or even a good-looking one, not a particularly clever man, but a man who had never harboured an unjust thought or even an unmerciful one, whose lips had scarcely ever spoken an unkind word to or of anyone, a man who would never fail her – the man whom she utterly loved.

She leaned her forehead on their joined hands, hiding her face from him.

'And—the others, Simon? Alison, John—Brian?' she asked in a low voice.

'Will never know, my darling. There is no need."

She lifted her face.

'Simon, why have I never really known you? Why have I never trusted you?'

He smiled, a saddened smile that was sad for her, not for himself.

'I didn't know. Why haven't you?' he asked.

She shook her head.

It was difficult to speak.

'I think—perhaps—because I thought it was too much to expect of anyone, even of you, to be forgiven for—what I did to you—about Brian, and about—Geoffrey.'

'Why do you say even of me?' he asked with that smile to which she clung as to an anchor.

'Because—because you're so unlike all other men,' she said slowly.

'Alison will have to know,' he said, breaking their silence again. 'Not everything, of course, but about Paraway having a wife.'

'Yes. It will hurt her. She made a god of him, as all women do of the men they love. But in the end, she will be glad, I think. She is getting over it already. She is taking an interest in things here, and she is very young, and there will be someone else. There is sure to be. It's made her grow up. She was such a child in many ways before, and she's got to learn, as we all must do, that life isn't a fairy-tale and that the—happy-ever-after isn't easily come by.'

'No, but when it does come, it's worth what it has cost.'

'Will it be worth it, to you, Simon?'

'It has been worth it,' he said.

'Oh, Simon—Simon,' and she bent her face down on his hands again. 'Darling, there's something that's still got to be told, something about—*him*.'

He knew, suffering fear and pain for her, what it was she felt she must still tell him, and he stopped her.

'No, my dear, there is nothing else,' he said. 'There are sometimes things that must not be told, things that will hurt in the keeping back far more than in the telling. That, I think, is often laid on us as the penalty – the need not to tell.'

She was silent for a long time. He knew what it was that she would have told him, what it was she must not tell, the secret that, for her penance, she must keep in her heart for ever, must not ease the burden of her knowledge by sharing it with him.

The truth about Giles Paraway's death must go with her to her grave.

She felt his hands tighten about her own and knew that she had accepted the burden, her penance.

His voice spoke to her softly.

'Do I need to ask you any more if you love me, Helena?'

She lifted her face to look at him. There was sorrow in her

eyes, the faith veiling within which part of her must for ever hide itself from him, but there was no faltering in her voice, nothing but gladness in the things she could say with no reserves.

'You don't *need* to ask me, but I want you to,' she said.

'Then do you, Helena?'

'Oh my darling—with all my heart, with all that I can ever be, with all the best in me if there is any good at all, with my blessing and my gratitude for all the years that have gone, and all the years which, please God, are to come, with what you have made of me, my beloved, out of your love, something I never used to be, never would have been had you not loved me.'

He lifted her up to stand with him, their eyes meeting each other's with love and knowledge and perfect truth between them at last.

'I haven't made you any different from what you have always been, from the first moment I saw you – the one woman I have ever loved and shall love as long as I live.'

They were silent, their minds filled with thoughts of the time to come, the adjustments, the careful steps, often the pain, through which in the end they would come back to each other again and more fully and completely than they had ever been.

A shrill whistle from downstairs pierced their ears.

'Mum! Stinky fell off a cow's back and cut his knee on a stone and you should see the blood!'

There was a note of ghoulish delight in John's loud voice.

Helena dried her eyes in which the tears had gathered and laughed shakily and went to the door and opened it.

'All right, dear,' she called. 'Go into the downstairs cloakroom. No, not up here, Johnno! I'm coming.' Simon caught her hand and she turned to him. He kissed her.

'Well,' he said, 'here we go again.'

'Yes,' she said, her voice quivering. 'Here we go again.'

Plaster Cast

An ambitious and talented pianist, Roland Wade, nonetheless lacks true artistic genius. This leads him into temptation and he publishes another musician's work as his own. Trapped by his actions, he needs help. His beautiful wife, Hermione, is not going to support him – she is cold and calculating. Might Gretel, who in contrast is warm and loving? However, she too has reason to leave him to his plight. Just how is this all going to end?

The Weir House

Philip wants to marry Eve. It is her way out - he is rich, not too old, and has been in love for years – but not a man she can accept. He has even secretly funded her lifestyle, such that it is. Eve feels trapped. Unlike her friend Marcia, who cheerfully accepts an 'ordinary' life without complaint, Eve has known better and wants better. A chance encounter then changesthings – Lewis Belamie pays her to act as his fiancée for a week. Adventure, ambition, and disappointment all follow after she journeys to Cornwall with him, where she eventually nearly dies after what appears to be a suicide attempt because of a marriage that has seemingly failed. However, the mysterious and mocking Felix really does love her. Just who is he; how does Eve end up with him; and what part does 'The Weir House' play in her life? Has Eve's restlessness and relentless search for stability ended?

Through Many Waters

Jeff has got himself into a mess. It is, on the face of it, a classic scenario. He has a settled relationship with one woman, but loves another. What is he to do? It is now necessary to face reality, rather than continually making excuses to himself, but can he face the unpalatable truth? Then something beyond his influence intervenes and once again decisions have to be made. But in the end it is not Jeff that decides.

Misadventure

Olive Heriot and Hugh Manning had been in love for years, but marriage had been out of the question because of the intervention of Olive's mother. Now, at last, she was of age and due to gain her inheritance and be free to choose. A dinner party had been arranged at the Heriot's home, 'The Hermitage' and Hugh expects to be able to announce their engagement. Things start to change after a gruesomely realistic game entitled 'murder', which relies on someone drawing the Knave of Spades after cards are dealt. Tragedy strikes and other relationships are tested and consummated – but is this all real, or imagined?

18706040R00121

Printed in Great Britain
by Amazon